According to Queeney

ALSO BY BERYL BAINBRIDGE

According to Queeney

BERYL BAINBRIDGE

CARROLL & GRAF PUBLISHERS, INC.
NEW YORK

TO ANDREW AND MARGARET HEWSON,
WITH AFFECTION AND GRATITUDE

First Carroll & Graf edition 2001

Carroll & Graf Publishers, Inc.
A Division of Avalon Publishing Group
19 West 21st Street
New York, NY 10010-6805

Library of Congress Cataloging-in-Publication Data is available.
ISBN: 0-7867-0773-9

Manufactured in the United States of America

CONTENTS

Prologue

ON THE MORNING of the 15th December, 1784, a day of
bleak skies heralding snow, a box-cart rattled into Bolt
Court and drew up outside No. 8. Three men entered the house
and presently emerged carrying a roll of threadbare carpet as
though it were a battering ram.

Mrs. Desmoulins, shawl tight against her, remained on the
steps of the house and forced tears from her eyes. Though she
felt grief she was too old, too used to death, to weep without an
effort. She stood alone, save for a black and white cat busy washing itself. A number of neighbours came out and waited with
bowed heads until the cart had gone from sight. From the open
window of No. 6 could be heard the jangling of a spinet. It
was not known whether Mr. Kranach, a man who summer and
winter wore a coat lined with the fur of a white wolf, was
serenading the departed or merely about his daily practice.

The conveyance turning into Fleet Street, a gaggle of urchins ran in pursuit and leapt for the tail-board, at which the driver flicked backwards with his whip. Frank Barber, walking behind, accompanied his master as far as the church of St. Clement Dane's in the Strand; then, the bitter cold of the early hour getting to his living bones, he ducked away and sought refuge in a tavern.

Arriving in Windmill Street the cart trundled into the yard of William Hunter's School of Anatomy. The carpet was carried to the top floor and laid on a dissecting table. A fire roared in the grate and the air was filled with an aroma of herbs, that of mint being the most pervasive. In the corner of the cosy room, a dog, half-flayed, hung from a hook in the ceiling; above, the grey heavens nudged the skylight.

Present that morning were the physicians Heberden, Brocklesby, Butter, Wilson and Cruikshank. Also in attendance were Mr. Wilson's son, Arthur, and a Mr. White, neither of whom were as yet qualified in the practice of medicine.

Mr. White unrolled the carpet and removed the winding sheet. Arthur Wilson made the first incision, cutting downwards from the thorax. A quantity of water spilled from the cavity of the chest and dripped onto the floor. Mr. White was told to throw more herbs upon the fire to disperse the stink of dissolution.

Dr. Heberden made the second incision, this time across the stomach. He was troubled with a cough, and once, bending over his departed patient, the force of his breath fluttered the dead man's eyelashes, at which Mr. White turned pale and swayed where he stood. Mr. Cruikshank, noticing his pallor, ordered him to swallow a measure of brandy.

Later, under the instruction of his father, Arthur Wilson wrote the following report:

Opened the chest. Lungs did not collapse as they usually do, as though power of contraction lost.

Heart exceedingly strong and large.

Abdomen appeared to have incipient peritoneal inflammation and ascites.

Liver and spleen firm and hard.

A gallstone size of a pigeon's egg removed from bladder.

Pancreas enlarged.

One kidney (left) quite good. That of the right entirely destroyed.

Left testicle sound in structure but with a number of hydatids (cysts) on surface. Right testicle likewise. Spermatic vein leading to it exceedingly enlarged and varicose.

Body, large in life, now somewhat shrunken, save for left leg swollen from the dropsy. Right leg, recently stitched following self-inflicted wound.

Left lung removed for perusal of John Hunter, also slice of scrotum and gallstone. Specimens transferred to jars. Mr. White pricked his middle finger when sewing up body. The following day had red lines running up arm and was laid low with slight fever

Afterwards, the fire dying and the candles lighted, Mr. Hoskins of St. Martin's Lane, sent to Windmill Street at the request of Sir Joshua Reynolds, mounted the stairs to undertake a death mask. When the wax had cooled and he pulled away the cast, the eyelids were dragged open; he was too engrossed in scrutinising the imprint of the face to notice the staring aspect of the original.

The candles extinguished and the door locked, the dead man and the dead dog waited in darkness, gazing upwards to where snowflakes, star shaped, now fell upon the skylight.

CRISIS

n.f. (krisis)
The point of time at which any
affair comes to its height.

This hour's the very crisis of your fate;
Your good or ill; your infamy or fame,
And all the colour of your life depends
On this important now.

—DRYDEN'S *Spanish Friar*

SOLITARY NGHTS were to be feared, for when darkness fell, the mind, like the eye, saw things less clearly than by day and confusions and perversions of the brain manufactured black thoughts. Which is why he contrived to stay out into the small hours, to shrink the time left until the light came back.

He was fortunate in that he had acquaintances who were willing to sit up with him, some of whom considered it a privilege to do so. He knew this to be the truth, not vanity. His introduction to the Thrale household had been made a year before, in gloomy January, through the offices of his old friend, the Irishman Arthur Murphy. "They keep high company," Murphy had said, by way of inducement, "and an excellent table."

He had known nothing of his host beyond he was a prosperous owner of a brewery in Deadman's Place, Southwark, and but recently married. There was also a mansion in Streatham with hothouses and chickens.

Murphy thought he had caught him by mentioning the expected attendance of the poetical shoe-maker, James Woodhouse, the literary sensation of the moment, but, truth to tell, it was the promise of a fine dinner that led him to accept.

On his return home he had found Mrs. Williams waiting up for him, the kettle on the boil. She led, of necessity, a reclusive life and was eager to hear his impressions of the wider world.

"Was it engaging?" she had asked. "Was it worth the effort?"

"At least we were spared musical entertainment," he replied, and then, in spite of himself, blurted out, "Mrs. Thrale is an unusual woman."

"How so?" countered Mrs. Williams. "In looks or in intellect?"

Had he thrown aside caution and spoken the words in his head, he would have confided that Mrs. Thrale had sparkling eyes, narrow shoulders, penetrating wit, scholarship of the female kind, a favourable interest in himself and a leakage of milk from her right breast.

Instead, he said, "James Woodhouse has an impediment of speech, which is all to the good, as what he has to say is of little importance. Though a poor versifier, it is probable he's a competent maker of shoes."

"How many at table?" probed Mrs. Williams. "What order of placement?"

"From an upper window," he said, "Mrs. Thrale pointed out the site of Shakespeare's theatre. She maintains there are several timbers still standing."

"And you saw them?" cried Mrs. Williams.

"I saw nothing," he said. "The night was too black."

After no more than a quarter of an hour, fearful of betraying himself, he had feigned tiredness and announced he was for his bed. A disappointed droop to her mouth, Mrs. Williams preceded him up the stairs; theirs was an example of the blind leading the half-blind.

Now, the new year well advanced, his visits to the Thrales' house in the Borough had become regular, namely every Thursday in the month. Since last September a coach had been sent to fetch him, and as the light waned and the weather worsened he had half a dozen times been persuaded to stop the night. Mrs. Thrale had even marked for his particular use a room above the counting house, and had shelves built to accommodate his books, should he wish to bring them.

He was not a fool. He knew full well his presence drew others to Southwark, and if the circumstances had proved different he might have absented himself, in spite of the fine dinners. The satisfaction, however, was not all on one side, for the Thrales had a child, a daughter not much above twelve months old. One afternoon, coming face-to-face with his boots on the bend of the stairs, she had neither screamed nor scrambled past, simply stared gravely up at him. She wore a bonnet, askew, from which a tuft of hair, the colour of damp sand, stuck out above her ear.

"Sweeting," he had said, and bowed.

"Da-da," she had crowed, and crawled onwards on hands and knees.

Until that auspicious moment he had always thought of himself as a member of clubs; now, he was inclined to believe he was part of a family.

And then, on the Wednesday evening of the third week in April, climbing to his bed in Johnson's Court, he became aware of the Black Dog crouching on the landing, the shadow of its lolling tongue lapping the staircase wall. The stench of its hateful breath seeped into his chamber. He wrenched up the window to let in the night air, but still the rank odour swilled about the room; he propped himself upright and dozed with his hand clamped over his nostrils.

The following morning he woke out of sorts. He would have stayed where he was and distracted himself with arithmetic if Mrs. Desmoulins hadn't clamoured for his attention; yet again she had fallen out with Mrs. Williams. His head ached and he had difficulty in breathing, but he calmed himself and spoke rationally.

That afternoon Thrale's coach waited for him in the alleyway. Twice he went out of his front door and came back. The third time, Frank Barber, spying him hovering on the top step, his books spilled from under his arm, took him by the elbow and forcibly thrust him into his seat. Dog-tired, he would have clambered out again, but already the carriage was bowling into Fleet Street; besides, his belly was growling.

He arrived and regretted it, for he did not acquit himself well. When Thrale's mother-in-law began her tiresome and habitual questioning, this time pestering him to give an opinion on the riots in Spittalfields occasioned by the imports of French silk, he'd lost his temper and answered harshly. Though in the right of it, he felt vexed at his lack of restraint; he'd brought himself down.

Midnight having passed, Mrs. Thrale urged him to stop until morning. She mentioned the new hangings, green in colour, she had bought for his bed. "Dark green rather than bright," she elaborated, "with an elegant display of tassels."

He refused to stay with more vigour than was necessary.

"You do not look well," she persisted.

"Madame," he countered, "I have not been well these last fifty years." When he went out into the dark, he heard the child crying in an upper room above the courtyard.

In spite of the hour, his household was still at war when he let himself in. It appeared Mrs. Williams had taken a tumble and hurt her knee, a mishap caused, so she said, by Mr. Levet leaving his bag of medical instruments at the foot of the stairs. Frank

Barber swore that Levet couldn't be the culprit, on account of his coming in by the cellar door past one o'clock and falling facedown on the scullery table.

"I am not given to untruths," huffed Mrs. Williams, fierce as a bantam cock.

"He is there now," Frank persisted. "Bag at feet, head on arms."

Then Mrs. Desmoulins had put her oar in, crying out that such recriminations served no purpose, that it was beholden upon them all to be kind to one another . . . in a general pursuit of happiness.

At which he had lost his composure still further and thundered, "Enough, Madame," and given them all a piece of his mind before stomping off to bed.

Alone in his room his rage subsided, to be replaced by an all too familiar lethargy of spirit in which his thoughts drifted like feathers caught in a draught. This near somnolent state—he was staring fixedly at the coarse hairs of his wig flung down in the window recess—was shortly followed by physical stirrings of an unmistakable nature.

By a supreme effort of will he fought off his torpor, striking his forehead repeatedly with his fist to beat away a loathsome descent into sensuality. Sufficiently recovered, he occupied himself in mending his coal box, which was split; in this he was not successful and only succeeded in splintering it further.

The following Thursday he sent a note to the Brewery by Frank Barber, pleading a prior engagement. It was a lie, but then, had the truth of his indisposition been spilled out he might have been thought deserving of pity. He had been an object of that detestable sentiment throughout his childhood and shrank from the recollection.

It was unfortunate that Mrs. Desmoulins let in Dr. Adams that afternoon, for he was no longer able to control his agitation of mind. He was aware of Adams regarding him as he walked rest-lessly back and forth, but remembered nothing of their conver-sation beyond his own assertion that he would consent to an amputation of a limb if it would lead to a restoration of spirits. As from a distance, he heard himself groaning, weeping.

When Dr. Adams had gone he placed half a grain of opium on a spoon and, holding it against the rim of a cup filled with cold tea, carried it down. He thought of dear, dead Tetty and how he had berated her for the same indulgent practice.

That night he dreamt an old dream, one in which he crouched beside his mother on her bed in the room above his father's shop. His infant brother lay sleeping in the crook of her arm. Mother was turning the leaves of a child's book on the doctrine of universal salvation. She said there were two places where people went after their death, a fine place called Heaven and a sad place called Hell. When she began to read, her finger under each word so as to keep pace, he knew the sense of the letters before she did, but pushed their meaning from his mind. On the opposite page was an engraving of devils toppling small figures into the eternal flames. "The Lord hath made all things for himself," Mother read, "yea, even the wicked for the day of evil, for the wicked shall know the wrath of God and be pun-ished everlastingly."

He cried out in terror, and woke instantly, his big toe throb-bing with heat. It was the gout, yet he shuddered. Then it was that the Black Dog, scenting fear, burst into his chamber and leapt on his chest.

"I CANNOT BEAR it," Mrs. Williams said, slopping her break-fast dish of tea down the front of her gown. She was putting it about that she was the most affected by the atmosphere in the house. Both women had risen shortly after dawn, though in the circumstances neither had reason to leave their beds. Mrs. Desmoulins, smarting from an earlier encounter, remained silent. The altercation had concerned a half loaf of bread. "You forgot to cover it against the mice," Mrs. Williams had scolded, sightlessly raking her fingers along the scullery shelf. Crumbs, pretty as snowflakes, sprayed the floor.

Mrs. Desmoulins had denied all knowledge and blamed Frank Barber. "It was him," she blustered, pointing a finger, but he, motionless at the table, had stuck out his pink tongue and stayed mute.

Mrs. Williams's shortness of temper, in evidence at the best of times, had increased tenfold. Even Mr. Levet, with whom she often and perversely saw eye to eye, had fallen from favour. Three days ago, coming across him lying in his customary position at the bottom of the scullery stairs, she had kicked him awake. She hadn't caused him an injury but it was an indication of her agitated state. He, ignorant soul, had crawled on his knees to the fire and, murmuring the word "Mother," dozed off again with his arms about the coal scuttle. Some minutes later, contrite Mrs. Williams had asked where he was. "Gone," Mrs. Desmoulins had lied, and embroidered, "He was bleeding at the mouth."

"I cannot bear it," Mrs. Williams repeated, but now her voice broke in her throat and her hand shook.

"You are not the only one bent under a burden," Mrs. Desmoulins told her. All the same, she reached out to cover those fingers trembling upon the tablecloth. In doing so she was conscious it was Samuel's influence that guided her; left to herself she might have resorted to spitting.

"My hearing, at least, is unimpaired," snapped Mrs. Williams. "Your constant wailing and sighing scarcely goes unnoticed"; nonetheless, she allowed her hand to be stilled.

Presently Mrs. Desmoulins went out into the little garden beside the house and sat on the bench beneath the sycamore tree.

The air was cold, which suited her mood, for anger warmed her blood. From the dwelling next door she could hear Mr. Phipps berating his wife. His was a house riven with discord . . . but then, wasn't that a condition common to all?

Phipps kept a mistress in Clerkenwell. Once, when Mrs. Phipps had been away in the country undergoing the lying-in of her sixth infant, he had brought home his flighty woman in broad daylight and escorted her for all to see across the Court. There had been a boy-child born between them who had died in his third year, one with the same beady eyes and cleft lip inherited from his father. Sometime, the child, aided by his legitimate siblings, had been seen in the adjoining yard attempting to spin a top.

Samuel, hearing of the child's death, had called on Mr. Phipps and offered his condolences. Returning, he shed tears. He said Phipps had cared for that lost boy more than all his other off-spring put together. Mrs. Desmoulins had adopted a serious look. "The poor dear man," she wailed. Inwardly, she felt exultant, seeing her dead husband had been just such a one as Phipps, and one she hoped still roasted in hell.

Sitting there, her feet turning to ice, she fretted over how much longer Samuel would stay in his room. His self-imposed confinement had begun five weeks before, on his return from the Thrales'. In the morning he had seemed his usual self. She'd had occasion to speak to him at midday owing to Mrs. Williams's accusing her of extravagance in the matter of candles.

Samuel had urged her to be charitable. The pernicious effects of education, he explained, namely that the world had a great deal to offer, an expectation taken from fiction rather than fact, had left Mrs. Williams under the delusion she could ride the rainbow. Mrs. Desmoulins had protested she was talking of wax rather than the colours of the spectrum. In vain; he and Mrs. Williams were two of a kind, both dazzled by words.

That night, returning from his customary visit to the Brewery, he'd raised a storm over some remark she herself had made. To the best of her recollection she had been trying to still a quarrel between Mrs. Williams and Frank, and had simply observed that a desire for happiness was human. In this she had blundered.

"Happiness," he'd thundered, "resides in self-reliance. A man should never depend with certainty on anyone but himself." In an aside, for he was always scrupulous in regard to sources, he acknowledged he was paraphrasing Aristotle. Crushed, it had nonetheless occurred to her how curious it was that, in order to express themselves, great men constantly relied on the thoughts of those long dead. He'd said other things as well, wounding things, but she'd fancied they were directed at Frank and Mrs. Williams rather than herself.

The next morning he'd risen early, which was a bad sign, he being awake and it not yet noon. None of them had slept well, for he had shattered the early hours with a persistent hammering. Frank, impudently entering his room, had found him engaged in carpentry. Though worn out, Mrs. Williams agreed it was fortunate he hadn't started on one of his electrical experiments, for then they might have found him crackling in his bed.

They heard him striding backwards and forwards all day, but he didn't appear, not even for his rolls and butter. Mrs. Williams said he hadn't yet recovered from his recent labours in putting Shakespeare to rights.

Then, later that afternoon, she'd remembered they were approaching an anniversary of Tetty's death, and indeed, that very evening, interrupted by groans, a recitation of prayers broke out in the room above the parlour. Mrs. Williams winced at this audible show of suffering and stuffed her fingers in her ears. Mrs. Desmoulins felt impatience, Tetty having been gone a good ten years, but held her tongue and endured. In her opinion, Tetty's demise had been a merciful release rather than a matter for regret; she had been tired of life and fuddled towards the end, and he who now groaned so loudly had been shockingly absent during her fading.

Since that display of grief, if such it was, he had kept to his room; nor would he see anyone, not even Mr. Murphy, or Mr. Reynolds, whom he loved and in whose house he had always been welcome. Once, Mr. Hawkins had called and, resolutely mounting the stairs, thumped on the door with his stick and demanded to be let in, at which Samuel, overheard by Mrs. Williams, had cried out, *Etiam oblivisci quid sis, interdum expedit*. Mrs. Desmoulins had no idea of what this might mean, but had observed Hawkins come down quite pale and depart without a word.

As for Mr. Thrale, he had sent several notes, all left unread. There had been a break in the friendship some time past, when Samuel, invited to their summer residence in Brighton, had arrived to find the house shut up and its occupant returned to town, but Mrs. Williams held this lapse had been forgiven following Mr. Thrale's explanation that he'd hastened back to London upon a sudden decision to stand for Parliament.

Bird droppings splattering the garden bench, Mrs. Desmoulins went back into the house and loitered on the landing outside Samuel's room. Suddenly, too abruptly for her to hide, his door opened and he thrust out his chamber pot. He was dressed, though without shoes and stockings, and she noticed the angry redness of his feet. He looked her full in the face, yet he didn't see her. The sight of his stubbled cheeks, brow furrowed and eyes circled with darkness, filled her with terror. He retreated in an instant; the thud of the bolt as he secured his door echoed throughout the house.

She ran downstairs, calling out for Mrs. Williams. It no longer mattered who had the greatest influence, who was deemed closest. Mrs. Williams was half-asleep in her chair by the parlour fire.

"You must go to him," Mrs. Desmoulins shouted. "He is not himself."

"He has often been so," Mrs. Williams retorted. "But he always returns. A woman's pleadings at this juncture will only add to his anxiety." Her round face remained placid; she was so fair in colouring she had no eyebrows to raise.

It struck Mrs. Desmoulins how useless learning was in times of crisis; Mrs. Williams knew French and Italian and scribbled poetry, yet failed to recognise madness. "He is not anxious," she screamed. "He is out of his mind."

"It is not our function to interfere," pronounced Mrs. Williams, and closed her eyes, though they saw nothing when open.

Mrs. Desmoulins scurried frantically up and down the passage, wringing her hands and keening. As she confided later to Levet, a man she did not usually address, she had been tormented by a dreadful vision in which Samuel wrestled with the Devil. "If," she said, "Mr. Delap hadn't chosen to call at that particular moment, we might have lost him forever."

Mr. Delap, arriving so opportunely, listened to her hysterical outpourings and was wary of intruding. He said Mr. Johnson had always been subject to hypochondria and no man liked to be seen at a disadvantage. He spoke to her bosom rather than her face, but then Samuel had the same habit. Mrs. Desmoulins pleaded with him; she went so far as to bar his way as he attempted to leave. Reluctantly he ascended the stairs.

To her astonishment, no sooner had he knocked than she heard the bolt being drawn. The door opened and remained so, but for some time the voices scarcely rose above a buzz and she could make nothing of the exchange. All at once Samuel spoke up, though in a manner so disturbed and with such a gabbling of words that sense was lost. Above his wild utterances his companion could be heard entreating him to be calm. Then Samuel shouted out, *"By Heaven, I'll hate him everlastingly that bids me to be of comfort anymore,"* and moments later, loudly and with great solemnity, Mr. Delap began to declaim the Lord's Prayer—at which Samuel mercifully fell silent.

Mrs. Desmoulins, crouching by the banisters, joined in the recitation, to be interrupted during her whispering of *Give us this day our daily bread* by a rapping at the street door. Almost immediately Frank ushered into the hall a tall man with a florid complexion and a small pale woman whose eyes glittered. Awake at last, Mrs. Williams came out from the parlour and greeted Mrs. Thrale by name.

There followed a most distressing scene, witnessed by all. Mr. Delap appeared at the head of the stairs, followed by Samuel, who cried out pitifully and repeatedly. There was nothing human in the sounds he made. Mrs. Desmoulins was reminded of the chained and tormented bear tethered in the square on market days in Lichfield—and on the instant, the sufferer dropped to his knees and bear-like, swung his head from side to side.

Appalled, Mr. Delap tried to drag him upright, but the distraught man was too heavy; he crouched even lower and clutching Mr. Delap about the legs began to entreat God to help him. "Merciful Lord," he cried, "grant me the continued use of my understanding." Below, the stricken watchers stood as though turned to stone.

Mr. Delap, finding himself under scrutiny, shook free as best he could and hurried down the stairs. His white stockings had been pulled from his breeches and lay in folds about his ankles.

Lurching upright, Samuel lumbered in pursuit. Unaware of those others who stepped backwards at his awful approach, he reached out and caught Delap by the coattails; again he sank to his knees, again he beseeched God to save him from a leaving of his senses. Mrs. Desmoulins was not alone in fearing it was possibly too late.

And now began a demented outpouring of self-condemnation, a listing of sins accompanied by such a savage beating of the breast as to shake his very frame. The terrible emotion in his voice, the fearful despair in his eyes as he shouted aloud this litany of misdemeanours, was too much for Mr. Thrale; stepping forward, he clapped his hand over Samuel's mouth. Mr. Delap, hindered by his fallen stockings, made his escape and hobbled out into the Court.

Mr. Thrale departed soon after, either from weight of business or from delicacy. Mrs. Williams said it was the latter; no honest man cared to gawp at the derangement of a friend. Before he went he urged his wife to carry Samuel to Streatham, where he might have her full attention and be away from the strains of city life.

Mrs. Williams busied herself making up a small bundle of clothing; there was nothing beyond a nightshirt and a Sunday coat with candle grease hardened on the buttonholes. Flustered, she excused the lack of clean linen, explaining Samuel had locked himself in his room for so long she hadn't been able to bring out things to be washed.

Mrs. Thrale said it was of no importance, that garments quite suitable for use had been left behind at Streatham by numerous guests, among them Mr. Langton, who, though thin to the point of emaciation, was not much above Mr. Johnson in height.

While these domestic arrangements were being completed the sick man sat in the parlour, watched over by Frank. He now appeared composed and wore a somewhat bashful look. Studying his swollen toes, he wriggled them, like a child paddling in sea water, and chuckled. Mrs. Williams went up to fetch his discarded stockings but found them much holed.

When all was ready, Mrs. Thrale's coachman was sent for to assist him into the alleyway; he went barefoot and didn't look back. At the last minute Mrs. Williams remembered his wig, and sent Frank running.

Mr. Levet came home early that evening, sober. Mrs. Williams and Mrs. Desmoulins vied with each other in giving an account of the happenings of the afternoon. Mrs. Williams described how she had been busy dusting the breakfast room when voices from overhead disturbed her. "I recognised Mr. Delap's voice," she said, "and thought nothing of it, beyond being surprised, and relieved, that Mr. Johnson had admitted him."

"You were asleep in the parlour," Mrs. Desmoulins objected. "You only showed when Mr. Thrale arrived."

"I could scarcely have slept," countered Mrs. Williams, "considering the noise made by yourself."

"I was on the way to my room," Mrs. Desmoulins said, "when Mr. Johnson came out onto the landing. He cried out, *I am in torment. You alone can help me*. At that moment Frank let in Mr. Delap. It was only natural I should give way, he being a man of the church."

"Natural indeed," agreed Mrs. Williams, and smiled without humour.

"If he hadn't come," continued Mrs. Desmoulins, "the Devil would have conquered."

She proceeded to describe how she had crouched on the stairs and accompanied Mr. Delap in the reciting of the Lord's Prayer, and how, in the middle of the line *Give us this day our daily bread*, the Thrales had called—here she knocked on the table with her fist, causing Mrs. Williams some alarm.

"A providential interruption," Mr. Levet remarked, "for Sam last ate on Tuesday."

Before retiring, Mrs. Desmoulins crept into the empty chamber. The bed was rumpled and a squeezed-out orange sat on the pillow. On the table by the window, arranged along the margin of an open book, lay curls of peel cut into segments; she put a piece in the pocket of her gown, for comfort. Climbing the stairs she spied the cat, mewling on the second landing. She kicked out, from jealousy, not malice; often the animal, seeing Samuel immersed in his books, leapt on his lap and purred away the hours. Soundlessly, the cat fled higher. I live, thought Mrs. Desmoulins, among people unworthy of my companionship.

A tree grew close to the window of her garret room. When the wind whipped its branches against the glass she fancied its scrapings echoed her own internal scourging. Lacerated both within and without, she sank into sleep.

Almost at once she felt his arm across her shoulder, one brown hand pressed against her nightcap so that she lay imprisoned on his breast. He said little that was intelligible, yet his chuckings and gruntings were proof of his regard. He was clumsy in his fondlings, but what did she care? She breathed in the bitter sweet odour of his skin and thought her heartbeats would wake the household.

And then she woke to the small hour chiming of the clock of St. Bridget's—a dismal awakening, for now he lay under another roof and all those tumblings of years gone by were but the stuff of dreams.

To Miss Laetitia Hawkins
2, Sion Row, Twickenham

Sept. 21st, 1807

Dear Miss Hawkins,

Your kind letter arrived on the 18th of the month, a birth date which, though he preceded my entry into the world by more than fifty years, you suppose— through no fault of your own—*that I share with Dr. Johnson. To the best of my belief, I was born on the 17th day of September, it being my mother's later conceit to pin my arrival to the more auspicious date.*

Yes, I do indeed recall the supper given by your father, Sir John, to cele-brate the Dr.'s 65th year. It was held, if I remember, three days early as my father and Mr. Baretti had planned a visit to Paris on the 16th. You and I were much frowned upon for the unseemly giggles that burst forth at the sight of Dr. Johnson dropping to his knees the better to examine Miss Reynolds's new shoes. That same evening I fell into a sulk provoked by a frank obser-vation made by your good self. Admiring our childish reflections in the hall mirror, you declared my face handsome but "chubby." The years fly by, but some events—vanity, all is vanity—remain engraved on the mind.

Your present intention of putting pen to paper regarding the Johnsonian Circle *is one worthy of success, yet I fear I can be of little help. I was not a year old when Dr. Johnson first came to dine at the Brewery in Deadman's Place and scarce a twelvemonth older when my father afforded him sanctuary at Streatham Park. Though reluctant to answer questions of a speculative nature—I have no wish to revive mem-ories which, owing to circumstances, arouse in my breast none but melan-choly thoughts—I will do my best to reply to your more factual queries.*

The cabinet you mention is in the procession of my mother, Mrs. Piozzi, as is the globe bought by Dr. Johnson to instruct me in Geography. There is a scribble in the region of the Americas executed by my brother Harry, for which my mother whipped him cruelly. Dr. Johnson was away at the time but upon hearing of the punishment said it was not well done. Mr. Baretti, being present, was bolder. I recall he seized the rod from the nursery shelf and stamped it underfoot.

Though Mr. Boswell and Mrs. Piozzi have frequently asserted that the pet name of Queeney was given me by Dr. Johnson, it is my belief that it was my dear father who first called me so. First I was his Queen Esther, then his Hetty, then his Queeney, the change taking place in about my third year.

The dog seated in front of my grandmother Salusbury in the painting by Zoffany was called Belle, on account of her beauty, though she was stout and by temperament irritable. It was she who committed the offence of devouring the Doctor's buttered toast while he was engaged in slurping his tea.

The titles of the books you refer to, also in the keeping of my mother, are as follows—the Poems of Metastasio *in six volumes, the* Comedies of Terence, *a Latin grammar and a Virgil. As to Mr. Baretti's* Dialogues, *it did indeed commence with an eight page dedication to myself, the concluding sentences later rendered into English verse by Dr. Johnson. Modesty prevents me from repeating the lines in full, sufficient to say it began,* Long may live our charming Hetty . . . *In her* Anecdotes, *Mrs. Piozzi quotes the verse while omitting any reference to its origin. As we bear the same name this has led many to suppose the dedication was intended for herself.*

Queeney's Covenant is in my possession, but I would not wish it to appear in print. It is in the form of a promise dictated by Dr. Johnson, that I would come down promptly every day to be taught Italian . . . I will be in the very best of humour, nor will I look about me with a vacant and weary expression, *etc., etc. It was signed by myself and witnessed by Dr. Johnson.*

My sister Mrs. Mostyn is well in health though alarmed at the prospect of my mother moving closer. It had been hoped she would be living at Streatham, but news has come that she is thinking of letting. Having her as a near neighbour would be irksome indeed. As somebody has remarked most truly, a fair proportion of the unhappiness of life consists in recollections of past, or dread of future, miseries.

Adieu, my dear Miss Hawkins,

Yours Sincerely,

H. M. Thrale

REINTEGRATE

v.a. (reinteger, Fr. *and integer,*
Lat. *It should perhaps be written redintegrate.)*
To renew with regard to any state
or quality; to repair; to restore.

The falling from a discord to a concord hath an agreement with the affections,
which are reintegrated to the better after some dislikes.

—BACON'S *Nat. Hist.*

Mrs. THRALE ROSE early, on Queeney's account, and spied from her bedroom window a lawn sparkling under dew. The dogs, loosed from their chains, scudded across the grass, spattering diamonds.

When she went to the nursery Queeney was still sleeping. Her mouth lay open and sweat glistened upon the bridge of her nose. Old Nurse said the child's breath still smelled sour. She had passed stools twice in the night, though without discomfort.

"And the pustules on her chest?" inquired Mrs. Thrale.

"Now scabby," Old Nurse said, though her eyesight could not be relied upon.

Mrs. Thrale examined the child's arm and was relieved to find it less swollen than before. Queeney had jerked in shock when Dr. Sutton had made the puncture, and the resulting scratch had turned angry.

The haze had lifted from the beech trees in the Park when Mrs. Thrale came down to breakfast. The rays of the sun caught the scarlet hangings on the second landing and splashed the stairs with crimson.

It was noticeable that both her husband and her mother had fallen under the influence of clear skies. Mrs. Salusbury announced her intention of delaying her return to town, and Mr. Thrale, having first visited the kitchens to give final instructions to the cooks as to the advancement of the dinner planned for later in the day, was moved to part from his wife with less reserve than usual.

"I shall return at four o'clock" is all he said, then, bringing his melancholy face close to hers, pressed dry lips against her cheek. It was the merest peck, yet it was not his habit to kiss her, and never when sober.

"Four o'clock," she echoed, and neither raised nor lowered by his gesture, wiped her face with her sleeve. He was a good man, one she had come to like, not love, a sentiment she felt contrary to the proper order of affections existing between men and women. Her mother, who lived on a diet of vegetables and water and could not be accused of emotions disturbed by either spirits or meat, often referred to the dead Mr. Salusbury as a "monster she had been fond of to distraction." At such times, Mrs. Thrale, observing the light of passion in her mother's eyes, felt envy. On Sundays, in church, she sometimes prayed, without fervour, to be persecuted by love.

At noon, Queeney awake and the weather still balmy, Mrs. Thrale told Old Nurse to carry the child outdoors. Mrs. Salusbury and she were about to follow when Mr. Langton came downstairs. After standing in the porch for some considerable time, languidly waving his hand back and forth to test the temperature of the air, he agreed to accompany them. By the time they set foot on the gravel, Old Nurse and Queeney were nowhere to be seen.

Walking with the extremely lofty Bennett Langton was tiring. In order to remain at his side his female companions, both short of stature, were forced into an unseemly trot. There was little opportunity to remark upon the heavenly blue of the cloudless sky, the glittering reflections of sun on foliage, to breathe in the sweet perfume of the full-blown roses lolling on their mound above the Ice House. Each inhalation was vital to sustain motion, if not life. True, Mr. Langton checked his loping stride from time to time and sought to regulate his step, but all too soon forgot. Peering upwards at him, the cloth of his hat mottled by the shadows cast by the beech leaves, it occurred to Mrs. Thrale that, should such an unlikely situation arise, she would be well prepared to keep pace with a giraffe.

Perhaps he read her thoughts, for presently he launched into an anecdote concerning himself and Mr. Garrick, who was expected that afternoon. "It was winter," he began, "and Davy and I had been invited to take dinner at the house of a mutual acquaintance. I was late . . . the weather was very inclement—"

Here Mrs. Salusbury exchanged sly glances with her daughter. Bennet Langton was always late for appointments. Those who knew him wisely took it into account. If guests were expected at five o'clock, Langton was told he would be required at three.

"When I entered the room Davy leapt onto a chair and asked me how I did. It was quite comical."

"And uncivil," cried Mrs. Salusbury, puffing.

"No matter. I believe I got the better of him. 'Thank you,' I replied, 'I am quite well . . .' Then no sooner had Davy got down from his chair than I knelt in front of him and held out my hand."

"He is, of course, on the small side," observed Mrs. Salusbury.

"And conscious of it." She came to a halt; holding her finger to her chin as though thinking the matter over, she fought for breath.

Mrs. Thrale remained silent. She had heard the story many times, indeed fancied she had been present on the actual occasion. To the best of her memory it had been Garrick who had turned the tables—quoting from *The Tempest*, he had promptly retorted, "*Give me thy hand. I do begin to have bloody thoughts.*"

At the recollection, she grew agitated, her own thoughts being far from serene. Not a twelvemonth had passed since the funeral of her second daughter, and though it was true the sickly infant had not lived long enough to leave any lasting impression, the experience had caused upset. Now, four months gone with a third child, she often tormented herself with gruesome images. She was sure Queeney had scrambled free from Old Nurse's arms and was at this very moment tottering towards the lake. Old Nurse, blinded by age and sunlight, mistakenly took her to be sitting at her feet, tearing the heads off cowslips.

"Queeney is now on the mend," she announced aloud, to reassure herself, and fairly scurried off along the path, although not ahead of Mr. Langton. Mrs. Salusbury gave up the race and, coming to an upturned bucket left by workmen engaged in extending the stables, collapsed upon it, back to the sun, eyes closed and hand pressed to her thudding heart.

Mrs. Thrale, thoughts jumbled, had no sooner descended the steps that led between the lilac bushes than she saw Mr. Langton and Old Nurse, the child in her arms, coming towards her.

"Queeney, Queeney," she called out, and ran to clasp her close. She met with resistance; no amount of tugging, or pinching, would budge the child. Face flushed with resolve, Queeney stared defiantly and tightened her grip about Nurse's neck. Her bonnet had slipped off and the glitter of the lake tipped her curls with silver. Relief replaced with anger, Mrs. Thrale would have

slapped her into submission but for the lofty presence of
Bennett Langton.

"The bond between nurse and child," he observed unwisely,
"is often stronger than the natural one we suppose to exist."

"The sun is too hot," snapped Mrs. Thrale. "We shall all be
more comfortable indoors." Retracing her steps she snagged her
dress on a lilac bush and could have wept with vexation.

MRS. SALUSBURY, DOZING on her upturned bucket, was disturbed by the sound of footsteps on gravel. Opening her eyes
she saw in the distance the portly figure of Mr. Johnson round-
ing the wall of the pigsty, an addition caused to be built by the
pork-loving Henry Thrale to house a Cheshire hog recently
slaughtered on account of it being virtually wild, without fat
and so savage as to be a danger to all within reach.

Mr. Johnson's advance along the path, though no less erratic,
was more convoluted than usual. He had abandoned his rolling
gait in favour of a zigzag progression, each diagonal embarked
upon the moment the appropriate foot met the grass verge.
Several times it was apparent he had turned too imprecisely, for
he walked back and started over again. But for good manners
Mrs. Salusbury would have swivelled the opposite way, to avoid
confrontation.

Mr. Johnson and she were not friends. When first he had
come to her son-in-law's table in the Borough, she had been
delighted to make the acquaintance of such an enlightened
man. She had so many questions to which he alone, being so
learned and yet so lacking in cant, would be able to provide the
answers. From the very beginning—she had sought his opinion
of the silk riots—he had put her down, and continued to do so.
His residence at Streatham Park, his every need catered to by
her daughter, Hester, had restored his health but failed to

improve his temper. Though he no longer woke the household in the dark hours with his mumbling perambulations along the corridors, excursions which drove the befuddled servants from their beds and obliged them into nightly stalkings for fear he put his candle down beside a curtain and set the house ablaze, he was still fiery in regard to herself. She had caught him out more than once in the invention of answers to her numerous enquiries as to his opinion of this or that political conundrum. At first she had laboured under the delusion that the chuckles that punctuated his replies, the frequent glances he cast around the table, the throwing of salt over his shoulder, were no more than displays of eccentricity. No longer; she now thought him ill-bred.

Her daughter held that the antagonism between them was the result of jealousy, on his part. He needed her undivided attention, seeing he was beset by demons and had not had the advantage of a mother's love of the sort she herself had known. Mrs. Salusbury knew this was sincere; she loved her daughter and to the best of her ability had not tried to mould her. Even so, she kept hidden her own feelings of jealousy occasioned by the encroaching influence of the ever-present Mr. Johnson, who at this very moment, burbling to himself, was on a zig-zag collision course with her person. She shut her eyes once more and slumped lower as his mutterings grew louder.

He came so close that his sleeve brushed her bonnet—she distinctly heard the curious words, *October good blast to blow the hog mast*—and then he veered to the right and was gone. She had taken the precaution of tucking her feet out of reach, though even if he had trodden on them he would not have noticed, of that she was sure. It was not poorness of vision that rendered her invisible, simply that she was of no more interest to him than the stone urns set at frequent intervals along the way. Turning, she saw his stout white calves were devoid of stockings and that he wore slippers. The slip-slap of his feet as he veered down the path grew fainter, fading altogether as he entered the shadow of the oak trees and melted from sight.

Gradually she became aware of other sounds, the shrill barking of Belle as she raced alongside the poultry yard, the hum of bees in search of roses, the rush of air as birds swooped overhead. She dozed again, hearing in the swish of wings an echo of the waves lapping the shore at Pwllheli where once, her shoes laced with salt, the argumentative Mr. Salusbury had knelt in the damp sand and asked for her hand. If one is not caressed, thought Mrs. Salusbury, one develops thorns. She was not entirely thinking of Mr. Johnson.

HE, FINDING THE grounds deserted save for Mrs. Salusbury, whom he had stumbled upon squatting on the path in the act of passing water, felt he had been abandoned. Rising from his bed he had come downstairs to a house empty of all but the servants, and now rehearsed in his head in what manner he would reproach Mrs. Thrale when next they met.

Dear Mistress, he would say—smiling to soften the rebuke— *I thought to see you at the breakfast table.* She: *My dear friend, the sunshine called me, seduced me, etc.* He: *My dear Madame, the sun will burn everlastingly. Our little illumination, I fear, will be extinguished in the time it takes for a leaf to fall from the tree.* Far from satisfied with this exchange, he lunged at the oak leaves with his stick.

Four months had elapsed since the day when, like sweet bells jangled out of tune and harsh, reason had forsaken him and he had been brought to Streatham Park. For five long weeks he had remained closeted in his room, seeing no one but Mrs. Thrale. They had neither nature nor nurture in common, yet in her alone had he confided the thoughts that caused him such unease. Not quite all . . .

Since that enforced seclusion he had sufficiently mended to resume his old way of life. Though he now spent the better part of each week in the country, he tried, whenever possible, to return to London on a Friday evening to give both companionship and succour to the troublesome occupants of Johnson Court. There, on Saturdays, he received callers and dined with friends. Sundays, he made sure the members of his household ate a hearty dinner, after which, gathering them around the coals in the parlour, he endeavoured to convince them of the common vicissitudes that bound them together.

Mondays were fraught, for at noon Thrale's coach arrived and either Mrs. Desmoulins or Mrs. Williams, often both, contrived to delay him by a listing of Dr. Levet's numerous faults. He fought to be without prejudice but his sympathies lay with Levet rather than with the blind Mrs. Williams and the all-too-seeing Mrs. Desmoulins. Levet never resorted to tears.

He returned *home*—he had come to think of Streatham in no other light—to a flattering regard for his well-being. He had only to mention that a broiled lobster or a game pie was to his liking, than it appeared on the dinner table. If in an aside, he remarked that the writing table in his chamber was good but small, a more commodious one was placed at his disposal within the hour. Aware that on such a bed of roses the weeds of indolence flourished, he dropped to his knees every night and resolved to mend his ways and rise early—so far without success. Midday generally found him still abed.

A stone having lodged under his heel, he stopped on the path to shake it loose and was surprised to see that he was wearing slippers. He supposed he had prudently left off his shoes on account of the silver buckles Henry Thrale had provided him with three weeks before.

He had cause, beyond footware, to respect Thrale, who had recently shown him drawings of the library he planned to build on to the west wing of the house. "Its design, Sam," he had said, "will be mine . . . but I depend on you to choose the books on its shelves."

Thrale's honesty, his lack of affectation—he was that contradiction in terms, an educated man who cared little for reading—was to be admired. Many wealthy men had been known to furnish a library and later blame others for its lack of excellence.

The task would require patience and diligence, a *Gothick* rather than a *Modern* library was desirable, but the request was only reasonable considering the hospitality, tempered with affection, so lavishly bestowed. No man loved another without expectation of returns.

Standing there, it occurred to him that he was feeling in excellent bodily health. His breathing was sound, his stomach easy, and he was free of those pains which afflicted his groin.

On an impulse, and to test his lungs, he lumbered into a run, which he sustained until he reached the lake. A solitary duck flapped its wings at his approach. Breathless, but not unnaturally so, he dug into his pockets and skimmed orange peel across the water, promoting ripples. The duck, obedient to laws, swam in widening circles.

He was about to turn back in the direction of the house when his attention was caught by an object trapped in the rushes. He took it for a log of wood, but closer scrutiny revealed it to be a roll of canvas tied with twine. Using his stick he attempted to poke it loose, at which it cast off and began to bob away.

Without a moment's thought, he tore off his clothes and plunged into the lake, only to find the water came no higher than his knees. He was in time to pluck out the package before it sank. Climbing onto the bank he examined the contents, which proved of no great interest, being but an ancient fan set with glass panels in which were embedded three round objects.

He fancied they might be coins, until, rubbing off the mud, he saw they were buttons, each one engraved with the image of a leaping dog.

He was wiping himself dry with his shirt, the beams of the sun striking fire from the gold amulet hung about his neck, when he spied someone advancing along the path. At this distance, judging from pace, he thought it to be one of the elderly Southwark workmen employed on extensions and improvements, yet even as he watched the figure turned tail and retreated with speed, arms flapping the air as though pursued by wild beasts.

I am not alone, he told himself. The world is full of madmen.

FROM LONDON THAT afternoon came Mr. and Mrs. Jackson, Miss Reynolds, Arthur Murphy and the Jesuit, Dr. Fitzpatrick, the last being an old friend of Henry Thrale, as was Humphrey Jackson, the chemist. Both had known him from his fox-hunting bachelor days when he'd kept a pack of hounds at Croydon. Garrick was to have brought Miss Reynolds, but at the last moment he had been delayed and Murphy had obliged. The reason for the delay, when explained, caused merriment all round.

"At three o'clock," Murphy said, "the manager of Covent Garden sent word to Drury Lane that Davy was to come immediately owing to Mr. Quin having suffered a calamity in the middle of his denouncement of Desdemona."

"What sort of calamity?" asked Mrs. Salusbury, who until that moment had been leaning back in her chair and wishing herself in bed.

"The comical sort," said Murphy.

"Tell, tell," squealed Mrs. Jackson.

"It appears," continued Murphy, "that for some years' past Quin's gums have been in a diseased state . . . "

"Which is why Mrs. Ford waves her fan so vigorously," put in Mrs. Thrale.

"He had enunciated with admirable restraint, *Iago, All my fond love thus do I blow to Heaven,* yet when the time came for him to make his exit such was his feeling for the drama that all caution left him and he fairly bellowed, *Damn her, lewd minx! O, damn her!* . . . at which exclamation his few remaining teeth lost their hold and flew across the stage."

"Flew," echoed Mrs. Salusbury.

"Like crumbs," said Murphy.

The laughter was prolonged, Mr. Johnson, in particular, positively shaking with mirth. Indeed, the story tickled him to such a degree that he strode about declaiming Othello's words several times over. He had caught the sun and his face glowed. Even Miss Reynolds allowed herself a half-smile at Quin's expense. This was unusual; due to domestic circumstances she generally leaned towards the underdog. In spite of the hilarity Mrs. Thrale was aware there wasn't one among them, herself included, who wasn't secretly engaged in running their tongue along their gums.

She was pleased the party was proceeding so well. It was not always easy to promote a convivial atmosphere before the wine had taken effect, and well-nigh impossible if Johnson happened to be out of sorts; when he was in a gloom the whole company fell under his shadow.

Bennet Langton not yet come down, and Mrs. Jackson politely enquiring after the health of Queeney, Henry Thrale demanded the child should be brought from the nursery. When she came he sat her on his knee, where she perched quite contentedly and accepted the attentions of the company with composure. She even allowed her mother to dab the perspiration from her scarlet cheeks.

"The inoculation against the smallpox is a success," Mrs. Thrale announced. "Dr. Sutton assures me all danger is past."

The compliments on her daughter's prettiness—such lovely eyes, such a winsome curve to her mouth—provoked her into boasting of Queeney's more important attributes. She said, "She knows the compass as perfectly as any mariner upon the sea, is mistress of the solar system and the signs of the Zodiac . . ."

"What a little marvel," babbled Mrs. Jackson.

". . . and is thoroughly acquainted with the difference between the Ecliptick and Equator. She is also able to pronounce the names of all the capitals of Europe, recite the Pater Noster, the three Christian virtues in English . . ."

"A little marvel," repeated Mrs. Jackson, who had no children of her own, and was glad of it.

". . . also the four Cardinal ones in Latin." Mrs. Thrale's last words were rendered almost inaudible by a tremendous clearing of the throat executed by Mr. Johnson. She looked at him and saw that he was frowning, and knew the cause, for he had once told her that as a clever child he had suffered much from being put on show by his father. All the same, she saw no reason to subdue her own motherly pride. Raising her voice, she said, "In the last few months she has learnt to recount, with neat perfect accuracy, the Judgement of Paris and the legend of Perseus and Andromeda."

At this Mr. Johnson gave vent to what could only be described as a warning growl. The dog Belle, wheezing at Mrs. Salusbury's feet, struggled upright and waddled to the door. Taking a book from his pocket, Mr. Johnson turned his back on the room.

"Do please get the child to read to us," pleaded the silly Mrs. Jackson.

"She cannot read," Mrs. Thrale admitted, and called for Queeney to be returned to the nursery.

At half past six o'clock, an hour later than planned owing to the tardiness of Langton—he protested the servants had failed to knock on his door—the company went in to dinner. Thrale had ordered the windows to be left open, and flies swarmed above the table. There was discussion as to whether the windows ought to be closed, but most held it was better to have air, and besides, there were sweet perfumes drifting in from the darkening garden.

Miss Reynolds said there was a positive plague of insects in town, and Mrs. Jackson said *Yes, yes, indeed there was,* and tittered shrilly. She couldn't keep her eyes from Mr. Johnson who, standing up and wildly dashing his glass back and forth in an effort to disperse the flies, spilled lemonade onto the cloth.

Mrs. Thrale felt a grudging sympathy for Mrs. Jackson, who was openly chewing on her nails. It was obvious she had not been prepared for an encounter with Mr. Johnson, and though her husband may have explained to her that she was to rub shoulders with a great lexicographer and poet, it was doubtful if he had thought to paint a true portrait. The reality of Johnson, in appearance and behaviour, the scarred skin of his cheeks and neck, his large lips forever champing, his shabby clothing and too small wig with its charred top-piece, his tics and mutterings, his propensity to behave as though no one else was present, was at variance with the elegant demeanour imagined to be proper to a man of genius.

It was left to Mrs. Thrale to direct the conversation during dinner. At the best of times her husband was a man of few words, and of none at all with a dish set in front of him. Nor could Johnson or Langton, beyond a monosyllable, be depended upon to make a contribution until the serious business of eating was got through. She looked to Arthur Murphy for support, he being a man of the theatre and fond of his own voice.

True to form, he launched amusingly enough into gossip concerning the Rev. Mr. Dodd and his scandalous affair with a woman who owned a pieshop in Frith Street. Mrs. Jackson screamed satisfactorily at each twist of the story. Dr. Fitzpatrick, at its conclusion, observed that Dodd would end badly, and would deserve as much.

"Not so, Sir," barked Johnson, but added nothing more.

To cover the sudden lull occasioned by this savage interjection, Mrs. Thrale asked Murphy if he was engaged in writing a new play. He replied he was not, which she already knew, but confided that only the night before he had finished reading an extraordinary comedy written by a young man living in a remote village near Dover.

"In what way extraordinary?" enquired Humphrey Jackson.

"Why," cried Murphy, "because he has never been to the city, is the son of a clergyman and by all accounts has led a sheltered life."

"There is humour enough to be found in the countryside," protested Dr. Fitzpatrick.

"And none more so than in this play," Murphy said, "for it is in seven acts and all the characters are slain in act three."

"Out of the ordinary indeed," agreed Jackson.

"Death by the sword, poison and strangulation," Murphy elaborated.

"How can that be?" asked Mrs. Jackson, baffled. "Who is left to speak the lines?"

"In the next four acts," Murphy said, "they appear as ghosts. The final mode of death is particularly horrid . . . by a heated prong thrust up the nostril to the brain."

"Enough," said Mrs. Thrale sharply, for the colour had drained from Mrs. Jackson's face and Mrs. Salusbury was sitting bolt upright, fork suspended in the air. Beyond the open windows pink clouds rolled through the blackening heavens.

Some minutes after nine o'clock, by which time David Garrick had arrived, the ladies went into the drawing room. The doors on to the grounds being flung wide and the lanthorns lit, the gentlemen gathered on the terrace to applaud Garrick's exuberant re-enactment of Mr. Quin's dilemma.

Mrs. Thrale noticed her mother was staring fixedly in the direction of the garden; her expression was watchful, as though she saw in the flickering night something other than shadows. Alarmed, she confided in Frances Reynolds. She said, "The brightness of her eyes when listening to Mr. Murphy disturbed me. Her own life has not been free of torment, my dear father being wild to the point of cruelty."

Miss Reynolds replied that perhaps she stood too close for impartiality. "To my mind," she said, her eyes watching the moths that spun above the candle flames, "Mrs. Salusbury appeared more *drawn* than terrified."

Mrs. Thrale trusted Miss Reynolds, whose manner, though friendly, was always tinged with melancholy, like that of someone who had suffered a great deal. The blame lay with her brother, who was in the habit of making her the butt of his caustic wit. Johnson liked her too, though for different reasons, namely that she had shown kindness to Mrs. Williams, his poetical friend.

Just then, Mrs. Salusbury said loudly, "Hester, I am not deaf. I assure you it was not the prong up the nose that affected me, rather the talk of ghosts . . ."

"Such things are mere superstition," cried Mrs. Thrale.

"No less a person than Mr. Johnson thought otherwise," retorted Mrs. Salusbury. "He was gullible enough to investigate the Cock Lane Ghost." She was referring to the unquiet spirit of one Fanny Lynes, who, some years before, had supposedly manifested itself to an eleven-year-old girl residing in Smithfield.

"It's true he investigated," Frances Reynolds protested, "for his mind is always open, but it was at the insistence of the Rector of Clerkenwell."

"He could have refused," countered Mrs. Salusbury.

"It is not in his nature to stand aside," Miss Reynolds said. "A curious mind must always be in search of the truth. Besides, he found the scratchings and knockings heard by the child could only have been made by herself."

"I heard no scratchings or knockings," said Mrs. Salusbury. "My ghost rose out of the lake, naked save for a shimmer of light that near blinded me."

Neither Hester nor Miss Reynolds heard her, for just then the gentlemen came in, Mr. Garrick riding on Bennet Langton's back. In the ensuing uproar, Mrs. Salusbury, unlamented, retired to her bed.

Towards midnight games were played, a favourite one being the choosing of a colour that might best express the character of each of those present. Miss Reynolds knew it to be a cruel entertainment, and steeled herself.

Mrs. Jackson was pronounced scarlet by her husband and pink by Henry Thrale, who, in sentimental mood, trapped her hand in his and now and then leaned his head on her shoulder. Mr. Johnson, by common consent, was dubbed purple, of the darkest hue, until Mrs. Jackson changed her mind and bravely declared him brown. "Of the lighter shade," she said, "like curled autumn leaves or the spots on speckled eggs." Johnson was so taken by this that he came and stood extremely close to her and fingered the stuff of her gown.

Thrale chose yellow-green as most befitting his wife, a shade vigorously disputed by Johnson, who held it to be sickly.

Next, they played the fool as to what plant or flower each most resembled. Mr. Thrale named Mrs. Jackson as an orchid of the rarest sort and Hester a dog rose. Mrs. Jackson was both flattered and disturbed by the comparison; she had no wish to cause discord between husband and wife. Blinking the powder from her eyes—in studying her dress Johnson had twice jolted her hairpiece—she stole a misty glance at Mrs. Thrale and was astonished to see she was smiling. Either she is deaf, thought Mrs. Jackson, or else saintly.

"Samuel is a nettle," Murphy said, "and Hetty a sprig of myrtle," inspiring Johnson to add gallantly, ". . . which the more it is crushed the more it discloses its sweetness."

Later still, by which hour Henry Thrale had slid under the cloth with a saucer of ices melting on his chest, Mr. Johnson announced that earlier that afternoon he had come across two items of small significance caught in the rushes of the lake. He and Davy Garrick would mime what he had found and the company would be allowed two questions each to guess what they might be. Accordingly, Garrick, hand on hip, minced up and down the room, waving his hand back and forth. At his side, on all fours, pranced Johnson, kicking up his heels, his wig falling over his eyes.

Observing him, Langton shouted, "Richard III . . . deformed, unfinished, sent before his time."

"That is a description, not a question," opposed Johnson.

"Is it Mrs. Ford attempting to be rid of Quin's breath?" asked Mrs. Thrale.

"It's that woman in Cheapside," cried Miss Reynolds, "the poor soul who set fire to the orphanage and danced among the flames."

"Wrong, wrong," sang Garrick, peeping at her through spread fingers and fluttering his eyelashes; all the same, he stood on his toes and pirouetted.

No correct answer being forthcoming, and Johnson finally collapsing onto his back, legs, beetle-fashion, feebly waving, the fan and the button were produced and passed from hand to hand. Mrs. Thrale argued that in mentioning Mrs. Ford she had been almost right, but Garrick said he couldn't allow it, at which moment Henry Thrale, emerging from beneath the table and staggering upright, demanded to see the button. First he examined it and then, striding to the open doors, flung it out into the darkness. Of a sudden, he jerked backwards; a gust of wind swept in from the terrace and sent the shadows racing. Mrs. Jackson clutched at her husband, mouth open in a silent shriek of alarm.

When Thrale turned back to the room he was rubbing the palm of one hand violently up and down his coat as though to relieve some irritation. All were startled at how diminished he appeared; a long shadow cast by the candlelight hollowed his cheeks and turned him old.

Garrick and Dr. Fitzpatrick helped him to a chair and a glass of brandy was fetched. Restored, though constantly scrubbing his hand across his knee, he attempted to explain, in his usual stilted manner, what troubled him.

A hundred years before, he told them, a young woman had been seduced by one George Farthingale . . . the heir to a fortune . . . and then abandoned. "She had a little dog . . . followed her everywhere. Weeks passed . . . young woman vanished. Little dog found trotting up and down beside the lake holding fan in its jaws."

"Bow-wow," barked Garrick, and hopped about, hands held up like paws.

"Rich man come to his senses," continued Thrale, "returned only to learn that the woman had drowned herself. Full of remorse . . . had buttons made for his coat with the image of the dog upon them. No sooner stitched to the cloth . . ."

Here Garrick, who, in lightning fashion had transformed himself from leaping dog to floating body, features first distorted in agony and then smiling beatifically, sprang upright from the carpet and began to thread an invisible needle with imaginary thread.

"... than the man ... in period of weeks ... sickened and died."

"And I suppose, Sir," said Johnson, "that the dog, snatching the coat from the corpse and wearing it, flung itself into the lake."

"Of the dog ... nothing known," Thrale said.

Soon after, Johnson, looking sombre and placing his feet as though the ground was unsafe, walked out onto the terrace.

"Why did Mr. Garrick look so merry when drowning," whispered Mrs. Jackson to Miss Reynolds.

"Possibly out of perversity," Miss Reynolds replied tartly.

There is always something behind what they say, thought Mrs. Jackson, and quivered with excitement.

Presently Mrs. Thrale went in search of Johnson. He was standing at the far end of the terrace emitting strange hooting noises. At her approach he held up his hand for silence, head cocked to one side. Beyond the buzz of voices coming from the drawing room she heard nothing, and said so.

"Shhh!" he bade, and out of the darkness came the answering call of an owl. Beside himself with delight, Johnson clapped his hands and did a jig on the spot.

When he grew calmer, she asked, "What did you think of the tale of the button?"

"Why, I thought nothing of it," he said, "for there was nothing in it that would engage the thoughts of a *sensible* man."

"My master thought different," she snapped. "It has made him quite ill."

"His illness is caused by an over-burdening of the stomach," Johnson said.

"There is a distinct swelling on his palm where he held the button."

"A swelling no doubt caused by the sting of a drowsy wasp. It is that time of year. As for his fiction, there was no lake here thirty years ago, let alone a hundred. It was an excavation begun by your father-in-law and only recently completed by Henry."

"There is a pond in the field beyond," she said. "What difference does it make . . . lake or pond, this year or last?"

"Tolerance," he chided, "in regard to matters of truth, merely pardons the weakness in ourselves. If you excuse the folly, instead of condemning, you will begin to imitate it. Dear Mistress, one must always be on one's guard, for as the Spanish proverb observes, a clattering hoof signifies a nail gone."

"Pff!" she exclaimed. "There are nails enough in this world."

He touched her cheek with his finger, as though ready to impale an unspilled tear, and gazed at her so fondly and with such compassion that she trembled; in his large eyes leapt the reflection of the lanthorn flame. "It is of small comfort," he said, "but it should be remembered that misery is an affirmation of life." Cupping his mouth in his hands, he emitted a low and tremulous hoot.

Save for Bennet Langton and Miss Reynolds, the guests left Streatham Park a quarter after three o'clock. Before being helped into his coach Garrick took Johnson in an embrace. They swayed together on the gravel, the small man pressing his cheek against the big man's chest.

"Sam, Sam," Garrick moaned, and for once was lost for words.

"There, there, dear Davy," soothed Johnson, "God bless you," and he stood waving until the carriage had crunched from earshot.

The noise of wheels woke the child in the nursery; she cried out, but Old Nurse slept on.

When Johnson went up to his room he shut the curtains against the light that was already spreading above the fuzz of the trees. He lay down and almost immediately fell into a dream in which he and Davy walked home from school across the market square in Lichfield. A cabbage lay in the gutter, leaves splayed out like wings, and he kicked it clear across the cobbles and over the railings into the basement of the bookshop. Descending the steps he spied through the window a man, head in hands, sitting at a table untidy with papers. Rubbing at the glass he peered closer and knew it was his father. Behind him stood Dr. Swinfen, practising the violin. He rapped on the window to make Father glance up, and when he did so his eyes were those of a dead man. He ran back up the steps and told young Davy to go home; he didn't want the boy to see those eyes. And now, the whine of the violin grew louder, intensified in pitch until it resembled a long drawn-out scream.

He woke on the instant, gaze fixed on the shelf above the fireplace; the spines of his books were stained with blood. The cause of such a delusion, he told himself, springs from an inward morbid discontent. Turning towards the window he observed how the sun beat against the curtains.

A SHOCKING INCIDENT took place two days later, an hour before Johnson left for London. Mrs. Thrale was coming down the second flight of stairs when she saw Queeney standing on the landing with Belle at her side. Something in the child's strange rigidity of posture made her pause.

"Queeney," she called, but the girl stared past her, eyes popping, face darkening. In a flash Mrs. Thrale remembered just such a distortion on the face of a cooper's boy who had choked on a fish bone. Terrified, she ran forward and bending the child double smacked her violently about the head. Suddenly Queeney coughed, then spat, then screamed; the button that had caused Henry Thrale so much perturbation flew from her mouth and fell to the rug. Overcome, Mrs. Thrale sank to the floor and burst into tears. Still screaming, Queeney scrambled up the stairs, the dog snapping at her heels.

After some moments, anger replacing fear, Mrs. Thrale sought out Old Nurse and boxed her ears, at which Queeney, restored save for an attack of hiccoughs, rushed from a corner and kicked her mother on the ankle. "Wicked, wicked girl," wailed Mrs. Thrale, limping from the nursery.

She was sure Johnson must have heard the hullaboo and would be waiting anxiously in the hall, but found him instead in the breakfast room, his wig perched beside the butter dish. "Such a fright," she shouted. "My heart was in my mouth . . ."

"There is something I must tell you—" he said.

"If I had not been there . . . if I had not come down at that exact moment—"

"Of the utmost importance," he persisted. "It will not have gone unnoticed that I have not been myself these last few days."

"There are many things that pass unnoticed," she snapped. "Some of them considerably more important than others."

Pushing back his chair he told her it would be best if they spoke outside. The weather still uncommonly warm, she protested it would be less tiring if they stayed where they were; he shook his head peevishly. All at once she wanted him gone. He wore her out with his daily demands on her time, his nightly insistence that she sit up with him into the small hours, pouring his tea.

"You cannot begin to imagine what I have just endured," she said.

"A man indulges his imagination while it is pleasing," he replied, "till at length it overpowers his reason." Brushing the crumbs from his mouth he left the room. Was there ever such a man for weighty pronouncements, she wondered, and was obliged to follow him.

Once on the gravel path, he said, "There is something of mine in the bottom right-hand drawer of my desk which I wish you to take into your care . . . it is for your eyes alone. Nor do I wish you to refer to it on my return . . . or indeed at any other time . . . not unless I broach the subject."

"What is it?" she asked, but he only entreated her most solemnly to swear she would never divulge his secret, a secret which soon she would share.

"I give you my word," she said, perspiration darkening the armpits of her gown.

Seizing her hand he covered it with kisses, looking up at her all the time with such distress in his eyes that immediately she forgot how troublesome he was and remembered only in what affection she held him.

When at last he had gone—the groom was sent back twice, once for his wig, and again for the basket of peaches left in the porch—she went into his chamber. A wasp was burrowing into the flesh of an over-ripe fig on his pillow. On his desk lay a single sheet of paper festooned with orange peel.

With difficulty, for his handwriting was disordered, she read—*Madmen are all sensual in the lower stages of the distemper . . . but when they are very ill, pleasure is too weak for them and they seek pain.* Beneath this was a space and then a single line of Latin, scored through—*De pedicis et manicis insana cogitatio.*

Thrusting open the window—the departed occupant of the room held to the notion that fresh air belonged on the outside—she hurled the orange peel into the stifling day, then, half alerted to what she would find, pulled out the bottom drawer.

To Miss Laetitia Hawkins
2, Sion Row, Twickenham

Dec. 3rd, 1807

Dear Miss Hawkins,

I am at a loss to know how best to reply to your most recent letter without causing offence. Believe me, my dear Miss Hawkins, I have no wish to incur your displeasure, but it cannot be repeated too often that circumstances surrounding my early life were such that certain events cannot be recalled without grave disturbance of spirits.

For that reason alone I must pass over your first two queries, and supply but a sketchy account of Mrs. Salusbury's supposed sighting of a ghost in the vicinity of the lake at Streatham Park. She had, so I was told, fled into the Park after a disagreement with my mother, and was therefore understandably prone to fancies. Her emphasis on the halo of fire surrounding the apparition was later ascribed by Dr. Johnson to a trick of the light, the illusion being caused by the rays of the sun striking the amulet—given him by Queen Anne when he was touched for the scrofula—worn on a chain about his neck. That same night, woken by what I curiously took to be the sound of a violin, I crept down the stairs and was leapt upon by my mother. She, as I afterwards learnt, jealous of my father referring to one of his guests as an orchid of the rarest kind, underwent a storm of the brain and, accusing me of stealing a button from his coat, set about me most roughly.

As you rightly observe, my mother was indeed diligent in regard to the education of her children. The weight of such instruction fell most heavily on myself, my brother Harry being less compliant. I have come to believe that my studious disposition as a child arose not so much from natural curiosity but rather from a fear of the whip.

Dr. Johnson often remarked that endeavouring to make children prematurely wise was useless labour. Suppose, he said, that they have more knowledge at five or six years than others of that age? What use can be made of it?

In his own early years he read very hard, and held it was a sad reflection, but a true one, that he knew almost as much at the age of eighteen as he did at fifty. I fear he was right, for it does not seem that I have learnt anything new these last thirty years.

I have no very strong opinions on the character of David Garrick. As a child, the animation shown on his face, and its quick changes of expression, confused me. One was never sure as to his exact feelings. He could make one laugh, but tears were not far behind. I believe that on stage he was considered natural, simple, affecting; it was only when he was off that he was seen to be acting. It was also said that he hated lending Dr. Johnson a book, for it was always returned in an unreadable condition, the pages turned down and the print discoloured from the juice of oranges. That he continued in the lending of them says much for his generosity of spirit.

I am sorry to hear of the death of your aunt. Generations, my dear Miss Hawkins, are but like leaves, and we now see the faded leaves falling about us.

I am obliged for your felicitations concerning my forthcoming marriage to Admiral Lord Keith, and remain, for one month more,

Yours Sincerely,

H. M. Thrale

I believe I do remember Mr. Goldsmith showing me how to play Jack and Jill with two bits of paper stuck to his fingers. Alas, I never liked him, his posturing being so extreme.

SWEETING

n.f. (from Sweet)

1. A sweet luscious apple.
2. A word of endearment.

Trip no further pretty sweeting;
Journies end in lovers meeting.

—SHAKESPEARE'S *Twelfth Night*

THE CHILD RAN out into the Gardens beyond the stables and, fleeing some way towards the mud banks of the river, whirled round with such vigour that her bonnet flew off. Cross, she wanted to put the world in a spin; if she twirled fast enough she might be rid of the image of her mother, spoon digging into a breakfast egg, the scar, caused by a fall from a horse, reddening above her top lip. When Mamma was in a temper the mark became prominent; sad, it whitened.

For two weeks their departure to Streatham had been delayed. Mamma had promised they would leave at the beginning of June, but only that morning she had announced it was out of the question on account of Sophia having sprouted a boil on her neck.

"It needs to be lanced," she'd said, belly bulging against the table, tongue flickering out to lick the egg yolk from her chin.

"I'm advised it would be foolish to undertake a journey, however short."

"Then I advise you to leave Sophia behind," Queeney had retorted, "you have abandoned me often enough," and jumping up from her chair she fled the room. She knew she was in the wrong but it was hard to be polite when Mother thought so little of keeping her word.

For a full month the atmosphere within the house had been discordant. Mamma spent most of her time closeted in the counting offices with Perkins, the chief clerk, or else sitting at her writing desk scribbling notes to Mr. Johnson, who was away in Ashbourne staying with Dr. Taylor. Not an hour passed without Mamma commenting on how sorely he was missed. She didn't miss Papa, who hardly ever came home, not even for church on Sundays. New Nurse said he was too busy playing cards and living the gay life.

Outside, though the air still hung heavy with the sour-sweet odour of fermenting grain, the thunderings and clatterings of the yard had stopped, and now, where once a dense head of steam had billowed to the city skies, only a thin scribble of vapour rose from the giant coppers of the Brewhouse. Even Papa's barges had ceased to move with the tide; empty of merchandise they sat idle upon the black jelly of the Thames.

Dizzy from spinning, Queeney sank to her knees and tugged pettishly at the grass. She did not care for Southwark; there were few trees to climb and the kitten Grandmamma had given her had chewed off its blue ribbon and turned into a wild cat who now stalked the barley stacks in pursuit of rats. There was no one to play with, not of her own age and interests, and the Italian teacher, Mr. Baretti, whom Mr. Johnson had found for her, had not yet begun to give her lessons. Mr. Baretti had a gruesome past—he'd been had up for murder by a stabbing with a fruit knife after undergoing the provocation of having his testicles

tweaked, and had only cheated the hangman through the inter-
cession of Mr. Johnson and his friends.

Curious as to what it would be like to be hanged, she put her
hands about her throat and squeezed as hard as she was able. It
had little effect, for her chest continued to rise and fall.

Soon, she knew, someone would come in search of her.
Found, she would be lectured on insolence, then kissed, then,
like as not, slapped. Mamma was contrary in all things.
Sometimes Mr. Johnson held it was because she had so many
things to worry about, at others that she had not enough to
occupy her. Once, during some disagreement over the correct
treatment for Lucy's ears, he'd likened her to a rattlesnake—
because she hissed so. When I am grown, the child thought, I
shall coo like a dove.

Presently, engaged in making little nests out of grass, she
heard Muggeridge calling her.

She had been christened Hester, after Mamma, but was
always known as Queeney. Mr. Johnson, her teacher, often
addressed her by another name, one which showed his tender
esteem—she was his Sweeting. He'd told her it was an old
endearment, one first used when she was but an infant on the
crawl.

"How?" she had asked, for the past mattered to her. "Where
. . . at what time?"

"On the stairs at Southwark," he replied. "As a sunbeam
pierced the window."

"Did I understand?" she had wanted to know.

"But, of course, Miss," he said. "You winked."

He liked her better than her three sisters, of that she was sure.
Lucy was quite ugly and cried incessantly from a discharge of
both ears, Susannah was clumsy, and Sophia, in spite of her boil,
too young to be of interest. As for little brother Harry, why, he
was in fear of Mr. Johnson because of the noises he made when

deep in thought. Mamma had assured him that such whistles and groans were common to men of intellect, but he had nightmares in which Mr. Johnson, hooting like an owl, pursued him down a dark tunnel. Besides, everyone knew it was Harry who, leaping downstairs too boisterously and colliding with Grandmamma, had bumped her into the cancer.

"Miss Queeney," Muggeridge shouted again. He had been employed at the Brewery in her grandfather's day. When young he had worked in the Millhouse as a grinder of husks; now old, his nose blue and corrugated, he emptied chamber-pots, trimmed candles and trailed children.

At his approach—he was dangling her bonnet by its strings— Queeney cried out imperiously, "Go away, I shall come back in my own good time." Then, watching his shambling retreat, she remembered Mr. Johnson's observation that no one lowly or lacking in education was ever treated with disrespect *except* by the truly ignorant. Belatedly, she called out "Please." She wasted her breath, for his hearing had gone.

A half hour later, fully expecting chastisement, she returned to the house to be met by New Nurse, who said that if she would be a good, *silent* girl the Mistress was prepared to take her across the river to visit Mrs. Salusbury.

"I will be good," the child babbled. "Very, very good and very, very quiet."

The rosy prospect of time spent with Mamma free of the younger siblings scratching round her like chicks about a hen filled her with such joy that she stood perfectly still and uttered scarcely a squawk while New Nurse wrenched the tangles from her hair.

IT WAS RAINING when they drove out of the gates of the Brewery. Such were the potholes in the road on the approach to

Pitt Bridge that by the time the Toll House was reached the windows of the coach were splattered with mud. Nothing could be seen through the pock-marked glass save for a glimpse of grey river beneath a rind of weeping sky.

Aware that earlier in the day there had been a falling out between Queeney and herself—though for the life of her she couldn't recall the precise cause—Mrs. Thrale endeavoured to engage her in conversation.

"Mr. Johnson," she said, "is thinking of buying you a cabinet in which to store curiosities, such as animal bones and shards of pottery. There is a monkey's paw, mounted on a base of silver . . ." Here, noticing Queeney's hand peculiarly clamped over her mouth, she anxiously inquired if the girl was afflicted with the toothache. Queeney shook her head but kept her hand in place.

"Grandmamma has the paw in safe keeping," Mrs. Thrale continued, "and does not care for it. It would look well in a collection . . . Mr. Hogarth gave it me . . . for sitting still while he painted my portrait."

She was met with silence, and tried again, this time seeking a considered estimation of young Harry's intelligence. Queeney's opinion, in spite of her tender years, was not without weight. Why, when she was but six summers in age, having been tested on the works of Dryden and Pope, no less an authority than the headmaster of Abington Grammar School had acknowledged that if the examination had been conducted in Latin she would have qualified for a degree from the University of Oxford.

"To my mind," Mrs. Thrale prattled on, "Harry lacks concentration. His pursuit of knowledge takes second place to his sword fights with the stable boys. You," she flattered, tapping her daughter's knee, "veered towards books from infancy . . . though it must be admitted you sometimes tore at the pages."

Still Queeney uttered not a word. Mrs. Thrale's heart fairly thundered in her breast. Heaven help me, she thought, I am intimidated by my own child.

She said, "It's as well we are not at Streatham Park. I am informed that the dust rising from the building of Papa's library would silt up one's lungs. The feathers of my bantams are turned grey and the goat is heard sneezing."

Eyes like winter glass, Queeney stared straight ahead.

Losing patience, Mrs. Thrale tugged away the hand covering the girl's mouth, and, after administering a spiteful squeeze to the fingers, kept silent for the remainder of the journey.

Their progress to Dean Street was hampered by the number of troops patrolling the streets in response to an alleged Jacobite plot involving the bishop of Rochester. Twice, the carriage was halted, once by a fresh-faced upholder of law and order—his mouth was damson-coloured and his manner offensive—and next by a ruffian with a patch over his eye. Of the two, Mrs. Thrale was inclined to think the latter more human, for, pulling open the carriage door and observing Queeney, hand yet again guarding her mouth, one-eye had promptly stepped back and ordered the coach to roll on.

Mrs. Salusbury's house had a front garden surrounded by paling. The border flowers, foxgloves and the like, were sadly neglected, and cow parsley ran riot. In the window boxes, primroses wilted.

Entering, Mrs. Thrale found her mother lying on a couch in the downstairs room, the dog, Belle, enthroned on a silk cushion, curled across her feet.

Mrs. Salusbury claimed that though poorly she was not in pain. "It is one of my good days," she asserted, albeit in a weary tone of voice.

Distressed, Mrs. Thrale pulled the bell for the housekeeper. The room was cold due to the fire having sunk to embers. When her summons was answered she ordered the scuttle to be filled with coals and that a basin of warm water be fetched; the corners of Mrs. Salusbury's lips were encrusted with spittle.

Queeney stood at the window, face pressed into the curtain. Last year Old Nurse had given up the ghost, along with Hawkins, the under-gardener, and a kitchen maid who had purged herself too strenuously in an effort to do away with an unwanted child.

Mamma had taken her to see Old Nurse in her wait to be transported to the grave, lying in her burial shroud in high summer on a trestle table in the store room at Streatham Park, a bluebottle spiralling above the black wart on her chin. Breath stopped, Old Nurse was but an empty vessel, cracked in places like the broken vase that nudged the scant hair on her shrunken skull. Past mending, Mamma had murmured, though she was referring to the pot rather than Old Nurse.

"Kiss Grandmamma," Mrs. Thrale urged. Reluctantly, the child approached and pecked the air above the sick woman's cheek; then, falling to her knees and seizing the dog in her arms, she smothered its snout in kisses. Belle smelled sweeter than Grandmamma, whose odour was that of death.

There followed a conversation between the two women concerning bank loans and chemical liquids. According to Mrs. Thrale, Mr. Perkins had behaved in a most exemplary manner, instructing the men to stop work until matters were taken out of Mr. Thrale's hands entirely. It was Mr. Johnson's considered opinion that but for Perkins's prompt grasp of the situation they would all be facing ruin. Things were bad enough, but at least the ludicrous attempt to brew beer without the addition of either malt or hops had been brought to a halt.

"Such a foolish enterprise," sighed Mrs. Salusbury. "One wonders what possessed Mr. Thrale to go along with such a notion."

"Perkins has also insisted on the immediate sale of the land in East Smithfield purchased for the benefit of that wretch Humphrey Jackson and his costly experiments—"

"I never cared for him," Mrs. Salusbury said. "His wife was an exceedingly vacuous woman."

"Indeed she was," agreed Mrs. Thrale. "Had Perkins or I been consulted we would have argued from the start that the preserving of bottoms by such means was doomed to failure . . ."

She was interrupted by Queeney, overcome by giggles. Exasperated, yet pleased the child was in a less sullen mood, she said: "The bottoms I am referring to, Miss, are those of ships attacked by worm . . . and it is scarcely a laughing matter, for the scheme has brought your deluded father to the edge of bankruptcy."

Still Queeney snorted.

"I would have thought," her mother said, "that you, more than most, would not find worms a fit subject for mirth."

Mortified at the mention of her affliction, the child turned scarlet. Dr. Sutton held she got too close to animals and that she should not let the goat eat from her hand or the cat lap from her cup, but what did he know? Whenever Mamma caught her squirming on her chair she dosed her with senna, which only succeeded in giving her an unpleasant taste in the mouth and a looseness of the bowel. When I am grown, she thought, I shall see-saw as much as I like.

At that moment there came a knocking at the street door, and shortly Miss Reynolds was shown in. Amid the exclamations of surprise and delight, the kissing and exchanging of compliments—a trifle forced on Mrs. Thrale's part, owing to the food stains on her mother's gown and the dull aspect of the furniture—no one noticed Queeney sidling into the hall.

Miss Reynolds was in some agitation, her carriage having being surrounded by a mob on its way to the Tower of London to protest against the arrest of George Kelly. Did Mrs. Thrale know Mr. Kelly, secretary to the unfortunate bishop of Rochester? He was a popular man afflicted with a frightful irritation of the skin . . . talking to him was unnerving because of his constant scratching. The cuffs of his shirt were often speckled with blood. She had met him when he had accompanied the bishop to her brother's studio in Leicester Fields. Joshua had abandoned the sittings because he too had begun to suffer from an itch and feared for his hands.

"My coach was stopped too," said Mrs. Thrale. "Fortunately the presence of Queeney secured our safe passage."

Mrs. Salusbury falling into a doze, Miss Reynolds confided it was her third visit to the house in as many days. As she informed Mrs. Thrale, with much hesitation and alteration of words, she had grown alarmed . . . worried . . . by the behaviour . . . attitude of the housekeeper, Mrs. Mountjoy . . . and the signs of neglect . . . lack of care . . . shown to Mrs. Salusbury.

"I see it, I see it," moaned Mrs. Thrale, pounding the back of the sofa on which her mother lay and watching the rise and fall of the dust.

Eyeing Mrs. Thrale's monstrous belly, the well-meaning Miss Reynolds assured her she was in no way to blame. "What with the problems of the Brewery," she murmured, "and your present condition . . ."

"There is nothing of more importance than the happiness of my mother," cried Mrs. Thrale. "It is my intention to take her to Streatham as soon as the business with the bank is settled. Please be so good as to sit with her while I speak my mind to Mrs. Mountjoy."

She had no sooner quit the room than Mrs. Salusbury woke; struggling into a sitting position, she said, "Hester means it kindly, but Mrs. Mountjoy and I understand one another. We are both past the age at which the shine on a table can bring ease to an ailing body."

How right she is, thought Miss Reynolds. The pain of existence could not be removed with a dusting-cloth.

HAVING LET HERSELF out into the street, Queeney had no clear idea of where she wanted to go, save it should be as far away as possible from Mamma, who had so cruelly taunted her on the subject of worms. Though the rain had stopped the thoroughfare was pitted with puddles and in no time at all the yellow fabric of her shoes had turned the colour of mustard.

She had been to Dean Street many times, but not for some months and was astonished at the number of old houses half pulled down and new ones half built up. There were ladders everywhere, and carts full of bricks, and on what had once been the pampered grass of the bowling green a boy was selling flat-fish from a stall anchored in mud. At No. 29, the branches of the mulberry tree, snapped by a fallen scaffold, hung in dripping rags. As for the windows of Sir James Thornhill's elegant house, why, they were quite clouded over, and, peer as she might, the parrot with the blue legs was no longer visible on its perch behind the glass.

Mamma had taken her to visit Lady Thornhill one morning in summer. She remembered the occasion because Papa, some days before, had given her an amber necklace, the very same which now lay upon the black lace mantle she wore about her shoulders.

When shown into Lady Thornhill's drawing room the parrot had rocked along its perch and squawked out she was a pretty girl. It had been caught in a jungle place in Brazil by a traveller paid to fetch exotic creatures for John Hunter, the medical man who, curious as to what constituted life, was forever anatomising them into death. Even he had admired the fiery plumage of the bird and, laying aside his dissecting knife, allowed Sir James to buy it from him.

Other visitors had tried to get the parrot to talk, but it had only opened its beak for Queeney. This, she reasoned, was on account of her not joining in the general pestering; she herself grew stubborn when put on show. Mamma, of course, had swelled with pride at its croaking declaration of regard, which only proved how ignorant she was, seeing Mr. Johnson held that birds saw only colours, not faces.

She was crossing Compton Lane when the rain fell once more. Had she not been wearing her straw bonnet with the scarlet ribbons she would have retraced her steps and returned to Dean Street; the bonnet was new and Mamma would be displeased if it grew sodden. Sighting the arched doorway of St. Anne's, she hurried to find shelter.

The interior of the church was dark, owing to brick dust powdering the windows. A dozen candles did little to disperse the gloom and at first Queeney thought she was alone. She didn't venture in too far, both on account of the darkness and because often such places gave shelter to poor people stricken with disease who had nowhere else to go. Once, taken by Papa to St. George's Church, she had witnessed an old man, crazy with the fever, attempting to climb onto the marble lap of a sea captain swooning in the arms of an angel. Too weak to reach his goal, he had slid off and hit his head on the stone step below. Papa said the old man would be taken to a hospital and made well, but she had seen how motionless he lay, chest no longer rising beneath his tattered shirt, and that pool of blood, cherry-red, spreading between the angel's toes.

When she had confided the happening to Mr. Johnson, enquiring whether it was not wrong of Papa to tell untruths, he said he had come, late in years and against former prejudices, to believe that it was a father's duty to shield his children from the horrors of life. Man, he told her, keeps the prospect of death forever in his thoughts, but is comforted by the hope of some future state. In this he differs from the brute, for whom hope is absent and who endeavours to avoid death instinctively, without ever knowing what it really is. "Without a knowledge of hope," he concluded mysteriously, "sorrow is unknown. Papa did right to protect you, for the miseries of existence will crowd upon you soon enough." After which dismal lecture, dashing his sleeve against the water that threatened to spill from his eyes, he had challenged Harry to a barefoot race across the grass.

She had taken scant notice of his words, it being her experience that even when the sun was a golden orb in the heavens and birdsong girdled the Park, old people took a bleak and melancholy view of the world.

Becoming accustomed to the dim light, she became aware of a figure seated further down the nave, crouched small and still. Dead, she thought, struck down by Providence, at which moment it rose upright and stepping from the pew, skipped with outspread arms towards the altar. She took the figure to be that of a boy, for its hair was cropped, but when it spun round at the rail and began a jigging return she saw it was a girl, not above ten years of age, her face round as the moon and vacant of expression. One eye was set lower than the other, and as she advanced up the aisle her open mouth emitted gurgling noises, as though she sucked from a cup that could never be emptied.

Queeney wanted to run yet her legs refused to obey; nor could she avert her gaze from that lopsided countenance. She knew it was ignorant to stare so, but something within her had locked fast and her head wouldn't shift. I am a pillar of salt, she thought, a pillar of marble . . . and now she and the idiot were level. From somewhere outside she heard the sound of hammer blows, and at that instant the amber necklace was plucked from her throat. Clutched in that fierce grip the circlet came away entire, then, as the creature put its fist to its mouth as though ready to munch on an apple, the string broke; beads popped from those clenched fingers and bounced like pips upon the stone flags of the porch.

For what seemed an age, heart pounding, Queeney waited in the shadow of the church door. Her fright was occasioned by what Mamma would say when her absence was discovered rather than by her encounter with the lunatic. She made no attempt to pick up the scattered remains of the necklace, and instead thought frantically of how best she might deflect her mother's anger. Perhaps she could relate, in a dull voice—as though her wits had gone—how, driven from the house by Grandmamma's sickly aspect, she had crossed the street to wave to her friend the parrot . . . just as the mob had surged round the corner. Distracted, she had fled in the opposite direction. If she kept her face free of expression, similar to that of the idiot dancing through the church, surely Mamma would quite pass over the matter of the lost necklace and instead spill tears of joy at her safe return.

Full of resolve and practising in her head the persuasive words she would employ, Queeney hurried back to Dean Street, and was standing on tiptoe reaching for Mrs. Salusbury's rapper when the door opened and Mrs. Thrale, noticeably animated, swept out.

"Make haste," she ordered. "Miss Reynolds tells me Mr. Johnson returned last night from Ashbourne." Propelling her daughter before her, she leapt with such vigour down the path that her skirt beheaded a foxglove lolling beside the wicker gate.

MR. JOHNSON LIVED in Johnson's Court, off Fleet Street, but a short distance from the house in Gough Square in which he had laboured over his *Dictionary*.

Mrs. Desmoulins opened the door to Mrs. Thrale, and kept

her on the step. She said Mr. Johnson was away again, at which moment Mrs. Williams, recognising the voice, cried out that Mrs. Thrale was most welcome and ushered her into the hall. Mr. Johnson was indeed not at home, having gone to his bookseller, but he would be back within the hour; Mr. Goldsmith and Sir John Hawkins were already waiting on him in the parlour. Smirking, Queeney trailed behind her mother.

Mrs. Thrale tolerated John Hawkins and thought Oliver Goldsmith clever and absurd by turns. Hawkins was dry and reserved, Goldsmith showy. Both men inhabited the room according to their character, the former remaining rigidly upright, stiff as the sofa he perched upon, the latter posturing at the fireplace, breeches strained across his nether parts.

It was in Mrs. Thrale's nature to put a company at ease, for she could not abide an atmosphere. Within minutes she had softened John Hawkins by kissing him on both cheeks and assuring him of the delight felt by his friends at the recent knighthood conferred upon him by the King. She was not being false; though a bore, Hawkins was an honest magistrate and a musical man to boot. As for Goldsmith, she coaxed him out of his affectations by appealing to his droll sense of humour. In no time, all three laughed a great deal and imagined themselves the best of friends.

Mrs. Desmoulins, seated in a corner of the room and saddled with the child, could not take her eyes from Mrs. Thrale. The woman's wit and intelligence, so often remarked upon by Mr. Johnson, was not strikingly evident, for her conversation consisted entirely of gossip. Speaking of Joshua Reynolds, whose unfortunate sister she said she had been with earlier that morning, she brought up the perishable nature of the colours it was rumoured the artist used, and quoted an epigram told her by Arthur Murphy.

The art of painting was at first designed
To bring the dead, our ancestors, to mind,
But this same painter has reversed the plan
And made the portrait die before the man.

The gentlemen applauded, which Mrs. Desmoulins considered cruel, seeing both had been the recipients of Mr. Reynolds's famed hospitality. Nor did she think Mrs. Thrale good-looking, her complexion being far from clear, her eyelashes sparse and her upper lip adorned with a scar. And yet . . . and yet, there was no denying she possessed a certain winning intensity of manner capable of seducing the onlooker. Sir John and Mr. Goldsmith, wearing foolish smiles, could fairly be described as spellbound. Mrs. Desmoulins felt her own mouth curving upwards, and despised herself for it.

Soon Mrs. Williams ushered in Frank Barber carrying the tea urn. Queeney didn't care for Mrs. Williams, who, dressed in a scarlet gown fashionable in a previous age and wearing a lace cap showing two stiffened wings of hair at the temples, appeared old and pale and shrunken. It wasn't nice being stared at by someone who couldn't see; it made Queeney feel as though she herself had disappeared.

She had never encountered Frank Barber before, though she knew he was servant to Mr. Johnson. He had come on errands to Southwark many times, but always at night, which made him difficult to be seen from the nursery window. As a child, at Mr. Johnson's expense, he had been educated at a school in Bishops Stortford. He hadn't proved to be clever, but Mr. Johnson loved him all the same. When he let go of the tray she saw the palms of his hands were the colour of her damp shoes.

Just as Barber was leaving the room, a fearful scream rang out from below stairs. Sir John, guiding Mrs. Williams to a chair, jerked in alarm. "It signifies nothing," Mrs. Williams said. "It is only Poll Carmichael." She gave no further explanation and commenced to pour out the tea, the tip of her little finger dipping into each dish to ascertain the level of the liquid.

Mrs. Desmoulins made an effort to be cordial to the child, Queeney, whom Mr. Johnson spoke of as a prodigy. The little Miss was very much the offspring of her mother, being both plain and mightily assured in spite of her limp bonnet with its bedraggled ribbons. When addressed she responded politely enough, but her eyes were mocking. On being asked if she had enjoyed her visit to town, she said, "Very much, thank you. Grandmamma is soon to die, but I am prepared for it."

Presently Mr. Johnson returned. He came in clutching a twist of bloodstained newspaper. On Mr. Goldsmith observing it was a strange parcel to bring back from a bookseller, he said his errand had been concerned with victuals for his cat; he did not wish Frank Barber to demean himself scurrying about on behalf of a quadruped. Mrs. Williams, chin in the air as though scenting smoke, told Mrs. Desmoulins to take the entrails down to the scullery.

Mr. Johnson fussed over Queeney, patting her hand and expressing the hope he found her well before turning to his other guests. He embraced first Goldsmith, then Hawkins, after which, without looking directly at her, he bowed to Mrs. Thrale. Queeney, watching her mother, noticed how pale she became and how she played with her gloves, first crumpling the fingers, then smoothing.

Mr. Johnson's conversation had to do with the hospitality he had enjoyed at Dr. Taylor's, who had once been his school-fellow at Lichfield. Dr. Taylor had deer in his paddock, pheasants in his menagerie, the largest horned cattle in England and possibly the biggest bull in the world.

"He is, by all accounts, a man of eccentric habits," Sir John said. "Proceedings in Chancery found his moral character not entirely consistent with his profession."

"Pff!" Johnson snorted. "I take him as I find him, and like what I find, though it is true, Sir, that he and I disagree on most subjects."

"How can that be?" asked Goldsmith. "One cannot form a true friendship with someone who has likings and aversions dissimilar to one's own."

"It would be difficult—" began Mrs. Thrale.

"Why, Sir, it is simple," scoffed Johnson. "You must shun the subject on which you disagree. For instance, I can mix well enough with Burke . . ."

"He is indeed an extraordinary man," put in Mrs. Thrale, and was again cut short.

". . . for I love his knowledge, his genius, his diffusion of conversation, but I would not talk to him of the Rockingham party."

"When people disagree on matters not to be mentioned," argued Goldsmith, "they will surely arrive at that situation in the story of Bluebeard, *You may look into all the chambers but one.*"

"I am not saying that *you* could live in friendship with a man from whom you differ as to some point," shouted Johnson, "I am only saying that *I* could do it."

"Will anyone take more tea?" asked Mrs. Williams, and received no reply, not even from Mr. Johnson who had been known to drink fourteen cups at a sitting.

After some moments of silence, Mrs. Thrale remarked, "Your stay with Dr. Taylor does not seem to have rested you, Sir."

"Madame," he retorted, "it was not rest I sought, simply diversion, and was not disappointed. Dr. Taylor's generosity far exceeds that of *any one* I know."

Queeney was startled at this implied criticism, and even more surprised at its effect on her mother. Far from appearing crushed at such rudeness, she ceased fiddling with her gloves and gazed at him with the utmost composure, and now it was he who seemed unsure of himself; turning away, he gave a bellow of laughter, of the sardonic sort, and banged his fist repeatedly against his breast.

Before he departed, Goldsmith stuck two bits of paper onto his thumbs and waggled them about for the benefit of Queeney. She giggled her appreciation, but was not diverted, being of the opinion that a game of Jack and Jill was best suited to those still in the nursery. Also, she did not like sitting next to a man whose parts bulged so obtrusively.

When the playwright had left, Sir John Hawkins said, "He is a great one for argument."

Mr. Johnson said, "Goldy talks so much merely lest one should forget he is of the company."

"For my part," countered Sir John, "I like well to hear him talk away carelessly."

"Why yes, Sir," Mr. Johnson agreed, "but he should not like to hear it himself."

When Sir John too had taken his leave, Mrs. Thrale pressed Mrs. Williams to take Queeney to seek out the cat. "She is very fond of cats," she enthused, "she has one in Southwark and three at Streatham Park."

"I prefer dogs to cats," Queeney said. "They are less independent and do not grow up so fast." She did not want to go off alone with old Mrs. Williams, who was possibly a witch, but she could tell Mamma wanted her out of the way. She had the curious conceit that there was no ceiling to the room, and above that no roof to the house, and that she sat beneath a sky whose whirling clouds constantly changed shape. Mr. Johnson stood at the fireplace, head swinging from side to side as though trying to clear his mind; Mamma was smiling. Neither spoke, yet thoughts passed between them. On the floor, like fairy footsteps, Mr. Goldsmith's bits of paper pointed to the door. Defeated, Queeney rose from her chair and reluctantly followed Mrs. Williams into the hall.

The stairs to the basement were narrow and twisted. Mrs. Williams descended the steps sideways, one hand stretched out, gown whispering as it brushed the wall. Mrs. Desmoulins was in the kitchen below, seated at a table opposite Frank Barber, who was scraping mud from a pair of boots, a lit candle at his elbow. In the fireplace corner an old man crouched coughing on a three-legged stool.

Mrs. Williams, smelling the burning wax, approached the table and blew out the candle. Mrs. Desmoulins pulled a rude face, but said nothing. The old man, now invisible, coughed again; the coals hissed as he spat out his phlegm.

"I have Miss Thrale with me," announced Mrs. Williams.

"So we saw," replied Mrs. Desmoulins, "until you dropped us into the dark."

"We are looking for the cat," Mrs. Williams said.

"My mamma wished me to see it," said Queeney, disconcerted by the shouts and hysterical laughter coming from the scullery beyond. "Then Mamma must be obeyed," murmured Mrs. Desmoulins, a note of sarcasm in her voice. All the same, Queeney liked her best, for she was the most ordinary, being neither blind nor black nor prone to spitting; she was relieved when Mrs. Desmoulins left the table to join in the hunt for the cat.

The animal was run to earth in the scullery, preening itself some yards distant from a young woman in considerable disarray who was dashing her head against the area door and wailing.

"Kitty, Kitty," called Mrs. Williams, sniffing the air, at which moment the young woman uttered a piercing scream, causing the cat to streak away down the passage.

"Poll," Mrs. Williams cried. "Behave yourself, we have company."

Poll took no notice; sticking out her tongue she again dashed her forehead against the door, and now the skin on her forehead split open and blood trickled down the side of her nose.

"What is wrong with her?" asked Queeney.

"Toothache," said Mrs. Williams tersely.

"Drink and men," contradicted Mrs. Desmoulins, eyes glittering.

Prodding Queeney in the back, Mrs. Williams propelled her from the room.

There are more ways than one of banishing bad memories, reasoned Queeney, fingering her throat in search of the amber necklace.

TWO DAYS BEFORE Queeney's birthday Mrs. Thrale was delivered of her eighth child. Though shut in the schoolroom Queeney heard her mother squealing on the floor above; the sounds were those of a sow caught by the hind leg. Bent over her Italian grammar, Queeney promised God she would be a patient girl forever if only Mamma wouldn't die. Mr. Baretti, noticing the child's pallor, sang very loudly a Corsican ballad about a milkmaid seduced by a goatherd.

At three o'clock Mr. Thrale came home, by which time the infant was two hours old. It was a girl, black in the face and unable to breathe properly, and it died before midnight. Mr. Baretti said it was not to be wondered at, given the worries Mrs. Thrale had been burdened with in the preceding months. "Your mother," he told Queeney, "has had the mending of the Brewery to contend with, the discharge from Lucy's ear and the nursing of your grandmother. You must endeavour to be thoughtful to her and not cause her agitation."

Queeney took notice of his words, for generally he was critical of Mrs. Thrale, thinking her too severe with her children and too frivolous in every other respect. Accordingly, when allowed to see Mamma, she had crept into the bedroom and kissed her most tenderly. Mamma smelt bad, but she stroked Queeney's cheek and murmured she loved her more than all the world. The dead infant, sprinkled with herbs, lay in its crib at the end of the bed, face covered with a muslin cloth. It was to have been christened Penelope, but would never hear its name.

For a full week afterwards Queeney was kind to her brother and sisters, even Susannah, who had crooked legs and an umbilical rupture which rendered her so irritable that she was known as Little Crab, though Papa on account of her pointy nose, called her Gilly from Gilhouter, the Cheshire word signifying an owl.

Mr. Johnson stayed away at Lichfield, mostly, so Mrs. Thrale said, because he reckoned she would be too weak to give him her full attention, but Mr. Baretti said he was working on a revised edition of his *Dictionary*. He did, however, dispatch Frank Barber to Streatham with the cabinet intended for the storing of curios which he had long promised his Sweeting.

It was a splendid piece of furniture comprising four large drawers within a door, topped by a smaller cabinet containing twelve compartments. Queeney had to stand on a chair to reach the upper cabinet; she filled two of the little drawers with shells gathered from the shore at Brighthelmstone. Mamma had not yet fetched the monkey's paw from Grandmamma's, but Papa gave her a tuft of hair believed to have belonged to Mr. Pope, and Mrs. Williams sent a poem written without the help of Mr. Johnson.

Queeney didn't care for either the poem or the snip of hair, the former being all about a sunset and relying too much on the colour crimson, the latter having the appearance of being plucked from the rump of a squirrel. After some thought, she rummaged in New Nurse's workbasket and taking out a length of ribbon labelled it as belonging to *Frances Thrale, born September 1765, died October 6th, 1765*. Once, she had indeed had a sister of that name, but so long ago that she now qualified as a curiosity.

In November Mr. Johnson wrote Queeney a letter, in which he asked after the health of his pet hen and acquainted her with the death of Miss Porter's black cat. *So things come and go*, he mused. *Generations, as Homer says, are but like leaves, and you now see the faded leaves falling about you.*

When Mamma read the letter she said that Mr. Johnson was merely being civil. Guests, she said, frequently engaged in correspondence with the children of their hosts; it was a means of conveying gratitude without too explicit a show of subservience. Strenuous expressions of gratitude implied need, something which no gentleman cared to demonstrate. His letter, she explained, was therefore to be taken as addressed to herself, in appreciation of the care he enjoyed under her roof. He would not expect a reply, far less want to be troubled with the scribblings of a child.

Mrs. Thrale having gone up to town to discuss Brewery business with Perkins, Queeney approached Papa in his study and inquired if it was not impolite to ignore letters from Mr. Johnson. Papa, purple in the face, two bottles of port at his elbow, was slumped over the remains of a large turkey; she knew it was the trouble caused by the bank that made him so hungry.

"What do you wish to tell Samuel?" Papa asked.

"That I am sorry about Miss Porter's cat," she said. "And to ask for things for the cabinet."

"And why is Mamma against it?"

"On account of his being important."

"No more than the truth," Papa said, wiping the grease from his mouth.

"So I should not send it?"

"On the contrary," said Papa, "it could be that you are of equal importance . . . which Mamma knows," after which he smiled, though his eyes did not look merry. Telling her he would see to it that Mr. Johnson got her letter, he filled his glass with wine and gulped it down as though but recently returned from a desert; it was the trouble caused by the bank that made him so thirsty.

Two weeks later a second letter arrived for Queeney. Mamma was displeased at its contents, though she pretended otherwise. Mr. Johnson complained that Mrs. Thrale had used them both very sorrily when she'd hindered Queeney from writing to him. He wrote that when he came home they would all have good sport playing together and that none of them would cry, not even Lucy, and ended by declaring himself to be her most humble servant.

IN DECEMBER JOHNSON left Lichfield and came back to London. Though he dined at Southwark with Henry Thrale and sometimes stayed the night in his old rooms above the counting house, he was not encouraged to return to Streatham. On the few occasions Mrs. Thrale visited the Brewery she seemed pleased to see him yet did not suggest he should come home and he was too proud to ask. He had to be content with her letters, which told him that Mr. Baretti and Queeney were the best of friends and that the Italian lessons went forward with satisfaction to both sides. At first Queeney had been given vocabulary lists; nouns, verbs, adjectives, prepositions and articles, but so rapidly had she improved that her teacher had now embarked on a series of dialogues to do with imaginary discussions between the goats and hens in the barnyard. On Baretti's calling these dialogues "bubbles of air," Queeney, wicked child, had

promptly bested him and proclaimed them "empty bladders all."
The letter also told him that Lucy's ear was worse and that Mrs.
Salusbury was now so ill that she could no longer be left in
the house in Dean Street and must be cared for at Streatham
Park. He took this to mean that his presence would be an added
burden, and was envious of Baretti for so quickly assuming
importance.

His lot in London was not a cheerful one, for his frequent
absences from Johnson's Court had made him less tolerant of its
bickering residents; Mrs. Williams hated everybody, Levet
despised Mrs. Desmoulins and did not love Mrs. Williams; Poll
cared for no one and was a stupid slut besides. In such company,
as the weeks passed, his spirits sank and his temper worsened.
His one solace was Dr. Levet, who, detested by all three women,
sat with him while he took his breakfast. Neither bread nor tea
passed the gaunt doctor's lips, his stomach generally in a turmoil
after imbibing the liquid recompense he received for his nightly
ministrations to the wretched inhabitants of Hounsditch. He
was not required to stand out or to make conversation, his purpose being closer to that of an old and once useful piece of furniture, which, settled in a fixed position and gathering dust, had
become so familiar as to fade from vision.

Johnson's visitors, those who called at the prescribed hour,
did not find Levet so easy to ignore, his appearance giving every
indication of a man scorched by life. Indeed, as Mrs. Desmoulins
once acutely observed, he could have sat for the portrait of an
alchemist's apprentice, his complexion mottled as if he had
breathed in the fumes of the crucible, his clothes singed as
though exposed to the sparks of a furnace. For a medical man,
his rasping cough fell short of inspiring confidence; neverthe-
less, Johnson was fond of him. He was poor yet honest, which,
as Goldsmith reminded the perplexed members of the Club,
was recommendation enough for Samuel.

One particular mid-day, noting Johnson's gloomy countenance and listening to his oft-repeated sighs, Levet enquired if he was dissatisfied with the book he was perusing.

"I cannot tell," came the reply, "for I am unable to take in its meaning."

"I have heard that knowledge can sometimes be a source of unhappiness," Levet said. He was not often stirred into speech, but concern forced him to find words.

"That knowledge in some cases can produce unhappiness, I allow," said Johnson, "but upon the whole, knowledge *per se* is certainly an object which every man would wish to attain, although, perhaps, he may not take the trouble necessary for attaining it."

"Why cannot you take in the meaning?" persisted Levet.

"Enough, Sir," shouted Johnson, "let me be," and almost on the instant jumped up from the table and, patting Levet on the shoulder, apologised for speaking so roughly.

"Write to her," urged Levet. "Tell her it is important you return."

"You talk in riddles," bellowed Johnson, and glowered with such lasting severity that Levet fell silent, and shortly after went about his business.

For a further month Johnson waited for a summons from Hester Thrale. He spent his days in the company of Hawkins and Arthur Murphy, or else supped at the Mitre Tavern and did battle with Goldsmith and Bennet Langton. He was not feeling well and fretted over an infection in his good eye. Besides, he was enraged by a scandalous item in the newspaper on the tables of the Turk's Head which stated that an *eminent Brewer was very jealous of a certain Authour in Folio, and perceived a strong resemblance to him in his eldest son.* Not one of the members of the Club was reckless enough to comment on this slander, not even the tactless Goldsmith, but he boiled within. Three rainswept nights in succession he perambulated about the town with James Boswell and saw nothing in the crowded streets that did not provide proof of the misery and decadence of humanity.

On the fourth evening, dining with Boswell at the house of General Paoli, he became entangled in a discussion as to whether the state of marriage was natural to man. It was his opinion that it was not, and he expressed it with some force, declaring that of the two inducements to marriage, the one being love, the other money, the first was unwise and the second ignoble. The General then proposed that the union of a man and woman in a state of nature would be more conducive to happiness than one conducted in a civilised society, for it would be free of the restraints deemed necessary to hold it together. This foolish supposition so irritated him that he cried out, "A savage man and a savage woman would be so unrestrained, Sir, that when the man saw another woman that pleased him better he would leave the first forthwith."

He was aware of the glances exchanged between Boswell and the General, and fancied they took his outburst to mean that he had been dissatisfied with dear, dead Tetty. In speaking so fiercely it was Levet he had in mind, who, following a dusky courtship in a coal-hole in Fetter Lane, had shackled himself to a woman later arrested for the picking of pockets. Lacking neither patience nor inclination to set his listeners straight, and angry both with himself and them, he quit the table immediately.

In Fleet Street he was overtaken by a horse ridden at such speed and with such disregard for those in its path that he was forced to jump for safety. Unbidden, a memory surfaced of his wedding day and of the ride to the church with his bride. Tired of her controlling the pace, first trotting ahead, then lagging behind, he had booted his horse's flank and, galloping out of sight round a bend in the road, waited in the shade of an oak tree; a gnat had bitten him on the little finger of his left hand.

When Tetty caught up with him he had seen the shimmer of tears on her sun-dappled cheeks.

Pondering on the sensitivity of women he continued on his way, and soon the image of his wife receded, replaced by thoughts of Hester Thrale.

Arriving at Johnson's Court he stood for a while on the steps of his house, peering upwards at the smoke-filled heavens. At Streatham Park the night would be full of stars, bright as the shine in his dear mistress's eyes. How he longed to bask in the light of her smile.

A cat, not his, stalked the Court in pursuit of a rat, belly scraping the cobblestones. With a sudden surge of terror he remembered what he had once written for the final issue of the *Idler* on the subject of endings—*In every life there are pauses and interruptions . . . points of time where one course of action ends and another begins; and by vicissitude of fortune, or alteration of employment, by change of place or loss of friendship, we are forced to say of something,* this is the last.

Entering the dark house he climbed the stairs to his chamber, where, abandoning pride, he put pen to paper and begged Mrs. Thrale to receive him. He could not wait, he wrote, to be with his Dear Lady, and hoped to give her some little comfort and amusement. A sudden draught extinguished the candle on his desk. He took it for an omen and paced his room in torment.

Not for the first time, it weighed on him that his progress through life had been ill-directed, that he had disappointed himself more than others. Fame would not be heard beneath the tomb. His days and years had leaked away in common business and common amusements, and he had suffered his purposes to sleep until the time of action was past. When he compared what he had done, those articles, poems, that poorly received play which Davy Garrick had struggled to promote, his criticism of

Shakespeare, the compilation of his *Dictionary*, with what he had left undone, he felt the effect which must always follow the comparison of imagination with reality—contempt for idleness, disgust at lack of resolve.

He would leave behind him no evidence of his having been, nothing which could be added to the system of life, had glided from youth to age among a flattering crowd, without any effort for distinction.

Worse, he had disregarded his father's wishes, squandered his time at Oxford, ignored his brother's pleas for help, spent Tetty's money, failed to attend his mother's funeral, allowed his mind to be polluted by impure thoughts, doubted the existence of a life beyond the grave.

Even now, as he got to his knees in an attitude of prayer, his body betrayed him and he experienced a stirring of lust he was powerless to subdue. Excitement mounting, he conjured up a flurry of skirts, a bulge of thigh, the exclamation mark of a scar above a pouting lip. As he gave way to this compulsion, raised hands lowering to pleasure himself, he discerned that it was not so much madness that disordered him but rather the human condition. Man's spiritual self, he reasoned, panting, trailed far behind the physical.

Mrs. Thrale sent her coach for him the following week.

MRS. SALUSBURY, THOUGH weak, her breast horribly swollen and black in hue, insisted on coming downstairs every day, an unsteady descent she often accomplished without the help of the servants.

"I am not yet helpless," she told her daughter, who, considerably alarmed and stepping backwards, went before her with arms spread wide. Twice Mrs. Salusbury fainted, though fortunately on the lowest step, where she was caught in the embrace of Mr. Baretti.

Johnson was not present on these tottering occasions, being abed until noon. He was suffering from a persistent cough and the infection in his eye had grown worse. For some years past he had been reconciled to Mrs. Salusbury, indeed, had grown fond, yet he could not help regarding her as a rival now that the attentions of her daughter were so diverted from himself. Mrs. Thrale knew the best of him did not want to be a trouble, but his was a need not sufficiently seen to in childhood.

Nor were there others in the household who could distract him. Baretti had been charged with keeping the younger children out of the way of their dying grandmother, and Henry Thrale, the only man who held sway over Johnson, detesting sickness in women, had absconded to Southwark. Save for a brief visit from Frances Reynolds and a tedious one from a rustic pair of Streatham neighbours, company no longer came to the house. Johnson continued to instruct Queeney in Latin, but the pain of his eye shortened his temper and he grew weary of begging her pardon.

He took to following Mrs. Thrale from room to room, endeavouring to engage her in conversation. If she did not answer him immediately or her gaze wandered from his face, he showed his displeasure by stamping his foot. When she hid in her chamber and did not answer his peevish knocking, he paced the passage outside, muttering aloud between bouts of coughing.

One warm afternoon when she was resting in the drawing room—she was yet again expecting a child and her back ached—her mother dozing on the couch and Queeney reading at the table, Johnson entered on tiptoe, finger to his lips, and made an elaborate dumb-show of searching for a book left in the recess of the window. Unaware of the sleeping dog, he trod full upon it, at which Belle let out a hideous howl, causing Mrs. Salusbury to start up in terror. Exasperated beyond endurance, Mrs. Thrale cried out, "This will not do, Sir," and burst into noisy tears.

She sought him out some hours later and made her peace with him. He was seated at his desk separating orange peel into heaps. She had thought he would upbraid her but he was pathetically pleased to be forgiven and covered her hand with kisses. She was not sure she liked him abject, for his roughness of manner and strong convictions were the qualities she found exciting.

Having instructed a servant to bring up a bowl of warm water, she bathed Johnson's eye most tenderly. "It is not," she said, "that I hold you in less regard than formerly, merely that I am preoccupied with my Mother and Lucy. My mother I know I shall lose . . . I pray that Lucy will be saved."

At this, his tears ran so freely there was no need of salt. When he was able to speak, he said he had written her a letter which he wished her to read when she was alone. It was not for careless eyes, and was in French.

"Why French?" she asked.

"The sentiments in it," he said, "are best conveyed in another language."

She waited until Mrs. Salusbury fell asleep before reading it. It was true she was not alone, Queeney sitting on the opposite side of the bed holding her grandmother's hand, but she felt that neither the young girl nor the old woman could be categorised as careless.

Johnson's words were not easy to make sense of, his sight having become so impaired that his handwriting was jagged. He began with accusations of neglect disguised beneath protestations of his own unworthiness and recognition of her sweetness of soul. As he did not want to be a nuisance, could she not invent a routine for him that would avoid putting the harmony of the house in peril? Seeing that he was expected *to spend several hours a day in profound solitude, should he prescribe himself to confined limits in the house?* It would be more befitting a *mistress*, if she herself took the initiative and spared him the necessity of constraining himself. He would keep to his chamber . . . she had only to turn the key in the lock twice a day. Her inconsistency of nature had led her to forget her promises of help and forced him into repeated solicitations for her attention, provoking in him an abnegation of pride which he found horrifying. He concluded with the hope that she would continue to keep him *in that slavery you know so well how to make happy.*

Having read the letter through, Mrs. Thrale felt first bemusement, then anger—she crumpled the paper in her fist—then sadness, at which emotion she smoothed out the page as though calming a bird with a damaged wing. Despite its bold phrases and dictatorial tone, it was the letter of a man struck down . . . though, on reflection, perhaps that of a spoilt child was nearer the mark.

She rose at once, determined to put his mind at rest, and no sooner had put foot to stair than he appeared on the landing ahead. It was now dusk and the servants had not yet lit the lamps; he was holding a candle in one hand and his shadow leapt the wall.

Queeney, curious as to her mother's abrupt departure from Mrs. Salusbury's bedside, followed her. She was astonished to see Mr. Johnson and Mamma struggling together on the landing. They seemed to be wrestling for possession of a length of chain attached to some metal object that knocked repeatedly against the wainscotting of the window.

Mr. Johnson shouted out, "You will use it," and Mamma shouted back, "I will not," and at that moment from the nursery above came the sound of desperate crying; it was Lucy, a martyr to the infection in her ear. Mamma dropped the chain and fled higher.

Queeney stared up at Mr. Johnson. He was holding the candle flame too close to his head and a small curdle of smoke issued from the top-piece of his wig. Dashing his fist against his forehead he turned and stumbled off to his room, the chain and its attachment, like a dead dog on a leash, bouncing behind him.

The next morning when Queeney asked what had disturbed Mr. Johnson, Mamma said he was unhappy for Mrs. Salusbury. "The thought of death frightens him," she explained. "His own as well as hers. I am trying to persuade him to accompany James Boswell to Scotland."

Though Queeney had not met Mr. Boswell she knew he was a lawyer who was in awe of Mr. Johnson, hung on his every word and desired he should go with him on a tour of his native Hebrides. Mr. Garrick likened him to the buffoon, Pantalone, and Mr. Goldsmith said he was of no account, but Papa held he should not be so easily dismissed.

Later that day Mrs. Thrale replied to Johnson and left the letter on her worktable while she attended to Mrs. Salusbury. As it was not folded, Queeney read it; she found it overdone. Mamma asked what more care could she give her dear Mr. Johnson that she did not already give, what tenderness that he had not already experienced? Diversion would be his best medicine and Boswell his best physician. Farewell and be good, the letter ended, and *do not quarrel with your governess for not using the rod enough*. Queeney reasoned this last sentence was meant to be humorous, for it was only children that got whipped.

All the same, she thought it an odd exercise, writing to someone who lived under the same roof.

To Miss Laetitia Hawkins
2, Sion Row, Twickenham

Dec. 6th, 1807

Dear Miss Hawkins,

You persist, and with each enquiry I am drawn back to years best for-gotten. I regret I can tell you little regarding the failure of the Thrale Brewery; I was but eight years old at the time and my dear father did not think it necessary to acquaint me with the facts. Sufficient to say, that, owing to my mother's desire for expansion, both at Streatham Park and the Brewery, my father was forced to borrow money at exorbitant rates of interest, a debt he did not shake off for a further nine years—which burden undoubtedly led to a decline in his health. At the time of the crisis, my mother, though it is to be presumed that she acted without malice, was peculiarly supportive of Perkins, chief clerk to the Brewery, who, seeking financial advantage, threatened to resign, thus causing my dear father further aggravation.

I cannot, at this distance, remember the name of Miss Porter's cat, the death of whom was commemorated by a candlelit ceremony con-ducted beneath the mulberry tree. Dr. Johnson did indeed have a pet hen. It was called Socrates, on account of its persistent squawking.

My grandmother died in her bed at Streatham, a day or so after my father had carried her in his arms to see the finishing of the library.

The argument you mention, the one between Mr. Goldsmith and Dr. Johnson on the subject of the regrettable peeling of oil paint—it was the colour crimson that was at fault—from the canvasses of Sir Joshua Reynolds, took place in Bolt Court. I have every reason to remember the occasion as only that morning my father had given me an amber necklace, which treasured possession I wear to this day.

I remain,

Yours Sincerely,

H. M. Thrale

I do not recall Dr. Johnson speaking of Francis Barber in other than the warmest of terms. Nor did he treat him as a low servant. Once, in my presence, Mrs. Desmoulins referred to him as a blackamoor *at which Dr. J, exceedingly vexed, told her to mind her tongue.*

YESTERDAY

n.f. (from **Ψεοτερδαψ**, Saxon.)
The day last past; the next day before today.

To-morrow, and to-morrow, and to-morrow,
Creeps in this petty pace from day to day,
To the last syllable of recorded time;
And all our yesterdays have lighted fools
The way to dusty death.

—SHAKESPEARE'S *Macbeth*

AFTER VISITING THE nursery to kiss little Ralph goodbye—his head was very large and his mouth drooled in spite of his not yet teething—Mrs. Thrale went down into the hall and stood inside the porch to watch her husband direct the loading of the carriage. Through the pale mist came the bleating of sheep and the trill of birdsong.

"There is something wrong with his understanding," she said, to no one in particular. She was referring to the child whose fat cheek she had just pecked and in whose eyes she had seen no sparkle of wit. It crossed her mind that his shrill cries were not unlike the twitterings of young thrushes . . . and who could distinguish the tweetings of hunger from those of vacuity?

She reasoned her fancies sprang from the strain of settling the children before embarking on her travels. Yesterday she had taken Sophy to lodge with her sister Susanna at Mrs. Cumyns's boarding school in Kensington. The death of Mrs. Salusbury, followed so swiftly by that of dearest Lucy, had chilled her heart; she felt herself less capable of affection than before and would not miss either girl too much, Sophy being petulant and Susanna not immediately likeable.

Harry was her main concern, for though he was content enough to attend St. Thomas's School by day, he refused to board nights and had threatened, should he not be fetched home to sleep, to run away to sea. He had inherited his father's inordinate appetite and she feared that in her absence he would take liberties in ordering his own dinners, thus overloading his belly. He had such winning ways she did not trust the servants to disobey him, though New Nurse, who had fast become Old Nurse, swore she would thwart him.

The carriage ready, Mr. Johnson had to be sent for twice. The footman reported that he was dressed but was having difficulty in deciding which books he should leave behind. When at last he did appear he descended the steps with speed, his face expressing great good-humour. Since his jaunt to Scotland with Boswell, and the completion of his journal of the Hebridean tour—only that week he had dispatched the first sheets back to the printers—he was in favour of motion and was looking forward to introducing his dear master and mistress to his home town of Lichfield. Yet, even as the occupants of the coach shifted to make space for him, he abruptly turned and made off in the direction of the library door at the side of the house. He was dressed in his Sunday coat, but his shirttail hung out at the back. This comical oversight prompted Henry Thrale to repeat, for the benefit of Mr. Baretti, one of Garrick's many anecdotes concerning Johnson's dismal efforts, in the early days of his marriage, to run a school in Staffordshire.

"There were but three pupils . . . Davy the oldest. Late at night . . . young gentlemen had the habit of peeping through keyhole of Johnson's bedchamber. One occasion . . . spied Sam at table . . . heard Tetty's pleas that he should come to bed. Aware of something dangling alongside his chair . . . Sam mistakes it for his shirt . . . tucks the cloth into his breeches and strides about, reciting aloud what he has just written . . . Tetty, shivering, tries to retrieve departing bedclothes . . ."

"I see him, I see him," cried Baretti, slapping his thigh in delight.

"Her complaints grow louder . . . Sam, misinterpreting feverish cries . . . discards shirt in flurry of expectation . . . shouts out, 'I'm coming, my Tetsie, I'm coming.'"

At this conclusion, Baretti laughed so loudly that Mrs. Thrale thrust her handkerchief into his mouth. She was not a moment too soon, for just then Johnson reappeared at a run, puffed past the carriage, climbed the steps to the porch and knocked with his fist three times upon the stone head of the griffin beside the door.

Mrs. Thrale thought again of the child in the nursery; no matter how vigorously one tapped there would never be a response.

On the journey to London, Henry Thrale and Johnson dozed on and off, neither being given to liveliness much before noon. Queeney coughed and wriggled a great deal. As they approached the river, she suddenly asked her father why Mr. Garrick had peeped through keyholes, and if it was not rude of him. Fortunately, Johnson was asleep and Thrale too drowsy to reply, although Baretti uttered a bellow of mirth wild enough to wake the dead. But for his presence Mrs. Thrale would have slapped Queeney.

Baretti was volatile, and had odd ideas on the nurturing of children. He was forever hiding the ivory whistle she used to summon the younger ones for punishment; nor had she forgotten his snapping the nursery rod in two after she had whipped

Harry for scribbling across Mr. Johnson's globe. Sometimes she reflected on how long it might be before the Italian, in one of his tempers, would resort to the fruit-knife that had so nearly sent him to the gallows.

Baretti said his goodbyes when the carriage reached Joshua Reynolds's studio in Leicester Fields. He was to sit for his likeness, one of a series of portraits of Streatham habitués commissioned by Thrale, of which those of Garrick and dear, lost Goldsmith were already completed and could be seen displayed on the walls of his library.

Johnson, shirt still dangling below the tails of his coat, insisted on alighting and accompanying Baretti to the top step, where, as Thrale observed, he shook his friend's hand as though they would not meet again this side of the grave. Miss Reynolds appeared briefly in the doorway; seeing the carriage, she darted out of sight, but not before Mrs. Thrale had taken notice of her dishevelled appearance; it was probable she and her brother had been indulging in yet another of their disagreements.

Intrigued by the strange roarings and shriekings coming from the garden across the square, Queeney scrambled down into the street. She grew excited and would have run off to investigate if her mother hadn't caught hold of her skirt.

Returning, and learning the reason for the child's animation, Johnson told her that John Hunter lived across the way and promised he would take her one day to visit him. The beast noises coming from the garden, he explained, were those of a tiger and a collection of gibbons, the latter being a species of monkey, grey in colour, almost hairless and possessing hind legs capable of leaping great distances. Had she been here the week before she would have heard the barking of numerous dogs, some of whose stomachs had been cut open and filled with warm milk before being hanged.

"Why?" questioned Queeney, wide-eyed.

"It was an experiment to ascertain the absorption of fat through the abdominal lymphatics into the thoracic duct."

"Why?" Queeney repeated.

"In the pursuit of knowledge, Sweeting," Johnson said. "The day after, by Dr. Levet's account, Mr. Hunter dissected an old man and observed that the veins of his intestines were filled with white fluid instead of red blood."

"Did Mr. Hunter hang the old man?" Queeney asked.

"Come," ordered Mrs. Thrale, frowning at Johnson and pulling Queeney into the carriage.

Seated and addressing Mrs. Thrale, Johnson acknowledged he was not acquainted with the anatomist, but had attended two of his lectures in the company of Levet and found both instructive. One had dealt with states of mind, in which it was proposed, and who could gainsay it, that the mind was often in opposition to itself, and that one state of mind, if strong, would always get the better of another state which is weak.

"How true," murmured Mrs. Thrale, thinking of Johnson's own mind, and in particular of its perilous state when overcome by melancholy.

"The second lecture," Johnson told her, "had to do with sexual selection. A man, according to Hunter, has an appetite to enjoy all women; but if the mind has formed itself to any particular woman, the appetite or enjoyment can be suspended until—" here, he caught Mrs. Thrale's reproving glance and broke off in mid-sentence. Moments later, as the coach turned out of the Square, he remarked, "The skin is affected by feelings of shame . . ."

"As in blushing," supplied Mrs. Thrale.

"Quite so. The secretion or even the non-secretion of the testicles takes place under certain states of the mind—"

"Enough, Sir," barked Henry Thrale, and instantly obtained silence.

They drove to St. Albans, where they halted to enjoy an excellent dinner with Ralph Smith, a first cousin of Thrale. Mrs. Smith went through the usual stages, disbelief followed by growing regard, experienced by those encountering Johnson for the first time. As she afterwards confided to Mrs. Thrale, what with that ill-fitting wig, those tremulous hootings, that untucked shirt—not to mention the convulsive jerkings of lower limbs—she feared they had brought an idiot to sit with them at table. It was with difficulty the party got away to continue on their journey to Lichfield.

The coach approaching Offley, Mrs. Thrale grew warm with memories of times gone by. It was hereabouts she had spent girlhood summers in the house of her father's brother, Sir Thomas Salusbury. As the carriage rolled down the country lanes and slowed to cross a timber bridge above a stream, she recalled going fishing with her father, perched on a grassy bank holding a willow twig from which dangled a length of cord with a hook tied to its end.

"Cast, cast," her father had bidden, only her throw was too feeble and the cord sailed backwards and fell across a tussock of weed. "Damn you, damn you to hell," shouted her father, shaking his fist at the horizon. She had taken to her heels in tears, thinking it was she who made him angry, until her mother had explained it was Sir Thomas, out hunting and hill-topping in a post chaise, whom he cursed.

"Stop . . . Stop the coach," Mrs. Thrale ordered.

"Are you ill, Hester?" called her husband, as she stepped out into the evening air. She didn't reply, at which he followed her, though merely to piss into the hedgerow.

Mrs. Thrale, staring upwards at the racing clouds, divined in their flight across the heavens a likeness to the fleeting years. She had been fortunate, she thought, for in their swift passing there had been nothing to cause her lasting despair, not even the harvesting of her children—for death was a natural event and in accordance with God's will.

She was cheerful when she returned to the carriage, so much so that she was moved to kiss the sniffling Queeney on both cheeks. Johnson was ready to explode; any unwarranted delay on their journey to Lichfield caused him agitation.

They spent the night at Dunstable, in an inn close by the parish church. The accommodation was far from pleasing, the rooms unclean and the food served up on scratched plate. The service too was tardy, owing to the landlord being deficient of a leg, which loss, so he would have them believe, he had suffered when the ship on which he had served his country had run aground near Providence, Rhode Island, and been attacked by patriots.

Queeney's cold now gathering strength—she coughed and sneezed in rotation—Mrs. Thrale was anxious to put her to bed. She had not brought female servants and was obliged to attend to the child herself. This was not as irksome as it might have been, for Johnson was wearying them all with his knowledge of the town, informing them that its name was derived from the wool market or "staple" established in the region of the chalk downs by Augustine monks in the twelfth century. Neither skirmishes in North America nor weaving in Bedfordshire arousing her interest, she retired, leaving the talkative Johnson in the company of a comatose Henry Thrale.

The following morning it was past ten o'clock before the party left Dunstable. Johnson, who the night before had insisted on a departure not later than six o'clock, failed to rise for a further four hours. Nor did he apologise, though Mrs. Thrale could tell by the way he left his breakfast roll untouched that he felt discomforted.

It was moonlit midnight when their coach clattered into the yard of the Swan Inn, Lichfield.

• • •

WHEN QUEENEY AWOKE, Mrs. Thrale brought her a dish of warm bread and milk. Owing to a prodigious sneeze, the milk slopped on to the quilt. Anxious to appear well—her mother was a great advocate of dosing and purging—the child subdued her cough and professed to feeling quite herself again. In spite of this, Mrs. Thrale swore she detected an obstruction in her breathing and warned that an application of goose-fat to the chest might be necessary.

Dressed, and about to descend the stairs, Mrs. Thrale was surprised to spy Mr. Johnson pacing the hall below. Seeing her, he bounded upwards, and, fiercely studying her garments, cried out, "No, no, it will not do." On her enquiring what was wrong, he informed her that the morning gown she was wearing was of too dark a colour, and that she must change into something more gay and splendid. For one so poorly sighted, and one, moreover, so slovenly in his own dress, it was astonishing how critical he could be of the apparel of others.

Cross, but bearing in mind that he wished her to make an impression on his Lichfield acquaintances, Mrs. Thrale did as he bid and presently returned in a hooped gown of blue silk edged with swan feathers. Her husband murmured that it was inappropriate, the weather being unsettled and the inhabitants of Lichfield more than likely rustic in attire.

"I cannot please everyone," she said, exasperated, to which Thrale replied, "It is fortunate I am a good-natured man."

No sooner were the words out of his mouth than Mrs. Thrale turned pale, the phrase having been used for the title of a play by poor Goldsmith, who had died, submerged in debt and in great torment of mind, earlier that year. Hand to her heart, she looked anxiously at Johnson. Conscious of her concern, he said gruffly, "I loved Goldy, but though I can *say* I miss him, I cannot swear to *feeling* it."

Much relieved at his attitude, for had he descended into a gloom their visit to Lichfield would have been past mending, the Thrales followed him out of the Inn.

They had scarcely set foot in the street before Johnson was waylaid by numerous passers-by, all of whom claimed to have known him intimately in his youth. Some had splashed with him in Stowe Pool or else daydreamed beside him on the school-bench; others had stood guard while he raided the orchard in George Lane, run whooping at his elbow as the cattle swayed home from the darkening meadows. He was clearly gratified at the respect shown to him, though in an aside he confessed he did not know from Adam many who so vigorously shook his hand.

To reward Queeney, who, in order to deflect Mamma's medical attentions was conducting herself with great fortitude, Johnson first took them to Mr. Green's Museum behind the Cathedral. Here they viewed a curious collection of natural and artificial rarities, chief among them the skeleton of an Oronuto savage from Ethiopia, his bones sprouting porcupine quills. This wondrous monstrosity, it was asserted, was the only one of its kind in the world.

Mr. Green was absent when they arrived. Word being sent he came on the trot and greeted Johnson with great civility, indeed, fussed over his visitors to such an extent that after barely a quarter of an hour Henry Thrale declared himself fatigued and was escorted to Mr. Green's inner sanctum, where he lay down on an ancient couch believed to have belonged to the Emperor Nero.

Queeney was enchanted with a statue of the dog Cerberus, minus two of its heads, seated beside an enthroned Hades, and insisted on fondling its chipped ears. According to her, the remaining head bore a resemblance to Belle, being equally bad-tempered about the snout. She told Mr. Johnson it was a pity her cabinet was not large enough to hold a similar object, Brighton shells and Mr. Pope's snippet being but poor substitutes for such rarities. He agreed and promised to search for something equally exotic, if smaller in size, when next in Oxford. Mrs. Thrale pinched Queeney for being so outspoken and hurried her away from the statue, for its accompanying written information dwelt in some detail on the lord of the underworld's rape of Persephone.

Johnson, although not in Mr. Green's hearing, grew heated at the labelling of the Oronuto savage as a monstrosity, wondrous or not. He argued that if the poor wretch had indeed had the misfortune to grow quills instead of hair, then it would have been better to have buried him six foot under rather than expose his remains to the gaze of an ignorant populace. Nor was he convinced of the authenticity of the exhibit, having seen the very same phenomenon on show at Mr. Leary's establishment in Hampstead. "It is a copy," he shouted, rattling the skeleton with his stick, "and one inferior in every degree."

He grew so red in the face that Mrs. Thrale felt alarm, the more so because she understood the reason for his outburst; hadn't Johnson himself, from an early age, been an object of curiosity? Tears filling her eyes at the thought of his boyhood misery she pretended an interest in the intestine of a sturgeon. Queeney, watching as always, noticed the way she clenched on her lip to avoid yawning.

Next they visited the Cathedral, where Henry Thrale, complaining of a stiffness in the joints, said he preferred to stroll about the Close and view the Bishop's Palace. Queeney begged to accompany him, but Mamma wouldn't hear of it.

"You must see inside the Minster," she said, "and gaze upon the spot where Mr. Johnson, when a child, nearly perished from a collapse of the roof. Imagine the scene . . . the din of masonry, the screams . . . the volume of dust billowing outwards . . . and small Samuel, hands like talons, scrambling upwards to leap from a window."

Hearing this, Johnson shook his head in mock despair. "As is the way of women, Sweeting, and of Mamma in particular, her account is beset with inaccuracies. The falling of a roof, or rather the dropping of a few pieces of mortar and stone, took place at St. Mary's Church in the Market Square—"

"This church, that church," cried Mrs. Thrale, "what does it signify?"

"—after which mild disturbance my father took me by the hand and walked me through the door."

"It is the nub of the story that matters," persisted Mrs. Thrale, an assertion which Johnson was strenuously about to dispute when he was approached by the Subchanter of the Cathedral, a sober gentleman who miraculously made no reference to a schoolyard encounter and merely evinced a knowledge of his reputation.

Queeney, trailing in their wake, presently lagged so far behind that she found herself alone. At once she turned tail and sped out of the doors in search of her father. At her headlong arrival into the Close crows lifted from the trees and soared croaking into the heavens. The clapping of wings was so clamorous that she stopped on the path and stuffed her fingers in her ears; in her head stones spilled from the skies. Just then she spied Papa, approaching from the west corner of the Bishops Palace. He was smiling. She ran to him; Papa had a beautiful smile, one that always took away her fright. He told her that he had met a comical old man, a beater of silver who vowed he was yet another friend of Mr. Johnson when young.

"Did you believe him?" asked Queeney. "Did he tell you that he had swum with him in the pool, or had shared the same grammar in school?"

"Neither learning nor water was mentioned," said Papa, "only that Sam was a prodigious climber of trees."

The sun sailing free of the clouds, he led her to a convenient seat, where they lolled companionably together in its golden rays and amused themselves with the recitation of nursery rhymes. Though she considered herself far too old for such childish entertainment, Queeney submitted to it for Papa's sake. It was not a chore, for he made her giggle when he stuck his thumb in his mouth and played at being little Jack Horner.

An hour later Mrs. Thrale and Mr. Johnson emerged from the Cathedral. Engaged in bidding farewell to the Subchanter, they dallied so long on the steps that Thrale, patience fast fading, shouted out brusquely, "Come, Hester, the morning is almost gone."

Mr. Johnson, with considerably more alacrity than Mrs. Thrale, hurried towards him. Puffing, he asked if curiosity would persuade him to view the house in which he had first drawn breath, to which Thrale replied kindly enough, "Love, not mere curiosity, will dance me there, Sam. Be so good as to lead the way."

They were walking the short distance to the Market Square when Queeney uttered a yelp of pain. Her mother, scurrying behind, had trodden on her heel. "Keep up," urged Mrs. Thrale, and forged on.

The street now becoming more crowded, Johnson looked round to make sure his companions were close. Seeing the hopping Queeney, he retraced his steps and asked what was wrong. Tearfully she told him Mamma had struck her shoe against her heel, and indeed there was a small stain of crimson on her stocking.

"Does it hurt?" he asked.

"Yes, it does," she wailed, "the more so because Mamma did not say she was sorry." She stared resentfully ahead at the figure of Papa weaving his way between the market stalls, chased by the bobbing feathers of Mamma's bonnet.

Mr. Johnson said, "Would the hurt go away if Mamma expressed sorrow?"

"No," she admitted, "but at least Mamma would know what she had done."

"What advantage is there if injury has to be spelt out?" he demanded.

"It is not you who have been trodden on," she retorted.

"That is true," he allowed, "which is why we must keep it from Mamma, for should she learn of the wound she will most certainly insist on returning to the Inn to attend to it. Such a fuss will hinder the excursion to my birthplace."

"It is not a wound," Queeney admitted, "merely a scraping."

"Quite so . . . and Mamma does not always have a gentle touch, particularly when anxious."

Observing him, Queeney was aware of the trembling of his large lips, of the expression of dismay in his oyster eyes. He was not, after all, as arrogant as he would have one believe.

She said, "Heaven forbid I should be a hindrance," and limping, followed him across the Square. He and Mamma have much in common, she thought, for both are selfish.

The house in which Johnson had been born faced St. Mary's Church and the Market Hall. It had been built by his father, the bookseller, and Johnson still held the lease. Miss Porter, daughter of Tetty by a previous marriage, had lived here until the death of his mother; inheriting money from an uncle, she had then moved to a residence of her own. It was presently occupied by an impoverished schoolmaster who, given notice of the arrival of his landlord, had seen fit to absent himself for the day.

Mrs. Thrale was surprised at the size of the building; she had understood Johnson came from humble beginnings. Unwisely, she said as much, at which he snapped, "In regard to myself,

Madame, the word 'humble,' implying acceptance of one's station, is not one I would choose. Straightened circumstances is the phrase best illustrative of my father's later years."

At that moment, fortunately for Mrs. Thrale, he noticed that a section of the railing encircling the cellar steps had rusted away. His vexation diverted, he stood there, muttering and gesticulating, as though such a loss of iron-work would cause the house to totter on its foundations. It was Thrale who took him by the arm and marched him to the door.

As he conducted his friends from room to room, Johnson regaled them with childhood reminiscences. For instance, on a certain step on the stairs his brother Nathaniel—little Natty—in pursuit of a mouse had tumbled over and bumped to the bottom, where he lay bleeding from a cut above the eyebrow. The blow was superficial, but he had feigned insensibility. On aping a return to consciousness his piteous moans and tragic glances had rivalled those of a Davy Garrick. This recollection was firm in Johnson's memory on account of his mother blaming him for Natty's mishap and shutting him in the coal-hole for several hours by way of punishment. He emerged, so he said, as dusky of hue as Frank Barber, and not only on the outside; in suffering such an injustice his heart had turned black.

In the cellar kitchen he pointed a finger at the self-same stool on which he had sat reading *Hamlet, Prince of Denmark*, and, coming to the scene in which the shade of the dead King appeared, had found it so scary that he had flung the book aside and rushed up into the street to be rid of ghosts. "Nightly in the adjacent room," he continued, "my father closed his account books and leaving behind an outer door rotting on its hinges, climbed the stairs to bolt the front entrance against thieves."

The recalling of these last two incidents, the one, as he acknowledged, induced by an excess of imagination, the other from an absence of it, caused him to shake with laughter.

"I do not think a heart can turn black," Queeney said, "not unless the blood is disordered."

Catching Henry Thrale regarding him with something like alarm—he was a man made uncomfortable by extremes of feeling—Johnson strove valiantly to control himself. Dashing the water from his eyes, he spluttered, "There is something in the cadence of the words, *Adieu, adieu, Remember me*, that to this day strikes a chill to my soul."

Mrs. Thrale, understanding the ambiguity of his mood, smiled reassuringly. Merriment often seized him inappropriately, due to a surplus of emotion.

She was glad his sight was deficient, for the place was in a sorry state, woodwork dull, ceilings stained with damp and not a rug on the floor free from the attentions of moth. As if he read her thoughts, Johnson said, "It does not appear that the schoolmaster is a man much given to the pursuit of cobwebs." Leaping into the air he struck out with his stick, and added, "But then, no more am I," which was indeed the truth.

"I have heard," said Mrs. Thrale, clawing at her cheek to remove a gossamer strand, "that spiders make very good mothers," a remark which tickled Queeney and provoked giggles.

In spite of herself, Mrs. Thrale began to feel uneasy as she traipsed about the house, a sensation which threatened to overwhelm her upon entering the room in which Johnson's mother had given him life. He had confided in her so many details of his beginnings that here the ghosts of yesterday came crowding in, for the bed was still there, the same on which he and little Natty had lain while their mother read to them of Hellfire.

Above the bed-head a square of wall was scorched, as though a candle flame had flared too close. Attempts had been made to rub it clean, and merely enlarged the discolouration. Gaze fixed upon the mark, it seemed to her that it took on the form of a child's face, mouth open in a wail of silent terror. Outside, rain fell, blurring the outline of the church in which Johnson had been christened; in the tiny spatterings against the window glass she heard the crackle of flames.

Turning faint, she sank onto a chair, one of whose castors was missing, causing it to lurch sideways. Johnson protested this was not the time for her to grow lethargic—she had not yet seen the upstairs rooms once inhabited by Dr. Swinfen, player of the violin and father of Mrs. Desmoulins.

Anxious to disguise her feelings, Mrs. Thrale told him she was taking in the sounds of the market place, as he must have done as a child.

"What sounds?" he probed.

"The bellowing of an animal in pain," she improvised, for just then Queeney succumbed to a fit of coughing. "Similar to the tortured bear in the market square."

"What bear?" he demanded.

"The one Mrs. Desmoulins spoke of," she said, "the time Dr. Delap fled down the stairs and we fetched you home from Johnson's Court."

"You talk in riddles," he thundered. "There were never bears in Lichfield Market, tormented or otherwise, only bulls."

They left the house soon after, being expected, so he told them, at Miss Porter's a little before noon. Mrs. Thrale demurred at going on foot in the rain, but Johnson said she would look foolish travelling so short a distance in a carriage. She protested he must at least allow her to return to the Swan Inn to put on overshoes. He said she couldn't; growing irritable, he flapped his hand at her as though shooing away a fly. She thought he was possibly agitated at the prospect of introducing her to Miss Porter, and held her tongue.

The number of pedestrians thronging the narrow thorough-fare forced the party into a straggling procession. Mrs. Thrale was much inconvenienced by the width of her hooped gown.

When the Cathedral bells rang out to mark the hour, crows pecking at the garbage-strewn cobblestones surged upwards and flew so close to her bonnet that she shrieked. Repeatedly she had to look over her shoulder to make sure Queeney was safely keeping to the wall; the child had refused to walk ahead and was limping, to draw attention to herself.

They found Miss Porter sitting at cards with three elderly ladies, sisters to one another, and a gentleman with a patch over his eye. The ladies openly studied Mrs. Thrale from head to foot; indeed, one was ignorant enough to rise from the table and encircle her.

Smiling graciously, Mrs. Thrale strove to be pleasant. She was curious to discover in the daughter something of the departed wife, the better to understand the attraction Sam had once felt. Save for Garrick, she knew no one who had been well-acquainted with Tetty; there was Mrs. Desmoulins, it was true, her companion for many years, but she, still smarting under the delusion that the Thrales had robbed her of Johnson, could scarcely be persuaded to be civil, let alone forthcoming.

Queeney was astonished at the antics of Miss Porter. From what Mr. Johnson had led her to believe, there was fondness between them, yet here she was, for the benefit of her Lichfield cronies, back turned to him, rolling her eyes and grimacing to indicate how odd she thought him—Harry couldn't have behaved worse. Fortunately Mr. Johnson was too busy bowing and kissing hands to notice.

The introductions over with, he gave his attention solely to his stepdaughter and the one-eyed gentleman, who, it transpired, he had known in his youth and who had travelled from Birmingham to renew their acquaintance. New people he never loved to be in company with, except young and fair ladies, into which category the sisters could not by any stretch of the imagination be said to belong.

The conversation that ensued had to do with changes in the town since Johnson's last visit, Miss Porter's aches and pains and the continuing scandal surrounding the widow Mearns, who was widely suspected, though it could not be proved, of poisoning her husband by means of honey cakes.

Mr. Johnson became animated; he said the first classical description of honey death was to be found in Xenophon's *Anabasis*, Book IV, Chap. VIII. On the march to Trebizond the soldiers found a large number of beehives . . . all who had eaten a little of the plundered syrup resembled drunken men; those who had eaten a lot were like madmen, and died mouthing obscenities.

"How unsettling," said Miss Porter, handing round the biscuit-barrel.

Queeney found some of the talk difficult to follow, as did Papa, who was considerably foxed by the broad vowels of the company. Mamma was smiling away and nodding, but she was surely putting up a pretence. They were familiar with Johnson's speech, the way he pronounced "once" as "woonce" and "there" to rhyme with "fear," but the gentleman with the eye patch had a language of his own. When offered a third glass of wine, he said something like, "I dare'st not, for I may then becoom joongle-brained and later an Admiral of the High Seas."

Papa said, "I do not follow. Are you an Admiral, Sir?"

"Nay," came the reply, "do I look it?" at which one of the old ladies said, "He means, Sir, that if he drinks overmuch he will likely vomit into your lap." Papa thought this funny and laughed out loud. Mr. Johnson looked gratified; he hadn't heard the exchange but was delighted that Papa was enjoying himself.

The rain having stopped, and, as she comically expressed it, the sun come out to play, Miss Porter suggested Queeney might like to see the little garden behind the house. "Mrs. Scase will go with you," she said. Queeney would rather have gone on her own, although Mrs. Scase did not seem as decrepit as her sisters; the hair drifting from her cap was red in parts and she walked without tottering.

The way into the garden was through a kitchen upon whose shelves, amid a clutter of pots and pans, was propped a glass case containing a fish, its shiny scales and bulging eye shimmering in a beam of sunlight. Mrs. Scase said, "At last we have found something here that makes you smile," and led her outside, where she was encouraged to sit on a bench made from a length of gnarled wood laid across two barrels, the one smaller than the other. Queeney perched herself on the higher end, legs dangling.

It was an unusual form of seating, but then, neither was the garden of the usual kind, being without flowers and its beds entirely filled with giant cabbages, their leaves much disfigured from some seasonal blight. Beside a drooping pot plant on the path lay a dead bird eaten about the breast.

Mrs. Scase was also not usual, in that she treated Queeney as an equal, seeking her opinion, without condescension, of the town, the people she had met, and of Mr. Johnson. While waiting for a reply the old woman leaned forward and looked at her lips rather than into her eyes, as though she needed to be sure where the words came from. Queeney told her that she found the town pleasant enough and as yet had not truly met anyone. As for Mr. Johnson, why, he was so much a portion of her life that opinions had long since been replaced by feelings, at which Mrs. Scase slapped her knee and cried out, "Well done, little Miss."

Mrs. Scase knew all about Mr. Johnson, or rather about the boy he had once been. An aunt, she said, long dead, was cousin to a woman who boasted of being on calling terms with Mr. Johnson's mother. Much of what she related was not new to Queeney, but Mrs. Scase had a singular way of painting pictures in the head. The scars on his neck and the side of his face, she explained, came from a tubular disease, an infection, according to Dr. Swinfen, caught from the babe's wet nurse, whose milk was tainted and whose own infant had been similarly afflicted. As she talked she stabbed the air with one plump finger by way of emphasis; at her side the blighted cabbages whimpered in the breeze.

Mrs. Johnson, in spite of pride in her exalted Ford relations—they were a cut above those of the bookseller, Michael Johnson—put it about that it was an inherited condition, to lessen the guilt she felt at having farmed him out so perilously. The marks on the child's face stuck out more when his skin was new, and if that wasn't enough he was partially deaf, all but blind in one eye and deficient of vision in the other. His aunt Ford, seeing him for the first time, said she would not have picked up such a poor creature in the street.

"It is a wonder he did not die," Queeney murmured, looking at the bird putrefying on the path. In the sunlight its black feathers shone blue. She thought of Lucy, who had merely suffered from a running of the ears, and of the dead Penelope in the cradle who had expired from nothing at all.

"His mother took him to London to be touched by the Queen," Mrs. Scase told her, and Queeney said she knew that and had often fingered the medal Mr. Johnson wore round his neck.

"Mrs. Johnson thought the touching had saved him, but Dr. Swinfen, being cautious, insisted an issue should be cut in the boy's arm to let out the infection, a wound which remained open until he was six years old."

Poor little arm, thought Queeney, ashamed of the fuss she had made of her scraped heel.

"He was clever even then," said Mrs. Scase, "forever learning things off by rote and scribbling verses and the like. Not that it raised much gaiety in him, for his home circumstances were blighted by reason of his father suffering under a sensation of gloomy despair, which mood was habitual to him. Nor was his mother, by all accounts, of much relief, for she had not the nous to understand either the child or the husband."

How common that is, mused Queeney, gazing at the mottled cabbages.

"As a child he was remarkable for a violence of temper, no doubt due to his brain being too large."

"He has a temper now," Queeney said, "though afterwards he often says how sorry he is."

"There was one time in particular," continued Mrs. Scase, "when he was but three years old. My aunt's cousin's neighbour was a witness to it, having set off to sell a piglet. The child attended a Dame's school not a hundred yards from Breadmarket Street, taken and fetched each noon by a servant girl. One May morning, placing the pot to boil, she burnt her finger on the coals and spent too long jumping up and down to cool it. Samuel set off home alone, closely followed by the Dame who was anxious for his safety . . . she was a widow woman who had lost five children of her own to the smallpox and ever after laboured under an impediment of speech. At the junction of the road, unable to see clearly, Samuel got down on all fours and, feeling his way by means of the kennel running along the middle of the street, began to crawl towards his father's bookshop. The blue jacket he wore was stained black above the elbow . . . from the blood seeping out of the cut in his arm. 'S-S-Sam,' called the Dame, 'S-s-stop.' A speckled hen, escaped from a market pen, strutted ahead of him, head jerking from left to right . . . my aunt's cousin's neighbour remembered the hen to her dying day—"

"Some hens are more memorable than others," said Queeney. "Mr. Johnson had a pet one called Socrates."

"The Dame, fearful he would be run over by carts, ran to haul him upright, at which he kicked out at her in a fury. When his mother took him to task for treating the Dame so shamefully, do you know what the little creature replied?"

Queeney shook her head.

"That it was difficult for someone sick not to behave like a scoundrel. There were tears in his eyes, even before his whipping."

"And the hen?" inquired Queeney. "What of the hen?"

"Nothing is known," said Mrs. Scase, "though I expect someone boiled it for dinner," and she licked her lips as though tasting chicken meat. This amused Queeney; joining in the mime she jumped up and flapped her elbows. Her sudden movement unbalanced the seating—the plank of wood slid sideways, depositing Mrs. Scase beneath the cabbage leaves.

The resulting cries of distress brought her sisters hobbling into the garden. It had not been much of a fall, but Mrs. Scase made the most of it and moaned pitifully as she was helped upright. She was a well-nourished woman and by the time her sisters had got her indoors both trembled from their exertions. Miss Porter was talking to Mr. Johnson and barely looked up, and Papa and the old gentleman with the eye patch now dozed, so it was left to Mamma to fuss over Mrs. Scase.

"Is it your ankle?" she cried, endeavouring to sound concerned.

"I have damaged my fundament," Mrs. Scase wailed, at which the old gentleman chortled. It was possible he was dreaming, for his eyes remained closed.

Mamma tried to break into Miss Porter's monologue. "It would perhaps be advisable," she said, "to send for a surgeon to check there are no bones broken." Miss Porter replied, "To the best of my knowledge there are no bones in the fundament," and continued to address Mr. Johnson. She was telling him about the Cathedral and how the Brethren of the Corporation were threatening to censure the Dean for allowing the roof to fall into disrepair. Mr. Johnson looked grave and made tut-tutting noises. All at once he rose from his chair and announced that they were to dine with Peter Garrick at four o'clock and must now take their leave. Mamma prodded Papa quite roughly on the shoulder; waking, he helped himself to the remaining crumbs in the biscuit-barrel.

Miss Porter accompanied them to the door. Halfway there Mr. Johnson turned round, murmuring that he had neglected to say goodbye to the sisters. Queeney, looking back as he opened the parlour door, clearly saw Mrs. Scase sitting bolt upright, head swinging like a bull about to charge, feet scraping the carpet. It was a passable imitation, albeit exaggerated, of the mannerisms exhibited by the visitor who had supposedly departed. Caught in the act, Mrs. Scase covered her face with her hands.

She need not have worried; Mr. Johnson, having taken one foot over the threshold, came under his sometime compulsion of having to spin in a circle before continuing, and observed nothing. Kissing the hand of each disconcerted sister he bowed his way out.

Once in the street he expressed his disapproval of Miss Porter. Mrs. Thrale, eager to learn the cause, hastened to keep pace with him. She had hoped it might be a personal objection, and was disappointed, for his vexation was apparently due to her criticism of the Dean. "If indeed lead is being removed from the roof," he said, "I do not doubt that it is a transaction undertaken for the benefit of the dispossessed."

Mrs. Thrale made no reply to this, having often remarked that Johnson had more regard for the poor than any man alive. Once, while walking with him past the cheap cookshops lining a particular alleyway in Covent Garden—they were to take tea with Davy Garrick—she had referred to the area as Porridge Island, at which he had snapped that she should not make light of what was serious to many. She had retorted that he misunderstood her intention and, stung by his tone, wondered aloud if it was not an affectation on his part, seeing his own circumstances were now so improved, that he should identify to such an extent with those less fortunate than himself. At this distance she could not remember his response, beyond his cheeks had glowed purple.

"I admired Miss Porter," she told him, not altogether insincerely, "though perhaps the more so when she checked my suggestion that a surgeon should be called."

"She has little of Tetty in her," said Johnson, "if that is your meaning."

Arriving at Dam Street, he pointed out the infant school he had attended. He added nothing more, save for remarking that it was here he had learnt his letters. Upon reaching the steps of a house some doors further, he stopped, and indicating the porch with his stick urged his companions to bow their heads and give thanks to God for a certain deaf mute named Dyott. A monument, he said, should be erected to the man, for in the Civil War it was he who had caused the death of Lord Brooke, leader of the Parliamentary forces, a stray bullet from his musket entering Brooke's visor and displacing his brain as he stood on that very step.

Queeney paid particular attention to the porch, even going so far as to rub a licked finger across the woodwork, as though hoping to bring it away bloodstained. Mrs. Thrale sharply rebuked her, but Johnson said he had performed the self-same gesture as a boy and that imagination must never be crushed.

Mrs. Thrale could not let that pass. "By degrees the reign of fancy is confirmed," she quoted. "Then fictions begin to operate as realities. They grow first imperious, and in time despotic. False opinions fasten on the mind, and life passes in dreams of rapture or anguish."

"You have it in the wrong order, Madame," he said, but could not help looking pleased that she remembered what he had once written.

On their return to the Inn Mrs. Thrale hurried upstairs to change her gown, its feathers bedraggled from the rain.

"Queeney," she said and sighed, peering into the looking glass on the dressing table, "it is a misfortune to belong to the weaker sex. We do not see either Papa or Mr. Johnson hastening to repair their clothes or attend to their complexions."

"Why is Miss Porter so old?" asked Queeney. "Mrs. Strickland has a daughter from a previous marriage and she is not yet seventeen."

"Mr. Johnson's wife," Mrs. Thrale explained, "was twenty years older than he and no longer young when they married." To which Queeney, studying her mother's reflection, said, "It is kind of him to like old women, is it not, for most grow cruel with the years."

In the glass Mrs. Thrale's eyes became sad. The child told herself she did not care; her heel had begun to throb.

JOHNSON CHANGED HIS wig for his visit to the Close. At Streatham, it was customary of an evening, on Thrale's instructions, for a footman to waylay him as he left his room and replace his everyday wig, much charred about the top-piece, with one more fit for dining in company. The night well advanced and Johnson at last persuaded to retire, the same footman was waiting to whisk it off his head lest he should hold the candle too close during his small hours' reading. For the rest, he had on his brown suit with the horse hair buttons and his shoes with the silver buckles.

Mrs. Thrale wore grey, and dared anyone to utter a word of dissent. Her husband, mindful of her temper, had her carried to Peter Garrick's in a chair, Queeney perched on her lap. Though the rain had stopped, a fierce wind tossed the chestnut trees in the stable yard. Thrale himself complained of feeling unwell, an indisposition Johnson held would be easily rectified by a brisk walk to the Close.

The market now over and the Square deserted save for scavengers, Thrale biliously opined that Lichfield lacked industry. Johnson robustly retorted that while Birmingham worked with its hands, Lichfield folk used their brains. Henry Thrale was amused at this, seeing their champion had found it necessary to desert his native town so early in life.

In Johnson's honour, Peter Garrick had assembled a lively collection of learned old friends, among them Erasmus Darwin, scientist and inventor, and Dr. James, for whose *Medical Dictionary* Johnson had written the preface. There was an atmosphere of accord in the house which Mrs. Thrale found relaxing. She was fond of her host, who had many times sat at her table in Southwark. He was not, it was true, as diverting as his brother, but that was all to the good; Davy could often be tiring, particularly after triumphing in some production at Drury Lane. The second Mrs. Garrick was also likeable, being somewhat simple in the correct sense of the word.

It was she who brought up the subject of Johnson's recent journey to Scotland. She said she had met Mr. Boswell two years previously and found him curiously affecting. He had told her, in detail, of his first case as an advocate in the Edinburgh courts, when he was required to defend a man accused of stealing a sheep. By his diligent efforts he secured an acquittal, thus saving his client from the hangman's noose. Eight years on, the very same man committed a similar offence and was this time found guilty. "Mr. Boswell," Mrs. Garrick said, "spent hours in the condemned man's cell, trying to give comfort to its occupant. He devised a plan to cut down the poor wretch immediately after the drop and arranged for a physician to be on hand to revive him. Alas, it was to no avail. He was much disturbed by the event, for he said the dead man's eyes remained open in death and that in them he fancied he saw his own reflection."

There was a moment's silence around the table, broken by

Thrale proclaiming that stealers of sheep must be punished, else there would be no mutton left in the land. A female cousin of Dr. James chirruped with laughter and went so far as to tap the table with her spoon.

"Mr. Boswell has no side," Mrs. Garrick said, and added somewhat quaintly, "all his sentiments come from a heart open to the heavens."

At this, first Garrick, then Thrale, then Dr. James opposed her; tripping over themselves to drag Boswell earthwards they stressed his vanity, his absence of intellect, his desire to shine. Mrs. Thrale was surprised they left out his drunkenness, but then, save for Johnson, there was not one among them who was not a sot. Johnson took no part in the discussion. It was never his habit to butt in unless addressed directly. Mrs. Thrale, knowing how he valued Boswell's friendship, and having had recent reason to be grateful for the attachment, turned to him and asked, "It is true, is it not, that you found him an entertaining companion and would gladly travel with him again?"

"Indeed I would," he replied. "As Mrs. Garrick rightly observes he is a man who calls forth love, and that in spite of faults, of which he has many."

"I thought you had little time for Scotchmen," Garrick said slyly.

Johnson took this in good part, merely remarking that he found Boswell the most unscottified of his countrymen. Garrick then pressed him as to whether it was true that Boswell was keeping a journal of their conversations together, and indeed of Johnson's discourse in general, and if so, did he not find it intrusive?

"Why, no, Sir. Why should I? It will not be accurate, for man's compulsion is to replicate himself. Think of painting—one has only to examine a portrait to see in the sitter a resemblance to the artist. And did not Mrs. Garrick say that Bozzy saw his own image in the eyes of a dead man? Besides, he does not expect me to read what he has written."

"What if others read it," persisted Garrick, "after you are gone? What will you think then?"

"Think then, Sir! Think then..." spluttered Johnson, "Why, Sir, I will think nothing, for if the 'gone' you refer to is the grave I dare say I shall have nothing to think with."

Mrs. Thrale, noting how manfully he was trying to subdue his temper, hastily changed the subject, inquiring of Dr. James his considered opinion of the health-giving properties of sea-bathing. She herself, she said, found the reverse to be the case, her outer self much in conflict with the briny following a child-hood encounter with a jellyfish. "I have only to put a toe in the water," she told him, "for a swelling to start up." She was exaggerating, but felt a diversion was necessary.

Fifteen lengthy minutes later, a considerate Mrs. Garrick guided the yawning Queeney up the stairs to her bedchamber, where she gave into her hands an illustrated book of fables. "Thank you," said Queeney, and allowed her head to be patted.

Left to herself, she got up and examined the contents of Mrs. Garrick's dressing table. There was a small pot of rouge, a bowl with a lid in the shape of a cat, and a bottle of fragrant oil. Inside the bowl lay an amber necklace, similar to one she had once owned. Returning to the bed she lay down and picked up the book; soon, a page or two turned, she drifted into asleep.

The guests leaving the table and the wine liberally poured, Thrale began to make sheep's eyes at the cousin of Dr. James. The lady, all of forty years old and as yet unmarried, responded beyond the call of etiquette. She had a dab of rouge on either cheek and her gown of sprigged muslin would not have gone amiss on a woman half her age. Mrs. Thrale, mortified, thought of mutton rather than lamb and smiled a great deal. Presently, Mrs. Garrick sat with her and after much inconsequential chat to do with Lichfield, the weather and the service at the Swan Inn, openly asked what she had made of Miss Porter.

"She is strong," Mrs. Thrale said, "and somewhat mischievous. The company she keeps is not up to her standard."

Mrs. Garrick agreed as to Miss Porter's vigour of mind. According to gossip, she had shown no animosity towards her mother's curious choice of husband, unlike her two brothers, who had been against the union from the start. "The eldest boy never forgave her. He went away to sea and never saw her again."

"A second marriage," murmured Mrs. Thrale, "must always be injurious to the children of the first, owing to loyalties."

"It is rumoured that Mr. Johnson's affections were first directed to Miss Porter, and only later fixed on the mother."

"I did not know that," Mrs. Thrale said. She did, but was in no mood to set Mrs. Garrick straight. The misunderstanding had centred around a love poem written by Sam many years before, in aid of his friend, Edmund Hector, who had been sweet on a girl in the neighbourhood of Birmingham.

"The younger boy," continued the loquacious Mrs. Garrick, "so I have heard, called once at the house in Gough Square and ran away before Tetty could be fetched downstairs . . . too upset to look on his dear mother's face."

Thrale's hand now creeping across the knee of Dr. James's painted cousin, Mrs. Thrale ground out, "We must accustom ourselves to knowing that men are fickle and have an appetite for all women. For myself, I do not mind, for I do not love any man." She uttered these last words with such vehemence that she flushed red. "Where is Queeney?" she asked, rising to her feet in consternation.

Mrs. Garrick took her upstairs. At their entrance the little girl clenched her fists to her chest, but did not wake. "Such a pretty child," whispered Mrs. Garrick, primping her hair in the looking glass. "What a comfort it must be to have a daughter."

"Yes," said Mrs. Thrale. "Though not as often as one might suppose."

This silenced Mrs. Garrick, if not for long. She commenced to babble her opinion of Mr. Johnson, declaring she had never seen him looking so well, and how it was doubtless due to the care he received at Streatham. He dressed better, his temper was less uncertain and he had altogether mellowed . . . it was obvious to all that Mrs. Thrale's influence was paramount, as was his fondness for her.

"The affection is mutual," Mrs. Thrale said, "though he is not always easy to live with."

Mrs. Garrick expressed it a wonder he had not married again. "My husband once told me that a very fine lady had once told him that Mr. Johnson was a very seducing man when he chose to be so."

Mrs. Thrale remained mute; there was something upsetting her, and it had little to do with the humiliating conduct of her husband.

"—though I understand he did consider marriage, and that in spite of his protestations of grief, a bare twelvemonth after his bereavement."

Mrs. Thrale stared at her. She said, "To whom?" so loudly that Queeney stirred in her sleep. Modifying her tone, she repeated the question.

"Why," came the reply, "none other than Anna Williams."

"Mrs. Williams!"

"The very same."

"Never. Not so."

"I have it on good authority," whispered Mrs. Garrick, "that at one time there had been more, much more, than a friendly attachment between the two."

"What authority?" demanded Mrs. Thrale.

"Why that of Mrs. Desmoulins."

"Fiddlesticks," cried Mrs. Thrale. "It is a travesty of the truth. Mrs. Desmoulins has been besotted with Samuel for twenty years . . . her word cannot be trusted." Agitated, and muttering excuses to do with the lateness of the hour and the advisability of getting Queeney back to the Inn, she shook the child awake and pulled her from the bed. "She is exhausted," she said shrilly, "and is suffering from a chill. See how she clutches her chest."

Hurrying her bleary-eyed daughter down the stairs she called to Peter Garrick to summon the sedan-chair. "Hester," her husband remonstrated, "she will rest here more comfortably. I, for one, was much bitten in the night."

"I am surprised you noticed," she retorted, "seeing you lay as one dead."

Johnson did not look up when she left, nor did he trouble to break off his conversation with Mr. Darwin.

The moon obscured by cloud, Mrs. Thrale kept tight hold of Queeney in case the pole-carriers stumbled as they jolted through the dark streets. She herself would not have minded an upset, particularly one that would have bumped the thoughts from her head.

When she arrived at the Inn and laid the little girl down, she saw in the candle glow the glint of tears on her cheeks. She asked what was wrong, but Queeney merely whimpered and pressed her face to the bolster.

Mrs. Thrale tossed and turned in her bed; she could not shift the crotchety Mrs. Williams from her mind. Johnson had twice brought the faded woman to dine at Southwark, professing it a kindness to include her. Both times Mrs. Williams had worn scarlet. On Mrs. Thrale politely admiring her choice of gown, she had said Mr. Johnson liked her to dress brightly. On each occasion, her sightless eyes turned to his face, she had chided him for wolfing his food, and he, with surprising meekness, had replied, "Yes, yes, you do right to check me," and made an effort to chew less ferociously. Was that not the response of a man much under the thumb of a wife?

Telling herself she was being fanciful, Mrs. Thrale pulled the bedclothes over her head and threw them off again at the sound of a commotion beneath the window. Rising, she peered down into the road. The sky had now cleared, and below, in the brightness of the moon, she saw Peter Garrick swaying on the cobblestones and Johnson, humped over, Thrale slung across his back like a bag of coals. After a prolonged thumping at the Inn door, the landlord descended and let in the inebriates. The cacophony continued, Garrick's voice being uppermost, and beneath it that of Johnson's, urging hush. Mrs. Thrale drew the bolt on her door, then released it; she did not want Henry accusing her of pique.

An hour or so later there was a further uproar on the landing, after which the door opened with some force and Johnson staggered in, supporting Thrale under the armpits. Propelling him forwards he came to the bed and tossed his burden down. He muttered something when he left, but it was in Latin and Mrs. Thrale, cowering beneath the quilt, could not make out the words.

The weight of her husband's shoulder pinning her to the mattress, she punched him. The blow was ill-judged; waking, Thrale rolled on top of her. His thrustings afforded him little relief and much exertion. He uttered not a word and neither did she, and when the unsatisfactory business was over she toppled him roughly from her. Just then the moon shone full through the window and in its cold light she was bewildered to see a froth of petticoats above his naked buttocks.

Queeney slept fitfully and woke at first light from a dream in which she had been captured by a highwayman and robbed of all her jewels. The highwayman wore a handkerchief over his nose and mouth, and when she pulled it away it was Papa's face underneath.

She got up and dressed herself, then practiced walking up and down the room. Her left shoe was not comfortable, but she adjusted her stocking so that the stain of yesterday's blood was visible. From her window she watched a barefooted boy creeping towards the goose-pen in the yard.

She went downstairs and let herself out into the grey dawn. The boy would have run away at her approach had she not called out she would not tell on him. He had been sent for, he stuttered, by the landlord. A lady who was lodging in the Inn wanted a letter delivered most urgently to a house in the Close. Queeney said, "Give it to me. I am just on my way there," at which he dug obediently into his pocket. One of the eggs he was hiding in his ragged shirt fell to the ground and splattered its yoke across his feet.

Queeney went back into the Inn and was about to return to her room when she was arrested by the picture hanging on the stair wall beneath the antlers of a stag. The painting was of an old man dressed in a black linsey gown and a snuff-coloured velvet coat with gold buttons. One hand was thrust into the bosom of his shirt, the other held out a letter with the subscription: "To Mr. Farthingale." She had looked at the picture before, but until now the letter had escaped her attention.

She was turning the bend of the stairs when she spied Mr. Johnson tiptoeing from her mother's room. He did not see her and continued in the direction of his own chamber, trailing a petticoat behind him.

AT MID-DAY, horses having been hired, Johnson and the Thrales, accompanied by Peter Garrick, prepared to ride into the countryside. Thrale was pale as a ghost, Garrick stupid and Johnson lethargic.

Very early that morning Mrs. Thrale had dispatched a note to Mrs. Garrick, apologising for the abruptness of her departure the night before and quoting, by way of excuse, the dear lady's own innocent and well-meaning reference to daughters being of comfort. *The subject is a painful one,* she wrote, *for though I have three living girls, my sweet, lost Lucy was dearer to me than all the rest.*

Now exhausted, she had intended to let the others gad off without her, but the transformation wrought in Queeney at the sight of the white pony waiting in the yard altered her mind. Such a shine on her face, such a pleasing curve to her pink mouth, lightened her heart. At breakfast the child had gazed at her coldly and when spoken to had twice pretended deafness.

In spite of the lack of sleep suffered by all, it was not long before the beauty of the day affected the mood of each and every one. The stormy weather having dissipated and the sun now serenely beaming in a blue heaven, it was hard to remain dull. Johnson went so far as to assert that sunlight was possessed of chemical properties, as yet undiscovered, similar to alcohol and conducive to a heightening of the spirits. "How else," he said, pointing at Thrale just then galloping ahead, voice raised in song, "are we to explain Henry's renewed energy. Four hours ago he had not the use of his legs."

"Nor of any other part," murmured Mrs. Thrale, recalling her rude awakening.

Trotting beside Stowe Pool, she was startled by a kingfisher thrashing among the rushes. "There, there," she cried, spreading her arms in imitation of its awkward wings. "That is nothing like," said Queeney, although her tone was free of scorn.

Mr. Johnson held the landscape much changed, and for the worse. His father's parchment mill had been allowed to fall into

decay. Even the ruins of it had vanished, obliterated under net-
tles and bindweed. The weeping willows, whose branches had
once swayed above the waters of the Pool, had been hacked
down. "In my yesterdays," he told them, reining in his horse and
indicating the lower reaches, "it was here my father taught me
to swim. In a mild voice he instructed me to breathe out,
breathe in . . . to wield the legs in the actions of a frog."

"Frogs have legs," said Queeney. "They are not like fish."

"Nor are we," Johnson said, "which is why they are worthy
of copy."

Continuing along a rutted path between fields of rough pasture
they passed into the shade of an ancient oak. Johnson dismounted
and bade the others do likewise. He wished them to look back at
Lichfield, at the spires of the Cathedral and the tower of St. Mary's
Church. "It is often advantageous," he said, "to view things from a
distance. Close up, we are apt to see a part rather than the whole."

Mrs. Thrale stayed on her horse; the ground was waterlogged
and she feared for her shoes. Upon Queeney jumping down,
mud rose up and spattered her dress. Johnson, staring into the
hazy distance, intoned, "He left a name, at which the world
grew pale, To point a moral, or adorn a tale."

"If I am not mistaken," said Mrs. Thrale, "you are speaking of
Charles XII."

"In this instance," he said, "I am remembering my poor
father."

His adult companions kept a respectful silence and looked
sombrely towards the town. It was rare for Johnson to refer to
his father, and rarer still for his memory to be recalled in such
an exalted manner.

Addressing Mr. Johnson, Queeney asked if he knew a man
called Farthingale. He repeated the name several times and then
shook his head. He asked why it mattered to her, and she
explained it was on account of the picture in the Swan Inn and

the letter in the old man's hand. "I had not noticed the letter before," she said, at which Mr. Johnson remarked that a similar thing had happened to him in regard to the painting, in that he had not been conscious of the old man's gold buttons until he had observed that one was missing.

"Missing?" said Thrale

"What old man?" asked Mrs. Thrale baffled.

"The third one down," Johnson said

Mrs. Thrale could make neither head nor tail of the conversation, and said no more.

Presently Queeney wandered off in search of wildflowers. Peter Garrick stretched his arms above his head and proclaimed it a capital morning. He acknowledged his wife was displeased with him owing to the bedraggled state of her petticoat, but she was not a woman to long hold a grudge.

"Perhaps I should make peace on your behalf," said Thrale. "I seem to recall it was I who wore it through the streets."

"You did indeed, and to great effect," Johnson told him. "In Bird Street, Sir, you were accosted by a ruffian who called you a pretty wench and offered you sixpence for a trembler against the wall."

"The moon was hidden," Garrick said, "which accounts for the proposition. You would have obliged, but I dragged you away lest he should squander his money."

Amid laughter, Thrale asked Johnson if he considered a pretty woman to be superior to one of a studious disposition, to which he answered in the affirmative. "Sir," he said, "a pretty woman may be foolish; a pretty woman may be wicked; a pretty woman may not like me, but beauty of itself is very estimable." At this, Mrs. Thrale spurred her horse forward and waited further off. She did not think herself pretty, nor ever had.

After some minutes Johnson came to her. He said, "We are having merry times, are we not, Hester?" She refused to answer him and busied herself flapping away gnats. He laid a hand on her arm. "Come, come," he said, "do not spoil the morning. We are all men in our own natures frail, and capable of frailty." "Frail indeed," she snapped, at which, chuckling, he murmured, "Dear, peevish little creature," and patted her hand as though humouring a child.

They rode in a wide circle back to Lichfield. Queeney had threaded meadowsweet into her pony's mane. Now and then she leaned forward and pressed her lips to its neck.

By degrees, conversation faltered and finally died. Entangled in separate dreams, the party swayed through the balmy morning to the hum of bees.

To Miss Laetitia Hawkins
2, Sion Row, Twickenham

December 14th, 1807

Dear Miss Hawkins,

You will forgive my somewhat abbreviated answers to your many questions, but as you rightly conjecture, I am much preoccupied with preparations for my forthcoming marriage to Admiral Keith.

My mother was indeed a great traveller; her numerous letters give proof of a singular curiosity and an aptitude for enjoyment, which virtues she retains to this day. I recall a letter she wrote from Milan stating her intention of returning to Verona and thence over the Tyrol into Germany, for the sole romantic purpose, as she put it, of washing her mouth in the Danube. Her letters to me often ended with the injunction that I must aim for happiness, movement and gaiety. Alas, I do not feel I have inherited her longing for fresh pastures, nor her capacity for happiness. It is hard to travel and be gay when one is burdened with the baggage of the past.

Of Dr. Goldsmith I remember little, apart from the game of Jack and Jill and the tightness of his breeches—that and a remark attributed to him regarding Dr. Johnson's ferocity of argument—"If he (Johnson) misses with his pistol, he hits you with the butt end." This was told me by my father. Dr. Johnson was distressed at Goldsmith's death; I remember he wept at the mention of his name when we stopped at Lichfield on our way to Wales in the summer of '74—but then, as was the fashion of the time, Dr. Johnson was not alone in finding it easy to shed tears.

On that same excursion we did indeed become acquainted with Miss Porter. She was somewhat coarse, but worthy. She referred to Dr. Johnson's mother, whom she had nursed when dying, as Grannie. I remember a fish in her kitchen and a dead bird in the garden. There was also a puff-headed mushroom under some cabbages, which burst apart

when an old woman fell on it. These bleak memories are possibly to the
fore on account of my mother having left behind at Streatham my infant
brother, Ralph, whose head was swollen and wanting a brain. My mother
loved but two of her many children, the one being Lucy, the other Harry.

To the best of my memory, the story of the drowned man, as told
by Dr. Johnson, was as follows. A man called Saltmarsh, by trade a
brick builder, was walking one Sunday through Hyde Park in the
direction of Kensington. He had with him his Newfoundland dog. Idly,
he threw a stone into the Serpentine, at which the Newfoundland leapt
in and re-emerged carrying a man's hat—a gentleman's hat. Laying it
down at his master's feet the dog dived into the river again and this
time brought out a wig. A third time he returned, and now he pulled
to the surface a man, or rather held the shoulder of a man gripped
between his teeth. The dog was not strong enough to carry the man out
of the river, but he dragged him into the shallower water. His master
was then able to wade in and bring the body on land. The dead man
wore a coat with silver buttons and there was nothing in the pockets
save for two sixpences and a gold box of French design in which
reposed a lock of golden hair—not his, for he was almost bald and
swarthy with it. No sooner had the body been laid down than the dog
began to drag at the coat, and though it was driven away several times,
it at last worried the sodden material so persistently that a piece tore
free and hung from its jaws, one silver button catching the sunlight.
Then the animal ran off, and reaching a patch of earth, scraped out a
hole, dropped down the rag, covered it over and lay across it, like a hen
on an egg. On enquiries being made, it was found that the drowned
soul was a Mr. Farthingale who had done some injury to a young lady
of a lower class than himself, and whose conscience was afterwards so
troubled that he threw himself into the river. At the close of the story,
Dr. Johnson observed, "Without buttons, we are all undone," which
remark caused some of the company to guffaw and others to weep.

Dr. Johnson's watch, which on numerous occasions he left under his pillow at Streatham and often required my father, at some inconvenience, straight away to send after him, cost 17 guineas and was encased in tortoiseshell. It was engraved with an inscription in Greek, the words later scratched out owing to Dr. Johnson thinking them ostentatious. On his death I believe your own dear father, Sir John, removed it from the bedside table, no doubt for safety, along with certain papers. Dr. Johnson's executors insisted on its return, after which I understand it was given to Frank Barber.

I have no explanation for my mother's fallout with Mrs. Garrick, who you say was offended by some rudeness done her without subsequent apology.

In haste, I remain,

Believe me, affectionately yours,

H. M. Thrale

REVOLUTION

n.f. (revolution, Fr., revolultus, Lat.)

1. Course of any thing which returns to the point at which it
began to move.

2. Space measured by some revolution.

At certain revolutions are they bought,
and feel by turns the bitter change.

—MILTON

THE FORTUNES OF the Thrale Brewery much improved due
to the exertions of its chief clerk, Perkins, Henry Thrale fas-
tened on the notion of going to France. The party would consist
of his wife, Baretti, Johnson, Queeney and two female servants.
Accordingly, the child's eleventh birthday and Johnson's sixty-
sixth were celebrated on the 15th September, three days early,
at the house of Sir John Hawkins. Frank Barber was not included, an omission which offended Johnson. Dr. Levet received an
invitation but failed to arrive on account of his dropping into a
pothole on his way home from Hounsditch, a mishap spelt out
in a letter from Mrs. Desmoulins awaiting them at Dover. She
wrote that Levet had lain on his back for some hours, but, judging from the raucous singing that accompanied his eventual
descent of the cellar steps, had returned none the worse for
wear. The veracity of this report caused Johnson some concern;

Mrs. Desmoulins did not care for Levet, though more so than Mrs. Williams.

It was generally agreed that the festivities in Twickenham were not so conducive to merriment as those annually conducted in the Summerhouse at Streatham Park. Hawkins was less than generous with the wine and Thrale woke in the night complaining of hunger. Mrs. Thrale flew out of sorts owing to Queeney, on some provocation never adequately explained, tugging at the hair of Laetitia, daughter of Sir John, and reducing her to tears. The next morning it was a disgruntled group that left for the coast in two coaches.

An enthusiastic Baretti had put himself in charge of all travel arrangements; for months he had been writing to his contacts in Paris in order that his friends should be well received. Mrs. Thrale, worn down by the birth of yet another sickly daughter and the death of Ralph, allowed herself to be swept along by events. She inclined towards Johnson's view that any thing was better than vacuity.

The party dallied so long in Canterbury, admiring the beauties of the cathedral, that they arrived too late to catch the tide at Dover. Baretti, who had gone on ahead to oversee the crossing, was considerably put out and fell into a sulk. He became more agreeable after Thrale expressed himself mightily pleased to have time to explore the fort and the castle. Johnson, flinging stones down into Julius Caesar's Well, said that the reverberations emphasised the truth that the echoes of men's actions, good as well as bad, were always susceptible to revival. He was thinking, though he did not voice it, of Levet's stumble in the dark and of his muddied calls for help.

In the evening, walking along the shore, they witnessed a blood-red sun sliding into the waves. One moment its rays splashed the cliffs with crimson, the next the world turned black. Mrs. Thrale cried out it was a wonder the sun's drowning was not accompanied by a gigantic hissing, as when a kettle on the coals jerked water from its spout. It was a domestic observation, yet apt.

The journey through France passed enjoyably enough, though Johnson became weary of the continual oohs and aahs of appreciation loosed by his companions at this or that aspect of the landscape. There was, he felt, little to distinguish one clump of trees, one stretch of pasture, from another, and nothing to say of either save that they could be seen. For himself, he would have preferred a vista of bookshelves.

He grew more cheerful when, crossing the Seine for the third time and approaching Vernon, he glimpsed his first vineyard. It was a delightful novelty to step from the chaise, take but a short clamber down the bank at the side of the road and fill one's hat with grapes. It was the next day, when approaching St. Denys, that things turned sour. It happened thus. Mrs. Thrale, in the butterfly way of women, was twittering on about the sunlight darting silver arrows from the leaves of a field of asparagus, when she suddenly brought up the name of James Macpherson, author of *Fingal: An Ancient Poem*. The night before, she said, she had dreamt that Macpherson had approached her with *fire in his eyes*. The implication was obvious, for she began to simper and fan herself as though grown hot. It was true the weather was warm, but the window of the carriage was let down and a breeze ruffled the pages of the book on his knee.

He said with admirable restraint, "I have never met Macpherson yet know him to be a scoundrel. His attack upon me regarding a passage in my *Journey to the Western Isles*, in which I state my opinion that the poems of Ossian are impostures of the crudest sort, was not the response of a scholar."

She, "Or of a gentleman—"

He, "I care not whether my opponent is a knight of the realm or a herder of swine, only that his intellect be sound."

She, "I believe he accused you of falling into the same error some twenty years since."

He, with less restraint, "To which error, Madame, do you refer?"

"Why, that of—" she began, and broke off abruptly, eyes widening in alarm as a distant clamour disturbed the air.

He said again, "What error, Madame?" though he was only too aware she alluded to the regrettable mistake he had made in writing a complimentary preface to a pamphlet published by the schoolmaster William Laud, alleging that Milton in his composing of *Paradise Lost* had been guilty of plagiarism. It was unforgivable of her to bring up the subject, and cowardly to feign deafness when challenged, for he had surely expressed himself loudly enough to be heard above the screams and whinnyings that now irritated the ear.

Just then the horses were reined in with such abruptness that the carriage shuddered on its wheels and tossed the servant girl, Mags Hewson, onto his lap; in other circumstances the encounter would have been welcome.

"Which error, Madame?" he repeated, thrusting the girl from him, but Hester was opening the door and dropping into the road without the aid of the step. He leapt after her, demanding an answer; she ran ahead, skirts stirring up dust, towards a horse rolling belly up, hooves pawing a sky thick with circling gulls. Beyond, stood a stationary carriage, much tilted.

Sitting down some yards distant he busied himself snatching red petals, without malice, from the heads of common leadwort growing amid the grass. He refrained from indulging in the futile business of she loves me, she loves me not, and instead engaged in an argument with Macpherson. The man had not a leg to stand on; his supposed sending of a letter offering to produce the original manuscripts of the Ossian poems was an outright lie. No such letter had ever existed. The impudent rogue had even gone so far as to threaten him with violence if he failed to publish a retraction. Boswell had advised him to purchase a stout new stick to replace the old one mislaid on his visit to Flora MacDonald—in case Macpherson should seek him out.

At the recollection, he could not help laughing out loud at the idea he would have needed anything more than his fists to see off such a nincompoop. It had come to nothing, of course; the fellow was a bladder of air. As for poor William Laud, without the provision of a preface he would have been imprisoned for debt. One would need a heart cast in iron to turn one's face from the suffering of others.

Glancing up, he saw the horse was now on its feet, albeit unsteady, and that Hester was running round in circles, squealing like a stuck pig. A moment later, he was astonished to observe Baretti staggering up from the side of the road supporting a ghostly Henry Thrale covered from head to foot in some white substance. On the grass verge, rocking back and forth, crouched Queeney, bonnet askew.

It was a full two hours before the journey continued, during which time a dozen or more peasants wearing hats quaintly woven of straw appeared from nowhere and attended to the torn traces and the buckled shafts. The postilion believed his leg to be broke, until, revived with a flagon of wine, he ran about with hardly a limp. Henry Thrale's complexion, to be sure, was bloodless, but that was on account of his roll in the dust.

Once on their way again Johnson tried to engage Hester in conversation, but she, tight-lipped, merely clasped Queeney closer in her arms and refused to answer directly. Once, she uttered the mysterious phrase, "Such indifference," and another time, "It is scarcely credible . . ."

It was not a comfortable ride. The sun was now at its height and a quantity of flies, drawn by the smears of grapejuice in his hat, buzzed relentlessly about his head. It was only later, when they reached St. Germain, that Hester deigned to speak to him, and then with such coldness that he would have wished her to have kept silent. It discomforted him to be spoken to so angrily in the presence of Queeney and Baretti.

His casualness, she upbraided, towards the fate of the occupants of the first carriage, namely Baretti, Thrale and Queeney, was, in her opinion, unworthy of a true friend, indeed, of a member of the human species. "I would not have believed you capable of such callousness," she said. "You . . . who take pride in doing good, who would give the clothes off your back to the lowest wretch in the gutter—"

"I take no pride," he began—

"To appear so unconcerned," she continued, pearls of sweat clinging to the pale and delicious hairs trembling above the scar on her lip, "towards the plight of those you have been pleased to call your family—"

"If you had not insulted me by ignoring my question," he protested, "I might have been more conscious of the gravity of the incident. As it was, I was preoccupied."

"Incident . . . incident," she shouted, though her voice was so high in pitch it approached a scream, "why, three of those closest to you nearly met with their deaths."

She was wrong; there was but one close to him, and she unhurt.

"The word incident," said he, "does not detract from the seriousness of the situation. My *Dictionary* defines it as fortuitous, casual, an accidental happening—"

"I am not concerned with definitions," she spat, "only with your lack of imagination."

"Imagination," he spluttered, "what part has imagination in this?" At which she gazed at him as if seeing him for the first time and then asked, why, as a child, had he fled out into the market square after dwelling upon the apparition of Hamlet's father? Before he could reply, she added scornfully, "Though on that we have only your word for it. Indeed, for all any of us know, it could have been the fable of Cinderella you read, and it was the turning of mice into footmen that caused you fright." Shocked, he turned to Baretti for support, but he, false friend, took her part and thunderously proclaimed that lives had been saved by the greatest providence ever exerted in favour of three human creatures.

Such nonsense rendered Johnson speechless, but Baretti was not yet done. Did Johnson not understand, he raged, nostrils flaring, dark eyes flashing contempt, that with the traces snapped, the carriage careering with dangerous rapidity downhill, one animal over-run, the other galloping them to destruction, that Henry Thrale, fearful for the safety of his daughter, had jumped out with the intention of averting disaster? By misfortune, his courageous leap had landed him on so steep an incline that he had been bounced sideways and deposited in a chalk pit. "The action your master took," he concluded, "one embarked upon with the sole aim of helping others, was the likeliest thing in the world to produce broken limbs and death."

Their combined hostility so unnerved him that he was reduced to muttering that it was not unconcern for Henry that had made him appear disaffected, rather anger at Mrs. Thrale for starting up a controversy and then shying away from its denouement. He spoke in a contrite tone of voice, though inwardly he bridled at the Italian's impudent bandying of the word master, an appellation which, used by any one but himself, reeked of servitude. Baretti's stance struck him as curious in the extreme; it was not often he saw eye to eye with Hester. Why, when Queeney, in spite of calm seas, had grown nauseous on the crossing to Calais, he had loudly attributed it to a proximity to her mother.

The next day, when they reached Paris and things turned out better than had been feared, Mrs. Thrale made her peace with him. "Sam," she bleated, "you will forgive me, will you not, for speaking in the heat of the moment?"

"Madame," he replied, "it is I who should ask pardon."

"When we heard you laughing," she said, "even Queeney spoke out against you."

"Laughing?" he echoed. "Who said I laughed?"

"There was no need for the saying of it," she replied, "for the sound travelled quite clearly from where you sat beside the precipice."

He had no remembrance of giving way to amusement, and might have argued the point had not sense prevailed; women had ever been against logic.

"The tormenting of flies so addled me," he told her, "along with thoughts of the rascally Macpherson, that I was scarce myself." At which Hester was gracious enough to acknowledge that he, being a man who lived in the head rather than the body, had behaved no worse than could be expected.

He was grateful for her forgiveness, and made amends by acceding to her wishes in regard to mixing with people he found uncongenial and visiting places which held no interest for him, such as dining with Madame de Brocages and running from church to church. The former outing was memorable for the close stool in the dinner room, a pewter pot in which to spit and a large and ancient cobweb trembling above the table. Mrs. Thrale said the food was poor, the dish of hare being not merely tainted but putrefied, the beans old and the sugar plums uneatable. He had taken the spitting pot for an ornament and noticed nothing out of the ordinary save for the presence in the hallway of a number of footmen playing cards.

Their circle of acquaintances grew as the weeks advanced, the Abbé François and the Benedictine Father Wilkes being worthy of mention. There were also two Italian Counts, one of whom, Manucci, introduced by Baretti, paid particular attention to Mrs. Thrale.

When they were not dining in or out, the company spent far too short a time inspecting the King's Library and that of the Sorbonne, and far too long going to operas, fairs and pleasure gardens. The amount of attention wasted on egg races, rope-walkers and shopping would have tried the patience of the Saints, most of whom appeared to have been interred in Paris.

Thrale suggested to Hester that she leave the "studious Mr. Johnson" to his own devices, but it had little effect. Wherever she went he felt obliged to follow, on account of his allegedly churlish behaviour on the road to St. Denys.

On one of their many excursions to places of worship they suffered a second falling out concerning his insistence that they should leave before the elevation of the Host. Had they stayed they must have got to their knees, a theatrical gesture which Mrs. Thrale professed herself perfectly willing to undertake and one for which he, rather than comply, would have gone to the scaffold.

His reasons for flight had not been as pure in motive as he would have her believe. They had sat close by the choir stall, so close that his hearing was undimmed; it was not the first time he had been disturbed by the effects of music on the emotions. The workings of the mind, he conjectured, were as aimless as the motes of dust drifting within the rays of sunlight illuminating the nave. As the angelic voices soared heavenwards, his thoughts had dwelt upon the mother who had failed to understand him, the wife he had neglected, the temperament that had condemned him to idleness. Dashing the sudden tears from his eyes, he had blundered his way from the church.

Hester had delayed following him due to her straying into a side chapel and coming upon the statue of an angel bearing a child in its arms, at the sight of which she had tripped, so she said, and hurt her foot. He had rebuked her for keeping him waiting, and she, eyes glittering, had termed him an *impossible man*. There was also some reference to Count Manucci and the recalling of an exquisite delicacy of manner.

Later that afternoon, when Queeney had gone with her father and Baretti to the theatre, she had softened towards him and described the terror she had experienced upon seeing the statue. At once, he warned her not to give way to such fancies, and urged her to talk out her fears.

"The child in its arms," she told him, voice unsteady, "bore a distinct likeness to Harry. As I approached, I almost fell . . . and yet there was nothing in the way to cause me to stumble. And it was then that I was seized with such a heavy sense of dread that I all but fainted."

"No doubt from the pain in your foot," he reasoned, but she cried out, "No . . . no . . . it was the thought . . . the premonition that some ill had befallen Harry. Why, when an old man passed by and I enquired to whom the chapel was dedicated, he replied that it was to the Guardian Angel of Children."

"Well, then," he said, "that is all to the good, is it not?"

"You have often spoken of bad omens," she protested. "Think of the time the clock stopped in Perkins's office, two days before the discovery of Henry's near bankruptcy . . . think of when Frances Reynolds threatened to break Sir Joshua's head with the bust of Pope—"

"They could scarcely be called omens," he interrupted, "the one being an example of mechanical failure, the other of a woman's temper. Besides, there are good omens as well as bad ones, and I would suppose a guardian angel to be among the former. Harry is a strong and healthy boy and you must rid your mind of such morbid thoughts." It had taken more of the same to restore her, but before nightfall she smiled again.

Afterwards, to show her renewed fondness for him she chose to take breakfast each morning—mercifully at a late hour—in his chamber on the second floor of the house in the Rue Jacob. She said it was the change of air that caused her to lie abed so long, and how companionable it was that both could now be classed as *Sleepy Heads*.

Together, they often leaned on the window sill to watch the spectacle in the narrow street below. So near was the house opposite that they could plainly see a man with a tuft of hair under his nose and a nightcap on his head, sitting up in bed. At first they had pretended not to notice him, but he had taken to waving to them in a cheery manner and had once, in full view, even made use of his close-stool, at which Hester had burst out laughing; both had agreed that the French were remarkably free of reticence in regard to bodily functions, and possibly with good sense.

Standing so close to her, elbow to elbow, he was enchanted by the dazzle of light on her bare arms, the primrose hue of her small mouth; as her breath with its odour of warm chocolate blew against his cheek he was convinced that he knew happiness.

One morning, watching her capering free of slippers about the room, he was moved to sink to his knees and seize her tiny foot in his hands, the better to examine it. It resembled, he thought, in its warmth and softness, a pink and newborn creature whose fur had not yet grown. She misunderstood his gesture, or else his lips tickled her, for she shook him off so violently that both lost their balance, he falling on to his back and she on all fours—at which moment Queeney entered the room complaining of a sourness to her breakfast milk.

ON OCTOBER 18TH Mrs. Thrale rose from her bed and immediately encountered vexations. Entering her daughter's room to make sure she was being dressed as instructed, she grew aggravated and alarmed at the child's constant squirming and scratching as she suffered the maid to brush her hair.

Until that morning their stay in France, save for the horrid accident on the way to Paris, had been remarkably free of upsets and petty quarrels. It was true that Johnson had caused them to spend many hours in dusty libraries, but he had declared himself more than satisfied both with his visit to the Sèvres porcelain works and his introduction to Mrs. Femore, Abbess of the Austin Nuns of the English Convent in the Rue St. Victoire, she who had known Mr. Pope and not liked him, though for what reason she would not say. He had been even more intrigued by the mechanical table they had seen at Choisie, which could rise up out of the floor and sink again. Count Manucci had told them it was for the use of the King when he wanted to dine in private with his mistresses, but Sam had argued that nothing so ingenious could have been invented merely to further the seduction of women. "A draft of wine," he had said, "and a finger up the petticoats would have sufficed," an indelicate summation which had astonished his audience, for he was a man known to despise talk of a bawdy nature.

"Worms," deduced Mrs. Thrale, studying the wriggling Queeney, and at once ordered that she be purged, followed by the swallowing of patent pills. Scarce five minutes later the sly girl ran to Mr. Baretti and told him of her ordeal, at which the Italian, wigless and wrapped in a morning gown of lurid colours, stormed into the Thrales' marital chamber and accused Hester of endangering the child's health by the administration of a physic he considered dangerous. "Those dam'ned tin pills are as likely to kill as to cure," he thundered. "The scales settle equally between life and death."

At such moments of conflict Mrs. Thrale detested Baretti, yet, in the arrogance of his manner and the quickness of his temper, she could not but affectionately recall her dead father. "I am in full charge of my own offspring," she countered, pointing a scornful finger at Henry, who lay in his bed as though ready for the graveyard, "and am prepared to take the consequences."

In the middle of this exchange, Johnson, attired in a night-gown much soiled from the spilling of some brown liquid down its front, appeared in the doorway demanding to know why she had not yet come to his chamber to break her fast. A week before, anxious to show her gratitude for a kindness he had done her, she had twice drunk chocolate with him, a ritual she fancied he now took to be fixed in stone. Pushing him from the room, she shut the door in his face.

It was upsetting that such a disagreement should arise before undertaking the coach ride to the chateau of Fontainebleau. King Louis and his court having retired there for six weeks of hunting, the estimable Count Manucci had obtained a pass for his new friends that would admit them to the royal apartments, a circumstance—so Mrs. Thrale excitedly babbled—beyond her wildest dreams. Now, with Baretti in a huff and Queeney disor-dered, she did not imagine the journey could be accomplished without storms, and was pleasantly surprised. No sooner had they rattled into the Rue de Richelieu than Baretti laid a wager with the occupants of the carriage as to how many hours they would spend on the road. She herself staked fifteen livres, Johnson a louis and Thrale treble the two amounts, which put the Italian in a good humour as he appeared mightily confident of winning.

They arrived in the hamlet of Fontainebleau in late afternoon, having travelled through countryside reminiscent of the approach to Tunbridge Wells—though more rocky—and took up rooms in an inn procured through the offices of dear Manucci. Had this wretched accommodation not been recommended by the charming young nobleman, Mrs. Thrale might have fallen into a sulk. As it was, she ignored the unclean linen on the beds and the scamperings of mice beneath the floorboards, and dined in high spirits. Henry, possibly due to an absence of other members of the female sex, paid her much attention, and Baretti, who had won his wager—there were those among them who suspected he had made the journey before—was sweet as honey.

It was he who turned the evening sour, though it was surely unintentional. Observing a fly drowning in his wine, he elaborated on the suicidal behaviour of scorpions, which, so he said, placed in a circle of coals in the squares of Italy, ran round and round in extreme pain, until, rather than suffer longer, like true Stoics they coiled up and darted stings into their own heads.

Johnson held this was nonsense, maintaining that the turning of a tail to the head was merely a convulsion brought about by heat. "No creature," he said, "has so miserable an existence that it seeks its own destruction, for what may follow is not to be contemplated." At this, Mrs. Thrale tried to divert the conversation, for talk of death would likely cause Johnson to dwell on his own extinction. "I believe," she began, "that the gardens of Fontainebleau are famed for their beauty—"

"I take it," said Baretti, "that you are in disagreement with Roman law and do not consider suicide to be a legitimate choice of rational men?"

"No man takes his own life in a rational state of mind," shouted Johnson. "The fear of death is so natural to a rational man, Sir, that the whole of life is but keeping away the thought of it." Here Baretti opened his mouth to argue further, at which his opponent bellowed, "No, Sir, let it alone. It matters not how a man dies, but how he lives."

Later that night when Hester had gone to her bed, Henry Thrale, sitting in candlelight with Baretti and the morose Johnson, confessed that he was feeling unwell. Baretti held it was not to be wondered at . . . had not the physician attending him at St. Germain expressed astonishment that he still breathed?

Thrale shook his head, and after much prevarication acknowledged that his disorder was possibly due to an old infection, one no doubt venereal, seeing a swelling of the right testicle could not wholly be explained by his unfortunate ejection into the chalk pit outside St. Denys. Johnson questioned him as to other symptoms, and after some thought made reference to a publication whose pages he had rifled through in a bookseller's shop next door to the saddler's in the Rue Jacob.

"In regard to a diagnosis?" asked Thrale.

"Not so," Johnson said. "It had more to do with the avoidance of ill effects, its subject being onanism and its subtitle, 'A Treatise Upon the Dangerous Effect of Excessive Venery.' I did not agree with its premise, as it appears to me that onanism has much to recommend it, in that it does away with the mingling of harmful fluids."

"It does away with many things," argued Baretti. "Not least a woman's heat."

"Such heat, Sir," rebuked Johnson, "is the root of the problem. It would be wiser to practice onanism rather than engage in other than lawful congress."

"Practice ... practice," cried Thrale. "I have been adept at the habit since my seventh year . . . and scarcely need practice. Besides, I was tossed enough on my way through France." A remark which provoked such an outbreak of merriment that Johnson burst the buttons on his waistcoat.

THE NEXT MORNING he found himself wedged between Thrale and Baretti amid a murmuring line of onlookers intent on observing a man and woman eating in the gilded chamber beneath. He was shocked at himself for watching so common a ritual with such a degree of reverence.

A procession of footmen entered from the left bearing silver platters and waited their turn while a major-domo lifted the covers and sniffed at the contents. Waved on, four other footmen approached the table and set about the serving. The first course consisted of five dishes, of which the Queen tasted nothing but a quantity of pie under a crust; her companion partook heartily of whatever was put before him, save for a mess of pottage which he poked with his knife and appeared reluctant to shovel into his mouth.

A buzz of excitement raged through the gallery at this exception, for though the actors on stage spoke not a word it was as if the spectators were privy to some play in which poisoning was suspected. A stink of fish, riddled with garlic, seeped upwards. Even Henry Thrale was driven to pinch his nostrils together.

Johnson was dazzled by the reflections of silver plate in the multiplicity of mirrors lining the walls. He could see that the King was stout, but could not discern his features. Marie-Antoinette, as far as he could tell, was pretty, in that she was slender enough not to spill from the confines of her chair. A stream of sunlight from the end window caught her elaborate hairpiece and spun it gold. But a few yards to the left of her chair, at the front of a gawping crowd, he spied Queeney and Mrs. Thrale.

Peering down at Hester, it occurred to him that it was impossible to have both affection and veneration for one and the same person, and that if it came to a choice the former sentiment must inevitably triumph, not least in regard to his dear mistress. There was, he pondered, much in her character to inspire love and little deserving of respect. Even as he scrutinised her, she said something to Queeney that caused the child to wilt. He could not make out her expression, but the girl's shoulders slumped.

Turning, he was confronted by an image of himself in the

vast mirror on the gallery wall, and did not recognise his features. It was as though the shaving glasses at Streatham Park and Johnson's Court, deceived by familiarity, had presented a false portrait, for here the mouth that he had privately considered generous appeared licentious in its fullness, and his large eyes, at home seemingly so expressive of candour, were lit with a sly regard, as of a man fixed on himself.

He would have nudged Baretti for a denial of such an interpretation had he and the Italian still ploughed the same furrow—following Thrale's brush with death, Baretti had been less than respectful; only the previous night, when buttons had gone missing, he had stayed sluggishly in his chair and neglected to join in the search.

Just then Henry Thrale took Johnson by the elbow and urged him to come outside. "I may fall asleep if I stay much longer," he grumbled. "That the King feeds himself with his left hand as we do, does not greatly add to my knowledge of his character, nor does it add to the gaiety of my stomach to see Marie-Antoinette refuse so many dishes."

Together they descended the stairs to the lower floors. They had intended to go into the back courtyard and the grounds beyond, but instead found themselves lost in a maze of passageways and steps. Once, during their many twists and turns, they came face to face with two ancient liveried footmen, both of whom proved too intoxicated to be of help.

After further minutes of aimless wandering, Henry thrust open the door to a store room whose casements overlooked a yard in which a number of horses could be seen at exercise. There being no other means of exit he promptly heaved open the nearest window and clambered out.

Johnson was about to follow when he noticed a bulky shape lying in the far corner, partially hidden under a damask cloth. Intrigued, he approached and tugging aside the covering saw it was the sculpture of a naked man, arms spread wide, the wrists manacled and lengths of marble chain trailing the dusty floor. He imagined it must be a likeness of Prometheus, though the rock was absent.

For some time, looking upon that face, mouth carved in a rictus of agony, his mind remained vacant; he saw rather than recorded. Then, like bubbles in a glass, his thoughts rose upwards, and with their surfacing the sculptured features began to dissolve and reconstruct themselves . . . and now he stared down at a different countenance, one known to him from long ago. Gradually he grew conscious of a dreadful emptiness, as though his inner being had been sucked from his body and what remained was hollow darkness. But for the thumping of his heart, loud as drumbeats, he might have imagined himself dead. With a gigantic effort of will he switched his gaze to the chain in the dust and, link by marble link, dragged himself back to life. At last, shuddering, he flung the cloth over those blind, accusing eyes, and quite forgetting the open window, stumbled from the room.

Once again he wandered the numerous passages, until, climbing some stairs and putting his shoulder to a door mercifully unlocked, he emerged into the dappled sunlight of a deserted avenue lined with stately trees, leaves ablaze in autumnal glory.

I too, he thought, am about to encounter the fire before the fall, and still in the grip of terror and remorse set off at speed towards the horizon. Above his jogging head, like sails in a blue sea, white clouds flapped the heavens.

THE SPECTACLE OF the royal dinner concluded, Mrs. Thrale, accompanied by Baretti and Queeney, spent an hour or more searching for her husband and Johnson. It was upsetting that she could not find them immediately, for she had momentous news to import—no less a person than Marie-Antoinette had commented on the prettiness of Queeney and asked who she was. This thrilling information had been passed on by darling Count Manucci who had given assurances that he had answered such an enquiry with the right amount of reserve and discretion. No, he had not supplied the address of their lodgings in the Rue Jacob, but he had let it be known that the Thrales were visiting France in the company of the eminent Samuel Johnson.

Mrs. Thrale was not surprised that her daughter had been noticed; she had observed the extraordinary crookedness of posture exhibited by the inhabitants of Paris, and the predominance of trusses and the like displayed for sale in shop windows. Deformities of the spine in such numbers, she reasoned, were to be explained by the French habit of putting children into stays as soon as they could stand upright. The resulting inhibition of limbs and retardation of growth had produced a population unable to walk in an easy manner. That here, as at home, Samuel was stared at in the street, was due more to his remarkable freedom of movement than to the dramatics of his rolling gait and his sometime revolvings.

Queeney herself was far from overwhelmed at being the subject of royal attention, but then, her looks had never been matched by a warmth of temperament. From infancy she had shown coldness, though it was true she had shed tears when Papa had flown into the chalk pit. "It is an honour to be singled out by the Queen of France," Mrs. Thrale remonstrated. "It would do you no harm to appear gratified." To which the child tartly retorted that her mother was showing enough gratification for both of them.

They found Henry tramping the straw of the royal stables. When told of the attention Queeney's presence had aroused he said it was no more than he would have expected, and that he had no idea where Johnson might be, save that like a man long incarcerated underground, he had sought the air.

Some quarter of an hour later it was Queeney, striding sullenly ahead of an exasperated Mrs. Thrale, who spied him in the distance seated on a bench beside a luminous stretch of ornamental lake. Mrs. Thrale told her to run on ahead and fetch him. "I am not a dog," the girl murmured, and deliberately slackened her pace.

It took some time for her to reach the bench. Mrs. Thrale watched intently, and was astonished to see Johnson remaining in his seat and Queeney returning alone. She was limping again, an affectation assumed following a lesson with her Parisian dancing master during which she swore she had suffered a stubbed toe, an injury requiring the temporary postponement of further instruction. Mrs. Thrale suspected the toe to be an excuse, the girl having run about quite agilely the following day when taken for an airing in the gardens of the Tuileries.

Queeney coming within earshot, she called out, "What is wrong? Why is Mr. Johnson not with you?"

"He insists he is not fit company," Queeney said, "and is saying his prayers."

Much perturbed, Mrs. Thrale hurried down the path. Johnson sat bent forward, leaning on his stick, eyes lowered. "Samuel," she shouted, "we are ready to leave . . ."

"Go about your business . . . I am best left to myself," he replied, in such tones of muffled despair that she stood momentarily aghast. Familiar as she was with his moods it was not always possible to find the correct approach. Sometimes he was so angry and out of sorts that it did no good to reason with him; at others it was talk he needed and a sympathetic ear. Glancing at his face, it was pitiful to see the misery etched upon it . . . and yet, the dying day was so lovely in its aspect—the purple shadows on the grass, the silver sheen upon the water, the flash of wings as birds swooped from the fiery canopy of the trees—that she could not feel his sadness, and with an honesty of spirit was compelled to tell him so. Seating herself beside him she placed one small hand on his stout knee, where it perched like the lid on a teapot. "Look up," she bade him. "Look up at the sky."

For some time he could not bring himself to obey her; patiently, she waited. Presently, voice hoarse as though from speechifying or weeping, he said, "I am not such a good traveller as I thought myself to be."

She knew this to be true, for she and Baretti had remarked on his lack of ease away from London, and in particular his refusal to speak French, which kept him out of the conversation when in the company of strangers; he would either talk Latin or not talk at all.

"The French are a silly people," he said. "They have no common life. Nothing but the two ends, beggary and nobility. Nor do they have any common sense, common manners, common learning . . . with them it is either gross ignorance or les belles lettres—"

"We shall all be glad to be in England again," she lied; she herself found Paris more stimulating than either Streatham Park or the Brewery in Deadman's Place. Still, she was touched by his obvious homesickness, and tapped his knee affectionately.

He looked up then, but she could tell he did not take in the radiance of the fading day; she had been in the right of it when sometime past she had accused him of being a man who lived in the head rather than the body.

Suddenly, he said, "I have had cause to remember my brother, Nathaniel—"

"Little Natty," she prompted.

"Little Natty," he repeated, and lapsed into silence again.

She watched the scarlet streaks flooding the darkening sky and thought of other things; of the Queen's gown made of gauze adorned with flowers and of the pearl bracelets on her wrists; of the French way of cruelly whipping their horses over the face; of the infants in the Foundling Hospital pining away to perfect skeletons and expiring in neat cribs with each a bottle hung to its neck containing a milk mess, which if they could suck on they might live, and if not, would die; of the anniversary of her wedding day some two days past and of Henry presenting her with flowers and stammering she had been a good wife to him. That she had never been in love was not a great deprivation, for what one had never known was scarcely to be fretted over.

"I have had reason to think of the manner of his death," said Johnson.

For a moment she could not recall who it was that occupied his mind, and then, remembering his dead sibling, asked what it was that had revived the memory.

What Samuel told her was incoherent, and besides, she who had suffered the loss of so many children could not be expected to waste much thought on a man who had been dead for nigh on forty years.

"He died but a few hours, a day at the most, after Davy Garrick and I left Lichfield for London."

"He was ill when you set off," she probed.

"No. Not so . . ."

"A sudden illness, then—"

"I had not seen his face, not even in dreams, until today—"

"It is strange," she said, "how an image can suddenly come into the mind. Some years ago, I remember I was—"

"He was lying in the dust—"

"The dust . . ." she repeated, distracted by the sight of Queeney whirling round and round on the path.

"In fetters in the dust."

At once, she gave him her full attention. When Samuel dwelt

on restraints it was a sure sign he was beginning to allow a morbid melancholy to overpower his senses.

"It was in my gift to have helped him," he said, "and I did nothing."

"He died in prison?" she asked, trying to make sense of it.

"Neither in a prison or a madhouse," he said, "and for that is now in a worse place than either," after which curious utterance he beat his fist against his breast with such force that she started up in alarm and attempted to tug him to his feet. "Sorrow," she cried, quoting one of his own metaphors, "is the putrefaction of stagnant life, and is remedied by exercise and motion." He laughed at this, but there was no humour in the sound. She shouted to Queeney to seek out Papa and Baretti; her voice was so charged with urgency that the girl sped off immediately.

"In the dust," Johnson repeated. "In the everlasting dust . . ."

"Samuel," she said, "there is little in my own life to keep me in that state of mind called happiness, but such is my trust in God that I do not question His will and am convinced there is a purpose to it all." At that moment, fearful for his sanity, she believed in her fairy tale. "You yourself," she continued, "have written that the antidotes with which philosophy has medicated the cup of life, though they cannot give it salubrity or sweetness, have at least allayed its bitterness and tempered its malignity. The balm which she drops on the wounds of the mind abates their pain—"

"—though it cannot heal them," interrupted Johnson, and reminded her that those were Seneca's thoughts, not his. "I am missing a button," he suddenly confided—"Mags Hewson found but two to sew on my coat—" and got to his feet. Giddy with relief, Mrs. Thrale linked her arm in his and guided him towards the distant windows glowing with first candlelight.

As they walked he endeavoured to conduct a conversation, but the sense of it was hard to follow, punctuated as it was by prayer. "The ducks on the lake," he said, "are very fine specimens . . . giver and preserver of life, by whose power I was created, and by whose providence I am sustained, look down on me with tenderness and mercy . . . but not so fine as those at Streatham Park—"

"They are indeed fine," Hester gabbled, "and of a rare breed—"

"Grant that I may not have been created to be finally destroyed; that I may not be preserved to add wickedness to wickedness . . . I have a mind to buy a new wig before I leave Paris—"

She said, "There is a wigmaker further along the Rue Jacob. Count Manucci told Henry he has a good reputation—"

"Repent me of my sins, and so order my life to come, that when I shall be called hence, like the wife whom thou hast taken from me . . . " Here Johnson stopped in his tracks and gazed about him with a face so expressive of despair that Mrs. Thrale fought back tears; to succumb to the emotion of the moment would have been of little benefit to her dear friend. "When I think of my dead father," she said, "which I often do, I take care to think of the times when we were in accord. I remember him taking me fishing—"

"Tetty had golden hair," he interrupted, "bright as though the sun shone on it—"

"Like Marie-Antoinette," she said.

"I was not a good husband," he groaned, and lumbered ahead of her down the path.

"Wait," she called, and watched as a single streak of gold leaked from the sinking sun and stained the sky.

"Gold as corn," Johnson called back, and allowed her to catch up with him. "On our wedding day," he said, "I taught her a lesson and rode on ahead . . . Almighty God, forgive me my transgressions—"

That night Mrs. Thrale told Henry of the anguish she had experienced. "He was not himself," she wailed, "and I am still in the dark as to what caused the disturbance."

Henry said there had been intimations earlier, when he and Johnson, lost in the cellars of the Palace, had witnessed an act of buggery in the archway of a wine vault. He himself had not been affected unduly, but Samuel had trembled with disgust at the sight of the coarse hairs sprouting from the buttocks of the perpetrator, and had afterwards hidden himself in a store room.

Mrs. Thrale climbed into bed and turned her face to the wall. Though her eyes were closed she could see her anniversary flowers dead on their stems.

THE THRALES LEFT Paris on the 1st November and arrived in the town of Lille a week later. The closer they got to the coast the higher Johnson's spirits rose. He became remarkably even of temper, so much so that Baretti, try as he might, was unable to provoke him into argument. When the Italian, in the course of an intemperate evening in an inn at Douay, impudently asked if it was not a disadvantage to remain sober, Samuel mildly replied that though the habit of drinking eventually led to a dysfunction of the intellectual mind, it was of considerable benefit—in that it released the appearance of thought—to those persons who had little in their heads and much to say.

Foolishly, Mrs. Thrale had turned on Baretti and told him that Johnson's sobriety had arisen from the best of motives, a wish to set an example to a wife grown dependant on brandy and opium. No sooner were the words out of her mouth than she regretted them, yet such was Johnson's tranquillity of mood that save for a lowering of the brows he gave no evidence of displeasure. Then, on the afternoon of their departure for

Dunkerque, an incident took place which convinced all who witnessed it that Samuel had lost his mind.

In the morning they had driven about Lille in a fiacre, the streets of the town being too dirty to traverse on foot. They stopped to visit a very showy church adorned with pictures of souls in purgatory and statues of Saints hung about with little silver ears and eyes. On enquiring as to what these trinkets signified the party was informed that various miracles had been granted to supplicants requesting restoration of sight and hearing.

Mrs. Thrale, anxiously viewing the scenes of purgatory, whispered to Baretti how fortunate it was that Johnson's eyesight was poor, at which he reminded her of their visit to the Bibliotheque du Roi, and how, when inspecting the incunabula it was only Sam who had been able to deduce from the appearance of the letters in several volumes whether they were printed from wooden or metal types. His deficiency of vision, Baretti observed, was generally most in evidence when he had no interest in the subject before him. True or not, on this occasion it was the money boxes fixed beneath each depiction of hell that appeared to vex Johnson, an irritation he showed by striking out at them with his stick.

Next, at Thrale's insistence, they visited a magazine of corn, a vast building with nothing in it save a heap of rice in one corner. Henry said the French had little knowledge of agriculture and failed to make proper use of their land. Mrs. Thrale thought the lack of industry had something to do with their frequent holy days which were scrupulously kept, though they appeared to have scant respect for the Sabbath. Monsieur Le Liever, Queeney's dancing master, had cried off on All Saints' Day but had been only too willing to attend her on Sunday mornings, a request dear Queeney had declined on the grounds that it was against her Christian principles.

On leaving the corn magazine Mrs. Thrale instructed the driver of the fiacre to take them back to their lodgings; Queeney had earlier complained of a pain in the belly and she was anxious to dose her with ipecacuanha.

They had gone a little way along a narrow street when their vehicle halted beside a house under scaffolding. Henry, stepping down to investigate the cause of the delay, found himself in the rear of a crowd silently peering at some object close by the front door. He was attempting to push himself closer when a low muttering began, after which, as though seized by a common anger, fierce shouting broke out accompanied by the shaking of fists. He was still trying to force his way forward when the crowd surged back a pace and stared upwards, and now hats were thrown into the air and cheers rang out.

Mrs. Thrale and Baretti, peering into the street, were astonished to see Johnson hauling himself up the front of the house by means of the scaffolding. Above him, at an open window beneath the eaves, could be seen a solitary figure who stood with arms held out as though ready to catch bounty from the heavens.

Even as she watched, the tail of Samuel's coat caught on a projection of rotten wood and he was jerked sideways. The spectators let out a hiss of alarm. Queeney started to laugh hysterically. Mrs. Thrale turned to admonish her; she moved too abruptly and the child lost her balance and cracked her head against the seating.

And now Johnson had drawn level with the attic window; he swung himself inwards, collided with its framed occupant, clutched him in a necessary embrace and tumbled from view.

Mrs. Thrale saw Henry reach the steps of the house. He was taller than those around him, and as he stood there, head bent, he brought his arms up, either in shock or to hold back the crowd pressing at his heels.

On Thrale's return he stepped into the fiacre without uttering a word. All his movements—the way he shook his head from side to side, the way his clenched fists drummed on his knees—expressed disquiet; as for his face, never before had Mrs. Thrale seen such horror in his pale blue eyes.

Baretti demanded, "What is the commotion about? Where is Samuel? What is happening?"

"A child," came the faltering reply. "A fallen child."

"Fallen," echoed Mrs. Thrale.

"Dropped," Thrale said. "Either by accident or from intent."

"A dead child," screamed Mrs. Thrale.

"A dead one now," he said. "I saw its auburn curls."

Mrs. Thrale began to weep. She knew it was foolish to shed tears over an unknown infant, but oh, the sadness of it—to spill like a fledgling from the nest.

Presently the door of the house opened and Johnson came running down the steps. Approaching the carriage, he shouted, "Money, give me what money you have." Taking off his hat he held it out like a begging bowl and urged them to hurry. The occupants of the fiacre obeyed him without question, and when the hat was heavy with coins he sped off, the torn pocket of his coat flapping at his side, and disappeared once more into the house.

The story Johnson told them later that day was a curious one. The object Thrale had seen was not the body of a child, but that of a small sack filled with river mud and bound about with rags. Some years before, the man at the attic window had been employed as a night watch in the courtyard of the Bastille; he had a wife and a little daughter. He was, by his own admission, a prodigious drinker, and for this reason was shortly dismissed from his work. One stifling Sunday in summer his wife had given him the child to hold while she went to beg food from a neighbour. The bells were pealing for mid-day mass, and he stood at the open window rocking the babe in his arms and dreaming upon a time when he would be able to provide for his family. I will provide, he thought, and on the thought opened his arms to embrace the future. Soon after, his wife drowned herself in the Seine.

Ever since, he had wandered from town to town, always living in attics, always standing at an open window to drop his burden, always waiting with arms held out lest by some miracle time reversed itself and God gave back his daughter.

"But I saw the child," protested Henry. "I saw the auburn curls above its rags."

"He snipped off her curls before they buried her," said Johnson, "and stuck them into a turnip head."

Mrs. Thrale felt a warm indignation. Though the original incident was dreadful, she could scarcely be expected to feel pity for a madman who dropped sacks of mud from windows and caused bystanders to grow faint.

"The money," she said, "I had thought it was to pay for a decent burial, and now I suppose it will be spent on drink."

"Would that drink could drown such misery," Johnson retorted. "Besides, I will repay every penny," which put Mrs. Thrale in the wrong and made her appear uncharitable.

Henry Thrale held tight to Queeney's hand. His grip was fierce, but she endured it; she sensed Papa wanted to keep her safe.

To Miss Laetitia Hawkins,
2, Sion Row, Twickenham

March 8th 1809

Dear Miss Hawkins,

You will forgive my tardiness in replying to your numerous letters, but I have been staying in Dumbartonshire with my husband Admiral Keith and have only recently returned. I am somewhat surprised that you are still engaged on your reminiscences of Dr. Johnson and friends. Such drawn out labour must be wearisome indeed.

I am afraid I can give no very satisfactory estimation of the character of Mr. Langton, for he was so very tall and I so short that we did not often look one another "in the eye." That he and Mr. Topham Beauclerk were both good friends of the Doctor I know to be true, though there was one occasion—I think at Bolt Court—when Mr. Langton, bemoaning the serious illness of his mother, was savagely rebuked by Dr. Johnson for not going at once to wait on her. My mother considered it hypocritical of him to speak so harshly as he himself did not see his mother for nigh on twenty years, not even when Miss Porter wrote to say that she was dying. Nor did he go to her funeral.

Mr. Beauclerk was interested in the Sciences, as was Dr. Johnson; the latter tried to persuade my father to set up a laboratory for chemical experiments, but, following a near explosion in the schoolroom at Streatham Park, the idea was abandoned.

Mr. Johnson was a prodigious swimmer. I often bathed with him in the sea at Brighton. Indeed, he was so strong in the action and such was the quantity of water he disturbed, that it was advisable to keep one's distance for fear of being submerged.

Mr. Perkins, the chief clerk, was killed at Brighton races by Lord Bolingbroke's horse, Highflyer. Agitated by some insect at the moment Perkins was passing, the animal lashed out and kicked the unfortunate clerk in the head. His widow, whom I remember for her habit of humming under her breath, lived at one time near my mother, though I do not know if she and the "bee" kept up their acquaintance.

I do not care to comment on my mother's relationship with Dr. Johnson; sufficient to say she needed an audience and he a home.

As to my own relationship with him, I cannot in all honesty say that I loved him—he was too large, too variable in mood, too insistent on the attention of my mother. His was a melancholy disposition, an affliction shared by his younger brother, who, it is believed, perished by his own hand. Still, I was fond sometimes, for he exhibited a remarkable understanding of children and their needs, a quality singularly lacking in my mother.

His preoccupation with orange peel was due to persistent indigestion, a malady brought on by his irregular eating habits; he either fasted or gorged himself. I believe he ground the peel and dissolved it in a spoonful of hot port wine. Though he drank heavily in his younger days he was abstemious after, or nearly so.

I remain,

Sincerely yours,

H. M. Keith

I remember little of my visit to Paris in '75, save for suffering the unwelcome attentions of a dancing master who treated me with untoward familiarity, an outrage my mother refused to acknowledge. That, and the amount of letters Dr. Johnson wrote—two to Mrs. Desmoulins and one each to Mr. Boswell, Dr. Levet and Frank Barber. I recollect the letters because he told me that Mr. Boswell was languishing under the onset of melancholy, and that before leaving England Mrs. Williams had fallen out with Mrs. Desmoulins, and Dr. Levet with both of them—on account of the latter disturbing the household following an encounter with a pothole. "I must endeavour," Dr. Johnson said, "to heal differences and allay fear."

I remarked that to quarrel was a "bad thing," to which, rocking back and forth at the table, he replied, "Not so, Miss, for the less we quarrel the more we hate."

As a child I scarcely understood the perception of this observation, but in adult years have found it to be true.

No, I do not remember your presence at Streatham Park that Christmas, and for good reason—my mother's tenth offspring, named after an earlier infant, having died some two weeks before the festivities.

DISASTER

n.f. (disastre. Fr.)

1. Misfortune; grief, mishap; misery; calamity.

This day black omens threat the brightest fair
That e'er deserved a watchful spirits care,
Some dire disaster, or by force or flight;
But what, or where, the fates have wrapt in night.

—POPE

O N THE 20TH March—it was a Wednesday—Mrs. Thrale
went to fetch her daughter Susanna from Mrs. Cumyns's
boarding school in Kensington. She took Queeney with her,
and on the way they quarrelled; it was a trivial matter of the
child's amber necklace hanging in a lopsided manner about her
neck. Reaching forward to pull it straight, Queeney impudently struck her hand away.

On the return journey, in spite of young Susan whining a good
deal and Queeney remaining sullen, Mrs. Thrale managed to control her temper. Heart quickening in anticipation, she thought of
dear Count Manucci who had travelled to England earlier in the
week and was expected at Southwark in the morning.

Arriving at the Brewery she had scarcely stepped down from
the carriage before Harry ran up and said he had seen an adver-
tisement for Arthur Murphy's play, *The Way to Keep Him,* and

that he *must* be taken to see it that very night. On being told he could not go he seized her dress and twirled her round with such vigour that she all but lost her balance. Pestered thus, she gave in, and made arrangements for one of the clerks to accompany him to Drury Lane that evening.

Henry took issue with her for having agreed to such an outing. Guests were expected for dinner and he was anxious to show off his son. Mrs. Thrale would have answered in kind but for further thoughts of the Count.

The dinner party consisted of Sir John Hawkins and his daughter Laetitia, Baretti, Lady Lade, sister to Henry, and Perkins and his wife. At first the talk was exclusively concerned with the visit the Thrales intended to make to Italy later in the year. The excursion to France having proved such a success, and Johnson more than willing to be included, Henry Thrale was content to leave all the arrangements for such a trip in the hands of Baretti. The Italian, puffed up with excitement at the prospect of showing his country to his friends, monopolised the conversation to such an extent that Mrs. Thrale grew weary. Finding his tone proprietary and overbearing, she said loudly, "We have had enough of Italy, and of Italian opinions."

The table fell silent, until, eyeing a dish in the middle of the table with a seated cherub on the lid, Mrs. Perkins remarked that the china embellishment must surely be cast in the image of Susanna. "Such a little angel," she cooed, looking from the dish to the child. A general murmur of agreement arose, to which Mrs. Thrale responded as a mother should. First she smiled in appreciation, then she jumped up and kissed the *little angel* on both cheeks, a showy demonstration which was copied by each of the guests in turn. Susanna, flustered, covered her face with her hands.

Seated again and still smiling, Mrs. Thrale suddenly stiffened in her chair. Without warning, a picture of the statue in the church at Lille, of the angel bearing a boy in its arms, swam before her eyes. She immediately left the table and went to enquire if Harry had yet come home. Returning, she made the excuse that she thought she had heard the cries of an infant.

"There are no infants in the house," Queeney said. "They are all dead."

"A mother's ears," retorted Mrs. Thrale, "are so governed by the heart that echoes are ever present."

At this, Baretti gave a snort of derision, so loud and unrestrained that Mrs. Perkins began to hum, a habit she resorted to when in the grip of embarrassment.

Within half an hour Mrs. Thrale again quit the table; this time Henry greeted her return with a frown. It was a mild enough rebuke, yet she burst into tears. Comforted by Lady Lade, she confided that she was sure something monstrous had befallen Harry.

"The clerk has abandoned him," she wailed. "At this moment he is wandering about Covent Garden . . . prey to every ruffian in sight."

In vain did Mr. Perkins seek to reassure her that the clerk in question was a responsible fellow, that he would entrust his own children to his care without a qualm. Mrs. Thrale would have none of it. Harry was now being carried off into some dark alleyway to be beaten and stripped of his clothing. The servant having recently served the damson pudding, she looked down at the crimson mess on her plate and shrieked so loudly that Queeney spilled her lemonade onto Laetitia Hawkins's lap, and now she too began to cry.

At midnight Harry came home, sound of limb and half mad with delight at the events of the evening. Mrs. Barraclough had performed well, if inaudibly, until, the occupants of the Pit creating a rumpus, she had opened her mouth wide and bellowed like a bull. The second act had been interrupted by a fight breaking out between two players in minor roles. The catcalls growing in volume, Arthur Murphy had clambered on to the stage and ordered the curtains to be lowered, whereupon both actors had set about him with their fists. Little had been seen of the resulting disturbance save for a savage billowing of the cloths accompanied by the sound of muffled shouts and curses.

According to Harry, this had greatly added to the enjoyment of the evening, though Mr. Crick, the clerk, had been all for leaving at once. Mr. Crick had said he would never again take on the task of escorting him anywhere, let alone Drury Lane, but when Mr. Murphy came up and expressed himself delighted to make his acquaintance, he turned pink and lost his bluster. Mr. Murphy had a cut lip and the beginnings of a purple shadow under his left eye.

This reminded Sir John of how the actor Charles Macklin had murdered Thomas Hallam in the Green Room of Drury Lane. "It was over a wig," he said, "borrowed without permission. When Macklin demanded an explanation Hallam called him a clod hopper and a buffoon and threw the wig in his face. Enraged, Macklin lunged at him with his stick and pierced him through the eye. He lived but three hours."

Not to be outdone, Thrale recalled that Quin had killed no less than two of his fellow thespians, though not at the same time—one in a duel at Hampstead and a second by bribing a flyman to drop a weight on his adversary in the middle of *Coriolanus*.

"Peckham," corrected Mr. Perkins. "The duel took place in the meadows of Peckham."

"Poor Quin," said Mrs. Thrale. "He lost his teeth while denouncing Desdemona."

"Poor flyman," argued Perkins, "for it was he, I recall, who went to the scaffold. Neither Quin nor Macklin suffered punishment."

"In mitigation," Sir John said, "it has to be taken into account that all actors are volatile. It is a disposition natural to the profession."

The resulting discussion raged for some time. Mrs. Thrale drank freely and went so far as to apologise to Baretti for having been short with him earlier. Now that Harry was safe most things could be forgiven.

The next morning Queeney woke with a pain in her head. She kept it from her mother lest she was left at home when the others went into the city to visit the Tower. Mrs. Thrale remarked on her flushed cheeks at breakfast, but was too agitated at the arrival of Count Manucci to pay exact attention. She was wearing a gown made from material bought in Paris; whenever the Count looked at her she laughed, high and shrill, like Susanna did when tickled.

While Thrale and Baretti were showing the visitor the complexities of the Brewhouse, Harry ran in with the news that one of the ships in the river was on fire. It had been bound for Boston with a cargo of Papa's beer. Mr. Baretti hastened off to see for himself and returned elated. The flames had not yet been doused, he said, and there was a pall of smoke billowing across the Gardens. Just then the chief clerk came up and assured Thrale that matters were under control. "You can see our Porter is good, Mr. Perkins," shouted Harry, "for it burns special well."

By the time they left Southwark for London Queeney felt herself better, if drowsy. Sometimes, when spoken to, the words seemed to come from a distance, as though there was cloth in her ears. All the same, she watched her mother closely, observing in her movements a giddy extravagance of gesture and in her voice an unnatural note of deference. She did not doubt this playacting was for the benefit of Count Manucci, who, equally false, hovered about her like a fly above a jam-pot.

As they passed through the western gate of the Tower, Harry began to recite passages of history he had learned by heart. "The

White Tower," he babbled, "was built by William the Conqueror
. . . and then Henry II turned it into a fortress."

"Henry III," interrupted Queeney, at which her mother
tapped her hard on the shoulder.

Undeterred, Harry told of Kings and Queens being imprisoned in the dungeons and of how the young sons of Edward V
had been murdered while they slept. "They were but a year or
two older than myself," he said cheerfully.

"They never put Royalty in the dungeons," contradicted
Queeney, stepping out of reach of her mother, "and the Princes
were the sons of Edward IV."

Descending the steps to the Menagerie, Count Manucci
went ahead of Mrs. Thrale and led her by the hand. Mamma
oohed and aahed in an absurd manner, as though adrift on a
mountainside and in mortal danger of slipping. When she
reached the bottom she thanked him with such simpering
regard that Queeney felt quite queasy; her head began to throb
again. She thought of Mr. Johnson's dictum that it was advisable
to acknowledge at an early age that life was a masquerade, and
that to mistake an impression for reality was to court madness.
It did not help much, and some minutes later it appeared to her
that the ground beneath her feet was not fixed.

She remembered little of what she saw that afternoon, save
for the lions padding back and forth and the flame of the lanthorn flickering in the opaque eyes of the brown bear sat in a
pool of its own piss. That, and the blackened appearance of
Harry as he whooped up and down before a cage of wolves,
face, hands, white stockings, blue coat smeared with gunpowder.

Something miraculous happened as the carriage crossed
Blackfriars Bridge. She was peering out at the Thames when
suddenly the smoke-laden clouds shifted, and for an instant the
rays of the sun shimmered in a glittering stairway from water to
sky. She had only to put one foot on to the lowest step—

Mrs. Thrale screamed when the door opened and Queeney lurched forward. Had Manucci not interposed his body between the child and the drop, the outcome would have been tragic indeed. The door secured and Queeney restrained in her mother's arms, the carriage rolled on to Southwark, where, following the administration of an emetic, Mrs. Thrale put the girl to bed and sent Old Nurse to fetch Mr. Lawrence, the family doctor. He, God forgive him, never arrived.

She spent that night in Queeney's room, rising frequently to see whether the child still breathed. At four in the morning, the tears coursing down her cheeks, she knelt at the bedside and addressing God begged that her first born should not die in punishment for her own iniquities. "Take me," she cried. "Spare Queeney and take me."

Pacing beside the chamber window—a half moon battled through tumbling cloud—she talked to the absent Johnson; he alone was capable of understanding her fears. She confessed she had not always treated her daughter in a fair and gentle manner, not least when dealing with the child's strong affection for Henry, but this was on account of the adoration she had felt for her own papa, the dead John Salusbury. She had not wanted Queeney to suffer the same disappointment. To love a daddy to excess was to render inadequate he who must one day take a father's place.

At the fifth hour—Mrs. Thrale counted the chimes of the clock sounding from the wall of the Millhouse—Queeney raised herself from the pillow and complained of hunger. On devouring a slice of cold mutton she vomited and fell back insensible.

BARETTI HAD NOT accompanied the Thrales back to Southwark, being expected for supper that evening at the house of General Paoli. The next day he called on Sir Joshua Reynolds, and it was there, some time in the afternoon, that Manucci's servant sought him out and requested that he return immediately to the Brewery.

He was let into the house by a weeping maidservant and shown into the nursery, where he saw Thrale, hands in the pockets of his waistcoat, seated on a child's chair, so stiffly erect and with such a ghastly smile on his face that all who looked upon him shrank back in horror. Close by stood a spotted rocking horse with a missing tail. Count Manucci and Old Nurse, both pale as ashes and panting for breath, were attending to Mrs. Thrale, who, when she was not sinking to the floor in one swoon after another, threw herself about like a madwoman.

Presently, Thrale put his hand on the nose of the horse and began to rock it up and down. It made a creaking sound, like the squeal of a child at play.

THE NEWS REACHED Johnson some three days later in Lichfield, when he and James Boswell were taking breakfast with Miss Porter. It being March, the monthly anniversary of Tetty's death, he was already gloomy. When he had read the letter—it was from Perkins—he sat for some time in silence, crumbling his breakfast roll. At last, sighing heavily, he said, "One of the most dreadful things that has happened in my time," and called for pen and ink to compose a reply. He wept as he wrote.

The phrase "in my time," was so portentous that Boswell thought something of a public or general catastrophe had taken place, such as the assassination of the King or a disaster comparable to the fire of London.

Mrs. Thrale, on receipt of Johnson's condolences, sat dry-eyed and not simply because she had no more tears to shed . . . *in a distress which can be so little relieved, nothing remains for a friend but to come and partake it. Poor dear sweet little boy . . . When you have*

obtained by prayer such tranquillity as nature will admit, force your
attention, as you can, upon your accustomed duties and accustomed
entertainments. You can do no more for our dear boy, but you must not
therefore think less on those whom your attention may make fitter for
the place to which he has gone.

Attention . . . attention, thought Mrs. Thrale, he is thinking
merely of himself, and stuffed the letter into a drawer.

JOHNSON CAME BACK to Bolt Court on the Sunday. He was in
a distressed state of mind. Mrs. Williams wept with him and Mrs.
Desmoulins did her best to appear in accord. He told them that
he had left Lichfield soon after learning the awful news and that,
stopping for one night only at Dr. Taylor's in Ashbourne, had travelled on to Southwark, where he had found Mrs. Thrale in her
carriage at the very gates of the Brewery, about to depart for Bath
with Queeney and Baretti. Dr. Jebb had advised that a change of
air was imperative if the girl was to remain well; the two younger
children had already been taken back to Mrs. Cumyns's school by
Lady Lade. Waving the carriage away with many a sad look he had
gone at once to comfort Henry. A servant had stopped him on
the stairs and said that his master wished to be left alone.

"Such discourtesy," cried Mrs. Desmoulins.

"Discourtesy!" Johnson shouted. "The poor man is distraught. If it had been I who had suffered such a blow, I too
would wish to be solitary."

Mrs. Desmoulins checked her tongue. Upon Tetty's death,
Sam had demanded company day and night.

From Perkins Johnson had learnt of the events leading up to
the fatal afternoon. There had been an expedition to the Tower.
Young Harry had been in perfect health and clambered so ener-
getically about the cannons and the mortar employed to defeat
the Spanish Armada that he had come to resemble Frank

Barber. When Count Manucci had complimented him on his knowledge of history and urged that he should be a soldier like himself, Harry had retorted, "I would not fight for the Duke of Tuscany because he was a Papist." Later, according to Baretti, he had taken pains to show the Count the instruments of torture used by the Spanish.

"Such a precocious child," murmured Mrs. Williams.

"His mother boxed his ears for it," said Mrs. Desmoulins.

It was Queeney who had shown signs of sickness. There had been an incident in the Menagerie when she had pushed her hand through the railings and rattled the chain of the bear. "Poor thing," said she, though only Count Manucci heard her, "you too are caught by the neck." Then, on the return journey across Blackfriars Bridge, she had attempted to throw herself out of the carriage, on the delusion that she saw a pathway to Heaven. Harry's sudden collapse a day later had come as a complete surprise. There had been no evidence of illness until a mere half hour before his demise.

"Not so," corrected Mrs. Desmoulins, who had been visited by Old Nurse and had all the sorry details at her command. "In the morning, the day after the visit to the Tower, he rose quite well, went to the Baker's for his roll and ate it in the company of the clerks in Brewhouse Yard. After this, he bought two penny cakes for Susanna and Sophy and tickled them so much that they ran about shrieking. Mrs. Thrale spoke to him harshly for it—"

"She was worn out," countered Mrs. Williams, "from sitting up all night with Queeney. A half hour on, he was playing in the nursery, banging his drum and generally behaving in a boisterous way, when he suddenly began to cry. Alarmed—he was not a crying boy unless hurt—Old Nurse hurried into the breakfast room to acquaint Mrs. Thrale. She rebuked him for the noise he was making and held up his sister as an example, for Queeney, much recovered, was insisting on pouring out tea for her papa and Mr. Baretti—"

"Mrs. Thrale was busy fussing over that Italian Count—" interrupted Mrs. Desmoulins.

Voice high and cracked, Mrs. Williams said, "It was then that he vomited, and Mrs. Thrale coming to see the change in him sent the servant off to fetch whatever physician could be found. Then she ordered a tub to be filled with hot water, and laid him in it, and gave him an emetic in wine, all the time crying out most pitifully. At last Dr. Jebb arrived and gave him more hot wine, then Usquebaugh, then Daffy's Elixir. Harry was now in his bed sitting upright and talking quite briskly, so much so that Mr. Baretti said he should be whipped for giving his mother such a fright. But then Mr. Jebb said he must go with the utmost speed to ask Dr. Heberden's help in the matter, which put all into a fright again—"

"Some two hours later," said Mrs. Desmoulins, and now her voice too began to waver, "there was a terrible shriek from those around the bedside. Harry had been thrusting his fingers down his throat, trying to make himself vomit; then he stopped and turning to Old Nurse said very distinctly—*Don't scream so . . . I know I must die.*"

"Enough," said Johnson, greatly affected. "I have heard enough and can bear no more."

He stood for a while at the window, looking out into the Court. Behind him Mrs. Williams continued to sniff. Outside, clad in his white wolf coat, Mr. Kranach walked round and round, finger stabbing the winter air as though conducting an invisible quartet. Life goes on, he thought, and pondered whether this was a *good thing*.

Neither Mrs. Williams nor Johnson being cheerful company, Mrs. Desmoulins descended below stairs to the kitchen. Frank

Barber had gone out to meet one of his sooty friends and only Levet was at the fireside.

"You," said she. "Idle as usual."

"You," said he, "ill-natured as always," and getting up left through the scullery door.

Sitting in his vacated chair she stared into the flames. How easily, she mused, one's sight registers alteration and how quickly the impression fades. She was thinking in particular of Samuel, of how when she beheld him after an absence she perceived him as old and tired, only to find in a blink of an eye that he had become the man she had known so many years ago.

"God willing," she said aloud, "it is the same for him," and knew it could not be, for her gaze was dimmed by love and his clear of such mist.

It had not always been so. Time was, when she had been companion to Tetty in Hampstead, in those lodgings in Church Row to which he came infrequently, he had looked upon her differently. Tell him I am unwell, Tetty had urged, when word was sent that he would come. Tell him I need you to lie beside me. It was not Tetty's fault; she was above twenty years older than he who would so urgently require her wifely embraces.

She had done as she was bidden, leaving Tetty giddy from laudanum, the expression on her face disordered, her nightcap askew. Then, all a tremble, she had filled his warming pan and thrust it between the sheets, and gone to crouch on the stairs for his knock at the door. How the small hour chimes of the church clock had quickened the beat of her heart! What shameful fantasies had swarmed within her head! When she twiddled her hand about in the candlelight, a rabbit nibbled the shadowy wall. Sometimes, Lord help her, she had opened the wig cupboard on the bend of the stair and touched the powder dust to bring him closer.

Hearing his thump upon the door was both dreadful and full of joy; seeing him stomping in, boots splashed with mud, wig sparkling under raindrops, large eyes so full of desire, caused her words to quiver. "Your wife is not well. It is best that I sleep in her bed tonight."

"It is not best that she keeps me from her bed," he retorted, "and I doubt if illness has much to do with it."

Later, when Samuel was in his nightshirt—he knew she was hovering on the landing—he called her into his chamber and persuaded her to lie down beside him. First, they indulged in pillow talk. She had pleaded with him to lower his voice, to curtail his feverish thrashings about the mattress; when he fondled her he was apt to shout in triumph at the discovery of a protuberance or a suspicion of moisture. But then, at the very moment when, in spite of God's teachings, she would have welcomed a final assault, he had thrust her from him and bid her quit the room.

A moral man, she had then thought, and revered him for it, but now—now that it was all too late—she was not so sure. Perhaps a cowardly man was nearer the truth. It was curious, was it not, that great men who compiled dictionaries, whose intellect enabled them to expound upon the state of nations, had not the words or the understanding to define the small business of love.

Rising from the table, Mrs. Desmoulins poked at the fire. The way the cinders fell and died on the hearth, leaving the young sea-coals to flare up anew, confirmed her worst fears. She was, she reasoned, a woman snuffed out by the abominable Mrs. Thrale.

It afforded her some satisfaction to discover Levet's shoes stood beside the scuttle. He, at least, would be tramping ice-footed through the mire of the world.

• • •

MR. BARETTI'S RELATIONSHIP with Mrs. Thrale had never been easy. They were too alike in temperament, both being fiery, and had fallen out many times in the past, yet such was his tenacity and her shrewdness—she had a high opinion of his qualities as a teacher—a patching of sorts had always been possible. Then, a mere week after she had fled to Bath to take the waters, a more serious rift occurred. It arose from a rumour, believed to have been spread among the servants by Baretti, concerning a letter she had received from Dr. Jebb. According to the Italian, Jebb had requested most urgently that she stop giving tin pills to her daughter, for the remedy might prove more fatal than the affliction. Mrs. Thrale had denied receiving any such letter and charged him with scandalmongering.

At the time, in spite of her liking for Mr. Baretti, Queeney had sided with her mother, who for a whole seven days had behaved towards her with unaccustomed sweetness. By day Mamma had taken to scarcely ever raising her voice in temper, and at night had got into the habit of lying beside her as she drifted into sleep; she said nothing, merely held her close, one hand clapping against her back in imitation of a heartbeat. It is true her dosing and purging had intensified, but this was understandable in the circumstances and but a small price to pay for such a display of motherly love. Then, Mr. Baretti having soured her mood, she reverted to her old self and once again became crotchety.

Mrs. Thrale spent the remainder of the year moving from Bath to Brighton and back again in the company of what she referred to as the ruins of her family. Sometimes Johnson joined them, though apart from sea bathing in Brighton he found both resorts dull.

In the New Year they returned to Streatham Park. Mrs. Thrale had made a new acquaintance, that of Dr. Burney, a man renowned for the teaching of music and one whose instruction she had long sought for Queeney. On meeting this eminent personage Baretti spoke boastfully of his own knowledge of the Art, and generally behaved in a boorish manner. Mrs. Thrale was annoyed; she feared he would prevent Dr. Burney coming to the house on future occasions.

There were other worries on her mind, the most serious being Thrale's state of health. Shortly after their return from France the previous year he had complained of a testicle swollen to an enormous size. She had thought only of a cancer and had pleaded with him to get the best help he could find. Far from calling on Jebb or Cruikshank, he had insisted on consulting a quack named Osborne, whose services were sometimes advertised in the paper and who claimed to have studied under Monsieur Daran, a physician famed as a practitioner in the venereal afflictions. And all the while Henry had gone on protesting it was neither a cancer nor an infection, but a swelling caused by his leap from the chaise between Rouen and Paris. During this fretful time Johnson was of considerable support, urging prayer, and more importantly, a trust in physic. He corresponded with Dr. Heberden, who recommended the rubbing of Mercury ointment into the skin around the affected area, and the taking of a nightly dose of Balsam Copabia, which stopped the running but not the inflammation. Thrale complained bitterly of a soreness of the mouth and a loosening of his teeth. Sometimes of a morning, tufts of his hair lay shed upon the pillow, a circumstance he insisted was natural seeing he was now in the fifth decade of his life.

"If he should die," wailed Mrs. Thrale, "we are all lost," an observation overheard by Baretti who retorted, "If he does, then it will not be long before Mr. Johnson stands in his place." This remark so disconcerted Johnson that he raised his stick as though to strike the Italian to the ground. Shortly after, due no doubt to the stream of prayers issuing heavenwards, the swelling abated.

Now, it returned. She had no sooner settled back at Streatham Park than she was required to get to her knees night and morning to hold poultices to the injured part. At such illuminating moments Mrs. Thrale could not help but recall the words of her father who had prophesied that if she married such a scoundrel as Henry he would give her the pox. Nor did she receive much thanks for her administrations, Thrale being sunk into self-pity and constantly berating her for being either too rough or insufficiently firm enough in her applications. He still protested that his sickness was brought about by his tumble into the chalk pit, and stoically refused to give up wine and the excessive eating of meat as advised by Osborne. Samuel, though in accord with the strictures regarding bloody beef and fatty cuts of pig, went along with the notion that Henry's swelling was merely a consequence of a jolting of parts. Poor fool that I am, thought Mrs. Thrale, it is best that I believe it.

What with the nursing Henry needed and Johnson falling under an attack of gout, for which he demanded sympathy and wearisome talk as to the causes of the complaint, she felt much put upon. It was not to be wondered at that matters at last came to a head between herself and Baretti.

The night before, he had bullied her into tears over the cancellation of the trip to Italy. Henry was at the table, but it was only she who was upbraided for what Baretti called the willful breaking of a sacred promise. It was a well-known fact, Baretti argued, that an alteration of scene was of benefit to those suffering from bereavement, and, in any case, was it not better to be miserable in Italy where the sun shone, than in England where rain never ceased to fall? He had made so many plans. His relatives had expected them; his friends had incurred expenses through the arranging of excursions and accommodation. Were they to be left under the misapprehension that he had invented such a visit, that he was a man given to untruths and fantasies? Henry, befuddled with drink, had said he would recompense him for the trouble he had gone to, but Baretti's eyes had fairly blazed with anger.

Then, the following morning, he over-reached himself in the presence of Miss Reynolds and Mr. Langton. Dr. Burney, who, in spite of his earlier encounter with the Italian, had accepted an invitation to dine that evening, was fortunately closeted with Johnson, who sat at his desk composing one of his many charitable letters. Queeney observed the confrontation.

Old Nurse, the tears coursing down her cheeks, came into the drawing room clutching a toy soldier which had belonged to Harry. She wanted to know what she should do with it.

"Burn it," Mamma cried, and snatching it from her flung it onto the fire. After a while there was a spitting sound as the paint began to bubble from the wood. Papa, pale as snow, stared into the flames.

It was then that Mr. Baretti said, "Would that the consuming of an object could eradicate a mother's guilt," at which Mamma flew into a fury and accused him of stepping beyond his position.

"My position, Madame," he shouted back, "is that of a man who wishes to save this family from further grief."

"What do you know of grief," Mamma retorted, "or guilt for that matter, you who stood trial for murder . . . ?"

"My murder," he retorted, "was committed to prevent my own life from coming under the threat of extinction—"

"Come, come," interrupted Papa, rising to his feet in agitation, "this goes too far."

"Did Dr. Jebb not write," demanded Mr. Baretti, stabbing a quivering finger in the direction of Mamma, "that if you continued your meddlings with patent medicines you would tear Queeney's bowels to pieces?"

"You forget yourself, Sir," she screamed.

"—And that if you persisted you would soon send the daughter to join the son."

At this dreadful reminder Papa left the room rather in the manner of Belle, head lowered and a growl coming from his throat. Mamma sank into a chair and Mr. Langton strode to the window, where he stood staring up at the mild sky. As for Miss Reynolds, she hid her face in her hands, either from shock or to hide a smile. It is not easy, thought Queeney, to feel something that does not directly affect oneself.

Some moments after, waving a piece of paper, Mr. Johnson bustled in. He announced he had finished his petition on behalf of the unfortunate Dr. Dodd, now approaching sentence of death for forgery, and was anxious to read aloud what he had written.

"My Lord Mansfield," he began, *"but a few days—and the lot of the most unhappy of created beings will be decided for ever! I know the weight of your Lordship's opinion. It is that which will undoubtedly decide whether I am to die an ignominious death, or drag out the rest of my life in dishonourable banishment. O my Lord! Do not refuse to hear what I in my humility dare to—"*

Glancing up from the page he saw that Mamma was gazing about her distractedly. "It is somewhat flowery, I agree," he said, frowning, "but it is written as if from the pen of the wretched Dodd."

"What do I care for Dodd?" wailed Mamma.

"What do you care for anyone?" sneered Mr. Baretti.

"What is wrong?" asked Mr. Johnson, perplexed and none too pleased at the reception given to his morning's labour.

"There has been a disagreement," Miss Reynolds squealed, a description Queeney considered less than adequate.

"Concerning what?"

"Concerning me, Sir," cried Mr. Baretti defiantly, and quitting the room slammed the door so violently behind him that smoke billowed out from the hearth.

Queeney followed. Her belly ached; she had been purged before breakfast. Had she stayed and run to comfort Mamma, as she wished, she might have faced rejection. Her mother was again expecting a child and was therefore unpredictable.

Johnson called out, "Sweeting," for he had noticed the girl's bereft expression, but she did not hear him. Nor could he get a word out of Mrs. Thrale as to the reason for Baretti's anger; she sat bolt upright, a vacant look in her blue eyes, as of one whose gaze, too long fixed on the fires of Hell, was now burnt clean.

Observing her, he became anxious on his own account, for it was he who had introduced Dr. Burney to the household and such an atmosphere of disorder would surely reflect badly on himself. The Doctor had come expecting intellectual harmony, not the settling of scores. Urging Miss Reynolds to attend to Mrs. Thrale, Johnson went out onto the terrace with Langton and sought an explanation.

Langton's version of events was puzzling. According to him, Baretti had accused Mrs. Thrale of being the cause of young Harry's death, from the too frequent administration of tin pills.

"Tin pills!" said Johnson. "Harry never suffered from worms in his life."

"I merely repeat what I heard," said Langton.

"A monstrous calumny," exploded Johnson, "and not the first to be spread abroad. Why, on the night in question, it was said that a clerk of the Brewery, after a visit to Drury Lane, had taken the boy to an alehouse and returned him home out of his senses."

"And was there truth in it?" asked Langton.

"Certainly not," Johnson exclaimed. "The clerk is a family man and one in whom Perkins had the utmost confidence." Agitated, he caught hold of a branch of lilac just then coming into bud beside the wall, and twisted it about so violently that it snapped off. His look of horror as he contemplated the broken wood in his grasp, and the groan that escaped his lips, followed by the words, "How simple it is to check growth," unnerved Langton, who blurted out, "My gardener is a great believer in the practice of pruning at this time of the year . . . now that there is no longer a danger of frost." He attempted to seize hold of the branch, for now Johnson had taken to whipping himself savagely about the legs, and failed. Anxious to distract him, Langton enquired if he believed the Reverend Dr. Dodd would escape the hangman's noose. "Your letter," he flattered, "will surely count for something."

"Not so, Sir," Johnson said. "He is to be made an example of and there's an end to it." Nor, said he, would the subscription raised by James Boswell and others, to secure a quick transportation of the body to the surgery of John Hunter, prove efficacious.

Langton disputed the point; he said that resuscitation had been successful some years before in the case of a felon—the name escaped him—hanged for sheep stealing.

"The name is not on your lips," Johnson countered, "because the sheep-stealer was of no account, and for that reason the highway was empty of spectators when his friends bore him away. Time is of the essence if life is to be restored. When they cut Dodd down, the length of the route to Tyburn will be packed end to end with those who pretend an interest in him, thereby blocking his chance of a return."

Studying the mutilated lilac branch, and finding it past mending, he tossed it over the wall. "Baretti," he suddenly observed, craning forward to watch where it fell, "would do well to remember that second chances are hard to come by. Purging would perhaps do him good."

"Purging?" echoed Langton.

"We must consider the meaning of the word in the original

sense—to expel impurities from the human body. The mind is subject to the same imperfections. For instance, ambition is a noble passion, and one requiring a certain degree of resentment towards those whose ambitions have already been fulfilled. But, as in the case of Baretti, when a man carries his ambition too far, we pity him . . . for he is no longer in control of his passions."

"Baretti is certainly colicky," said Langton.

"Whereas you, my dear Lanky, have no such impurity—"

"I am, I confess, singularly lacking in ambition," agreed Langton cheerfully, at which Johnson, spluttering with laughter, commented that such a lack was no doubt a consequence of inherited wealth. Still guffawing, he descended the steps into the garden and set off in the direction of the Summerhouse, a rustic structure a generous Henry Thrale had built for his use some years before.

A genius, thought Langton, is one whose nervous power and sensitivity is largely in excess—and let him go. In London, Samuel could not bear his friends out of his sight, but this, the Literary Club reasoned, was because Mrs. Thrale was not of the company. The Sam of Streatham Park was a different being from the Samuel of Bolt Court and the taverns of Fleet Street. The latter was a personage who welcomed intellectual stimulation in the company of men who recognised his genius, and who, on rare occasions, could best him in combat; the former, one content to wallow in the capricious sunlight of a woman's affections.

As Johnson receded unsteadily into the distance he still appeared shaken by mirth. At intervals the snort of swans alighting on the lake echoed his whoops of merriment.

For the remainder of the day Baretti kept to the schoolroom. Nor did he join the guests at dinner, and instead requested food be brought to his chamber, for which relief Mrs. Thrale gave heartfelt thanks. It enabled her to pay proper attention to the discussion of a new work to be undertaken by Johnson, for which a committee of the most reputable booksellers in London were proposing to pay him two hundred pounds. The publication would consist of accounts of the lives of the English poets and criticism of their verse; Sam was honeyed enough to declare, in the presence of Dr. Burney, who had been persuaded to stop the night, that he would appreciate her help. His exact words were, "Your judgement, my dear, is of value, for you are not burdened by excessive scholarship and your perception is fresh."

Mrs. Thrale immediately insisted on the inclusion of Milton and Gray, the one, in parts a favourite of them both, the other, in her opinion, a poet vastly over-rated, "The Prospect of Eton College," in particular, suggesting nothing which every beholder was not capable of thinking or feeling for themselves. "Gray's supplication to Father Thames," she elaborated, "to divulge who drove the hoop or tossed the ball, is useless and puerile."

"Well said, Madame," cried Johnson, and patted her fondly on the head. Some weeks before, troubled with an infestation of the scalp, she had left off wearing her wig. Both he and Henry had applauded the change in her appearance and gone so far as to claim they saw moonbeams dancing in her hair.

She spent a disturbed night attending to her husband, for he spat out a tooth in the small hours. There and then she resolved as soon as possible to return with him to Brighton—sea bathing would possibly bring about a cure for his ills. She came down to breakfast nervous of encountering Baretti, having decided he must be left behind. He appeared half an hour later, and wished her good morning in so loud and defiant a tone of voice she was convinced he was about to insult her again. Sitting down, he asked if she did not think it was a pleasant day. Had she noticed the young leaves beginning to sprout on the chestnut trees in the avenue?

"I have not yet been out, Sir," she said, and head lowered mashed away at the shell of her breakfast egg.

"'The whole garden," said he, "is coming into life, as it should be at this time of the year, unless stricken by blight.'"

He was smiling, but she detected a sinister undertone to his remark, and stared at him coldly; in her mind she recalled Hamlet's judgement on the murderous Claudius—*One may smile and smile, and be a villain.* Baretti looked startled, and for a moment she imagined she saw hurt in his eyes; the next he put down his cup with a clatter and rising from the table went out into the hall. There—for Mrs. Thrale sent Queeney to spy on him—he picked up his hat and his stick and left the house. Miss Reynolds, hard on Queeney's heels, reported seeing him striding away along the drive without a backward glance.

That mid-day Queeney walked to the ornamental gates of the Park and looked out into the lane, in case her teacher should come back. From the elm trees came the call of wood-pigeons, and in their melancholy purring she heard Mr. Baretti crooning to her in the schoolroom, the day the small Penelope got born, and died.

Weeks later, Mamma said Mr. Boswell had told Mr. Johnson that Baretti had informed him that he had been treated with such contempt in the presence of strangers—it was believed he meant Dr. Burney—that he had had no other course than to leave Streatham Park forever. Hatred one can bear, he had confided to Boswell, for it comes from the heart . . . contempt from the head.

When he sent for his clothes and his books, Mamma murmured, "Good riddance," though not entirely with conviction.

JOHNSON, FOR THE third time in as many minutes, asked Mrs. Desmoulins whether Frank Barber had polished his shoes. "If you are enquiring," she replied tartly, "whether Frank has been told to clean them, the answer is yes. Has he done so? . . . No. They remain on the scullery table much bespattered with mud."

"Take no heed," cried Mrs. Williams, "she is out to vex you. I felt them myself an hour ago and they were smooth to the touch."

Mrs. Desmoulins swept out of the parlour and tripped across the cat, who fled yowling; she was annoyed with herself for having been caught out. Samuel had been invited to a party at Dr. Burney's. Of late, he had taken to showing more concern for his appearance, at least when Mrs. Thrale was to be present; when he went to the Literary Club he was not so fussy, but then, no one there looked lower than his mouth. By all accounts, Mrs. Thrale was now firm friends with Dr. Burney, who was teaching music to the indulged Queeney; a week before, the spoilt girl had been bought a harpsichord.

Mrs. Desmoulins went to her room and waited in the dark until she heard the thud of the front door. Then she scurried onto the landing and looked down into the Court to watch Sam depart. It was a bitterly cold night, and as he walked his shoes crunched on cobblestones sharp with frost. How lightly he turned his back on his home! With what little feeling he strode away from those who held him dear!

Dr. Burney lived in St. Martin's Street in a household of motherless daughters. The accommodation was not large and Burney had wisely decided the party could not be on the scale usual at Streatham Park. His principal guest, apart from Johnson, was to be his patron, the wealthy and high born Fulke Greville, whose emaciated wife was the celebrated author of *Prayers for Indifference* and something of a bluestocking. Both Grevilles had long wished to meet Johnson. Seward, the anecdotist, an old friend of the Thrales', had also been asked. All the same, Dr. Burney had not felt quite easy at the prospect of Greville encountering the tradesman Thrale and the sometimes irascible Johnson, and had taken the precaution of hiring an Italian contralto named Piozzi to entertain them should conversation begin to flag or else grow too heated.

The evening began well enough, though it was difficult to keep the drawing room warm due to the different times at which the guests arrived and the necessary opening of the front door. When at last everyone was assembled, Fanny, second daughter of Dr. Burney, sensibly had an old carpet rolled up and placed at the foot of the door to combat draughts. Hot punch was served and a quantity of sweetmeats passed round on platters, one of which Henry Thrale mistakenly took to be for his sole use and whose entire contents he rapidly devoured.

The first harpsichord interruption was listened to quietly enough, save for an outbreak of coughing from Johnson. When it was over there was a mild clapping of hands, above which Mrs. Thrale could be heard boasting of her recent visit to Court and of how the King had said she did not come often enough up to town. Mrs. Greville held up her eye-glass and studied her quite openly.

Fanny Burney took an instant liking to Queeney, who, though only fourteen years of age to her twenty-five, appeared quite able to converse on equal terms. Fanny went so far as to confide that she was an inveterate scribbler, particularly of plays, to which Queeney replied that she herself lacked imagination and was thankful for it, but admired the quality in others.

Mrs. Thrale, made uncomfortable by the stiff atmosphere— Mr. Greville was too grand to start up a conversation and Samuel never one to initiate talk unless challenged—began to laugh a great deal without obvious cause. Mrs. Greville went on studying her, which made matters worse, for she was as tall as Bennet Langton and twice as thin, and Mrs. Thrale could not help noticing the skeleton outline of ribs beneath the expensive silk of her gown.

It was not, as she later told Henry, that she had found Dr. Burney's guest a figure of fun, merely that it had struck her as comical that it was herself, rather than Mrs. Greville, who had become an object of scrutiny. Hence, she protested, she had been unable to stop tittering.

Dr. Burney, alarmed, signalled to Piozzi to start singing. This time Johnson's coughing got so out of hand that Mr. Seward felt obliged to beat him repeatedly between the shoulder blades, provoking Mrs. Thrale to laugh louder than ever. Worse, to divert the company, she suddenly began to mimic the singer, gobbling like a fish and gazing popeyed at the ceiling.

Outraged, Dr. Burney shouted, "Madame, this is not polite behaviour," at which Johnson, scowling at Mr. Greville, who had planted himself in front of the hearth, cutting off all heat except to his own backside, leapt to his feet and bellowed, "Sir, if it were not for depriving the ladies of the fire, I should like to stand at the hearth myself."

Mr. Piozzi, seemingly deaf to the uproar, continued to render "Sally in our alley," a popular refrain from *The Beggar's Opera*, and when finished turned to bow to his unruly audience. Mrs. Thrale clapped louder than anyone else; Johnson thought she did so from guilt at being the instigator of the disturbance. Not so Queeney. Mrs. Thrale's expression had turned tender, lips parted as though to utter endearments. Piozzi was small in height, fair of complexion, and his eyes, light in colour, looked only at Mamma.

Soon, thought Queeney, she will want him to instruct me in singing.

To *Madame d'Arblay,*
54, rue Basse,
Passe,
France

August 4th, 1810

My dear Fanny,

I read your letter with amusement and not a little relief, for now that Miss Hawkins has turned her energies towards yourself I have every hope that she will leave me alone. She is, as you have already found to your cost, remarkably persistent.

Over the years her letters to me have rained down like autumn leaves, and neither evading her many questions, not a few of them of an impertinent nature, nor ignoring her correspondence, has procured the desired result, namely that she let matters rest.

The letters still come, and I fear her enquiries as to the general order of things at Streatham Park stem more from a wish to settle old scores rather than from a genuine and creative impulse to add to the gaiety of nations. Mrs. Piozzi's published anecdotes concerning Dr. Johnson and his circle cannot but have served to stoke the fire of Miss Hawkins's anger, for Sir John was not treated kindly, and though it is generally agreed that my mother is a mistress of inaccuracy, her comments on his meanness undoubtedly touch the spot. There was the unfortunate matter of the missing watch, and the removal of certain private papers belonging to Dr. Johnson.

I beg you, my dear Fanny, to be cautious in your dealings with Miss Hawkins. You, who, when I was too young to know discretion, became the confidante of my childish fears, know full well that which I would prefer to remain hidden, not least the events of a morning in Paris when Dr. Johnson and my mother rolled about the floor, and an earlier occasion in Lichfield when I spied him dragging my mother's petticoat from her chamber.

At the time, you were steadfast in support of my mother, and for my own peace of mind urged that my imaginings should not be allowed to run away with me. I had, as you remember, boldly declared that I was lacking in imagination, and it was not until later, when my mother embarked on her final degrading and selfish course of action, that you took my side and confessed to a regrettable blindness.

In your letter you kindly ask after the well-being of my sister, Mrs. Mostyn. Recently I had the pleasure of a visit from her. She is so changed, so plump, such a picture of robust health that you would not know her. She and I spent many a night talking until the sun came up, an indulgence my husband, Admiral Keith, took in good part. There is more virtue in my sister than could be expected from the strange education she got. We have agreed that we were both exposed to injuries from a quarter where it was least to be expected in the common course. She is convinced that our mother's original and persevering dislike of her children arose from a hatred of our father, and certainly her general conduct to the whole family—when she received news that my sister Harriet was dying of the whooping cough she stayed on in Bath until the child expired—savours of that nature.

Forgive me, dear Madame d'Arblay, for dwelling on myself and not enquiring before now as to the health of your husband, the General, and your dear son, Alex. Had I been born into a family unacquainted with Dr. Johnson, whose reputation as a man of letters appears to burn ever brighter, I would not be forever facing myself. The attention given to the numerous emendations to Mr. Boswell's Life, and the spate of reminiscences and contradictions trailing in its wake, constantly resurrects memories I would wish lost in the mists of time. For one so cold of temperament, an affliction my mother laments I inherit from my dead father, it is surprising how my emotions sea-saw. I understood as a child that age brings forgetfulness, and am considerably inconvenienced to find that the multiplication of years renders the past more real than the present.

You mention your affection for Dr. Johnson, and seem puzzled as to my own lack of engagement. It is not that I had no fondness for him, rather that I was wary of allowing my fondness to grow, a state of affairs much helped by his disgusting manners at table and the often strong odour about his person. That being said, I do know he was a man of rare sense and that his belief in God was genuine and free of cant. When I was but ten years old I asked him why, if God was so infinitely good, did He find it necessary to condemn human souls to the fires of Purgatory—I was thinking of the probable fate of my mother—to which he replied that God was infinitely good on the whole, but that for the good of the whole, some individuals had to suffer. Though now the logic of such a statement is open to question, at the time I took it to be a reasonable explanation and did not so often cry myself to sleep.

I dreamt of him when my sister was staying with me, doubtless because he shambled through our talk of days long gone. I was in France again, in the dining hall of the Royal apartments at Fontainebleau; Dr. Johnson stood in the gallery above. I was twisting about between my fingers a button he had lost from his coat the night before, and my mother, aggravated by my fidgeting, stabbed me so savagely in the back with her fist that my grasp loosened and the button fell to the floor; above the buzz of the spectators watching the King and Queen at table, I heard Dr. Johnson cry out, "My wife's hair was golden." I looked down to follow the spiralling of the button across the flagstones, and of a sudden it changed into the bouncing head of Marie-Antoinette, mouth curved in a smile, the sunlight leaping through the gossamer web of her wig. At this horrid moment my sister shook me awake, for I was crying out in my sleep.

You write of your wish to renew your friendship with my mother, but as you rightly observe, though you have seen and judged characters all your life instinctively, hers passes all calculations and combinations.

God bless you, my dear Madame d'Arblay,

Ever yours,

H. M. Keith

Dreams are curious things, are they not? On Harry's first going away to school Dr. Johnson composed him a prayer, after which recitation he stood in the drive to watch the carriage depart. Suddenly he turned to my mother and said, "Make your boy tell you his dreams; the first corruption that entered my heart was communicated in a dream." "What was it, Sir?" she enquired. "Do not ask me," he replied, with such violence in his voice that she turned pale.

DISSOLUTION

n.f. (diffolutio. Lat.*)*

1. Breach or ruin of anything compacted or united.

2. The art of breaking up an assembly.

3. Looseness of manners; laxity; remissness; dissipation.

An universal dissolution of manners began to prevail,
and a professed disregard to all fixed principles.

—ATTERBURY

HENRY THRALE WAS a changed man. That reserve of manner and good sense which had endeared him to Johnson had evaporated. There was, for instance, the matter of Sophy Streatfield, who had recently joined the Thrale circle and with whom Henry gave every sign of having fallen hopelessly in love. It was not a risqué liaison, for Miss Streatfield was virtuous and he too ill to carry it to extremes, but Mrs. Thrale found his infatuation humiliating. It was as though he deliberately courted disaster; though not yet fully recovered from the effects of a second stroke, fortunately mild, he insisted on standing for re-election to Parliament, and lost. It was a blow to his vanity; he had represented Southwark for fifteen years.

Mrs. Thrale and Johnson thought his defeat had been brought about by his altered appearance and demeanour. Upon the death of Harry something had broken within him, and in

his lacklustre eyes and slurred speech the damage was apparent
to all. He still hunted, rode about the countryside, gambled at
cards, but his enjoyment of these pursuits had waned. His one
passion—Miss Streatfield apart—was food, and now his
appetite, always ferocious, increased to an extent that was truly
alarming. As Johnson remarked one morning after counting the
discarded shells of no less than seven eggs on his breakfast plate,
"Sir, you will soon surpass Falstaff in girth."

A cause of more serious anxiety was the neglect of his business,
which was exacerbated by a mounting extravagance. Once again
the stables at Streatham Park were undergoing enlargement; a
dozen peacocks had arrived to stalk the terrace; several marble statues had been purchased from Italy to stand along the drive, two of
which had fallen to the dockside on disembarkation and now lay
in halves in the shrubbery; to crown it all he was in the middle of
negotiating the lease of a substantial property in Grosvenor Square.

Johnson, fearful of a financial collapse, spoke privately to
Perkins, suggesting that the clerk should endeavour to persuade
Thrale to place the entire running of the Brewery into his own,
more capable, hands.

Perkins took his advice and wasting no breath on prelimi-
naries came straight to the point, indeed, some way beyond it.
He said, "Mr. Thrale, Sir, I have been thinking for some time in
terms of a partnership in the business. What do you think?"
Receiving no immediate answer from the astonished Henry, he
continued, "I would be willing to study the operative part of the
trade and concern myself more with our exports . . . and as you
are shortly to give up your house, my wife and our growing
brood would be quite content to take up residence here."

When Henry told Mrs. Thrale what the chief clerk had said,
she felt anger. Perkins had several healthy sons, and it was not
tactful of him to refer to their sturdy growth. Nor, though for
years she had longed to quit Deadman's Place, did she care to be

edged out by a mere clerk. She too had suffered disappointment, for at the time of her husband's first stroke she had been
delivered of a boy-child, perfectly formed yet stillborn. Henry
had scarcely noticed such an unfortunate outcome, and but for
the sweet support of Mr. Piozzi, Queeney's singing teacher, she
herself might have gone into a decline.

"His insight into a woman's nature is almost feminine in its
comprehension," she confided, unwisely, to her eldest daughter.

"I allow he flutters his eyelids," retorted Queeney.

"I have not noticed his eyelids," countered Mrs. Thrale, "only
his understanding."

"Last year, and all the years before," said Queeney, "it was Mr.
Johnson who knew best what a woman felt."

Mrs. Thrale, endeavouring to extricate herself, found she
stammered, even in her head. I have h-harmed Queeney in
some way, she thought, not least by loving her too much . . . and
must p-pay for it.

It was Johnson who finally convinced Henry it would be
advisable to relinquish the management of the Brewery to
Perkins, a function the clerk was already performing, in practice
if not in name. He softened the suggestion by terming it a temporary arrangement. "When you are fully restored in health," he
said, "you shall take up the reins again." Observing his master's lips
shiny with the grease of roast pig, brow dripping with perspiration, he reasoned such a time was gone forever. Mrs. Thrale was
pleased at Henry's retirement; she had grown tired of her role as
"Lady Mashtubs," a title bestowed on her by the dead Mrs.
Salusbury. When she left the house in Deadman's Place she presented Mrs. Perkins with its contents, save for Johnson's desk sent
on to Grosvenor Square, and the nursery furniture which she dispatched to an orphanage in Greenwich. As she explained to Mr.
Piozzi, she had no desire to take with her that which would only
serve as a reminder of irksome happenings.

Johnson was not happy at the thought of leaving his old rooms in the tower of the Brewery. He had reached an age when change was unwelcome, and beneath all the activity and talk of Grosvenor Square being more at the centre of things—Mrs. Thrale held it was better for her husband to be closer to his doctors—he had the niggling premonition that he himself was being nudged further off. In involving himself in safeguarding the future of the Thrale business, he had neglected his critical essays on the Poets, and now returned to the task, though without energy.

The Thrales had no sooner settled in town than Henry revived his notion of going to Italy. Worse, he said that the breach with Senor Baretti must be mended, for no one else was capable of arranging such a trip. Mrs. Thrale was in despair at the thought of being united with a man she hated and one who had spread scurrilous stories about her. And how were they to drag Henry across the continent, a man who could not keep awake for more than three hours at a stretch and who could scarce retain his faeces? When she turned to Piozzi for sympathy, he said Baretti was possibly not a bad man at heart, simply one whose earlier experiences had thinned his skin; the singing teacher's grasp of English was so convoluted that Mrs. Thrale had difficulty in making sense of this.

Johnson, informed of the proposal, looked grave and said what Henry needed was more convivial company, more gatherings of like minds. So perturbed was he at his master's deterioration that his knowledge of medicine deserted him; he was able to delude himself into thinking it was Thrale's mind that was the root of the trouble. It was a subjective diagnosis.

Thus a round of parties began, both in London and Streatham Park. Fanny Burney was now a great favourite of Mrs. Thrale's, and Johnson included her in his Latin lessons with Queeney. One morning when Sir Philip Clerke and Sophy Streatfield were visiting, Mrs. Thrale persuaded Sophy to perform her *party piece* at the breakfast table. Fanny, who was not yet aware of Thrale's feelings for Miss Streatfield, but had heard of the young woman's ability to shed tears at will, was taken aback at the rudeness of the request.

"Sir Philip," Mrs. Thrale began, "has heard so much of your tears, Miss Streatfield, that he would give the universe to have a sight of them."

"Indeed I would," agreed Sir Philip.

"Well, you shall . . . you'll oblige, won't you, my dear?"

"No," squealed Miss Streatfield, "no, pray no—"

"Oh pray do, Miss Sophy! Pray let him see a little of it," coaxed Mrs. Thrale. "Consider, you are leaving tomorrow, and it's very hard on him if you won't cry a little."

Suddenly, two tears came into Miss Streatfield's eyes and rolled in crystal pear drops down her cheeks; she was smiling quite beatifically. Mrs. Thrale clapped her hands in admiration and cried out, "Such tears manifest a tenderness of disposition while increasing a beauty of countenance."

Fanny marvelled at Miss Streatfield's stupidity. Was it not obvious that Mrs. Thrale was out to make sport of her? Then, at dinner that evening, Miss Streatfield proved herself not such an innocent after all. Mrs. Thrale was sitting at her usual place at the table when Mr. Thrale shouted out to her that she must change places with Sophy, for "she has a sore throat and may be injured by sitting so near to the door." Instantly, Miss Streatfield rose from her chair, at which Mrs. Thrale cried out, "Perhaps it will not be long before the lady is head of your table," and burst into noisy tears, a display which, unlike that of the fair Miss Streatfield, did little to enhance her countenance. With that, she fled the room.

Much later, when Fanny and Mr. Johnson went into the drawing room, they found Mrs. Thrale composed but still smarting. The moment Johnson set foot over the threshold, she asked,

"Was I to blame for what happened?"

He replied, "Why, possibly not; your feelings were outraged."

"Yes, and greatly so," she spat, "and I cannot help remarking with what blandness you witnessed the outrage. Had this transaction been told of others, your anger would have known no bounds . . . but towards a man who gives good dinners and allows you the freedom of his library and home, you were meekness itself."

After this tirade Johnson looked discomforted, and said not a word. He confided to Fanny the following day that it was Mrs. Thrale's worry over her husband's breakdown in health, rather than his foolish cavortings with Sophy Streatfield, that had caused her outburst. When Fanny told Queeney what Mr. Johnson had said, the girl observed it was merely what he wanted to believe. "Mamma gives not a fig for Papa," she said, "and is concerned only with herself."

Queeney too was changing: she was neither so quick to take offence, nor so secretive. On occasions, in intuition and changes of mood, Johnson thought her very like her mother. One morning, when he was sitting drinking tea in the back parlour in Grosvenor Square, she rushed in from her singing lesson and proceeded to twirl about the room. She did not often give way to high spirits, and Johnson, who had caught snatches of her warblings, went so far as to liken the sound to the trilling of a songbird. Truth to tell, he found music intrusive, but Queeney's lightness of heart was infectious. He wheezed as he flattered, being more than usually troubled with his habitual asthma. Queeney urged him to stand upright and throw back his shoulders, something Mr. Piozzi bid her do during instruction in breathing. "It is important," she babbled, "for the lungs to expand to their full extent."

Captivated by her gaiety, he stood and adopted a military stance. "Breathe in," she ordered . . . "deep . . . deeper." He attempted to obey and was promptly seized with a fearsome attack of coughing. Some moments later, leaning back in his chair, he rebuked her for thinking the act of breathing was the same for all. "It is as hard for me," he complained, "to maintain a shallow intake of air as it would be for you to inhale a whirlwind."

"Papa will not die will he?" she suddenly asked.

"In time," he said, "we all must die . . . but not yet."

"Mr. Garrick died before his time. I heard you say so—"

"That I did," he said, "and meant it, for we were young together and I miss him."

"Do you miss Mr. Baretti?"

"He is not dead—"

"No," she agreed, "but you do not see him, which is almost the same. You thought him worthy of friendship, did you not?"

Parrying her question, though understanding the reason for it, he said it was a good thing to hold people in affection, whatever the general and opposite opinion.

"Mamma was wrong, was she not, to forbid him the house?"

"Mamma did not forbid him. It was Mr. Baretti who turned his own key in the lock."

Queeney fell silent. Her face was so altered, its expression of animation quite wiped away, that Johnson felt pity. Thinking to distract her, he said, "Mr. Boswell considers himself a composer of songs. They have little in the way of melody, yet the words are catchy to those of a melancholy disposition. Last month he recited the beginnings of one. He has got no further than two lines, and those not good—"

"Tell me," she said, albeit reluctantly.

"'Tis o'er, tis o'er,'" intoned Johnson, "'The dream is o'er, and Life's illusion is no more . . .'"

"Is there not more?" Queeney asked.

"No, Sweeting. What more could there be?"

She said, "Mamma is good at turning keys in locks, is she not?"

He looked at her sharply, and replied in some agitation, "Mamma is good at many things, not least at loving. You would do well to think of that."

"I do not wish to think she loves Mr. Piozzi," Queeney cried, at which Johnson stood upright and, muttering to himself, head shaking from side to side as though to be rid of some stench beneath his nose, left the room. Queeney knew it was not rudeness on his part, more that being old he had doubtless remembered something previously forgotten.

"'Tis o'er, tis o'er,'" she sang aloud, and once more danced about the room.

JOHNSON WAS WALKING along Fleet Street, his gaze directed towards the ground, when his eye chanced upon the muscular tail of a rat protruding from a litter of old newspapers blown against the doorway of a pie shop. He was thinking at that particular moment of Dryden, of whom he had written, *The power that predominated in his intellectual operations was rather strong reason than quick sensibility*, a sentence he had reworked several times, for it seemed to him that he was dissecting himself rather than his subject. Distracted, he stopped to observe the emergence of the rodent. Out it came, snout sniffing the air, forepaws raised. It saw, or sensed him—and was gone in an instant.

Almost at once he was hailed by James Boswell, yesterday returned from Scotland and on his way to Bolt Court hoping to find him at home. Puce with excitement, Boswell cried out, "Sir, I am happy to see you," and wrung his hand.

When they had tripped through the politenesses, Johnson said, "The sight of an animal going about its business, seeking its food, foraging for its young—what a strange pleasure it affords us."

"True, true," Boswell affirmed, though he could see nothing but birds strutting the gutter.

"There is only one mendacious being in the world," continued Johnson, "and that is man. Every other is virtuous and sincere."

"True, true," repeated Boswell, and begged to be allowed to walk with him, for, he said, he had now read a great proportion of the manuscript of *Critical Observations on the Poets*, and longed to have talk of it. Johnson replied that he was just now in a reflective mood, but, if it would please him, he would be welcome that evening at Bolt Court.

As they parted, he said, "The main reason we take so much pleasure in looking at the lower animals is because we like to see our own nature in a simplified form." This observation appeared to him so apt that he began to chuckle at his perspicacity, an outburst that got the better of him and developed into full-throated laughter, upon which the pigeons rose in a disordered flock and swirled about his head.

Mrs. Desmoulins opened the door to Boswell; she was somewhat flushed. Sir Joshua, Arthur Murphy and Mr. Allen, the printer, were already in the parlour, but as yet Johnson had given no sign that he wished her to withdraw. The preferred Mrs. Williams was there, and Levet too, the one sitting by the fire in her faded scarlet, the other in the far corner, holding a cup out of reach of the cat perching on his bony knee. Mrs. Desmoulins sat down beside Levet, something she would not usually do, but then, she and he were not often present when Samuel entertained visitors.

At once Boswell began to praise Samuel's manuscript of the *Poets*. He argued that two hundred guineas was but poor recompense for such a mighty work of genius. "It was not guineas," corrected Johnson, "but pounds . . . and it was not, Sir, that I was paid too little, rather that I wrote too much."

"It is a work of infinite scholarship," gushed Boswell, and proceeded to recite whole passages from the essay on Pope. He spoke so long and so fulsomely that Johnson growled, "Enough, Sir. I wrote it in my usual way, dilatorily and hastily, unwilling to work and working with vigour and haste. Say no more, for it is not yet in print and your recommendations, which arise from prejudice, are not to be trusted." He then poured out brandy for his guest, which silenced Boswell for the moment.

Sir Joshua talked of having called upon poor Topham Beauclerk, who, he feared, was not long for this world. "His habit of taking opium has wasted him," he lamented.

"I have heard," Mrs. Williams ventured, "that after he stayed the night at Mr. Langton's, his bed linen was so infested with vermin it required burning." At this Samuel looked angry, but held his tongue. Had I spoken so cruelly, thought Mrs. Desmoulins, I should have been shown the door to the cellar.

Boswell brought up the subject of a lecture he had recently attended at Coachmakers' Hall. It had dealt with the resurrection of the Saints following the Crucifixion, and with the accounts of those claiming to have seen such a phenomenon. Mrs. Williams thought it an interesting subject and one she would like to hear discussed, at which Johnson argued that it could not be interesting because there could be no proof. He was not disputing the fact of resurrection—"The question simply is," he reasoned, "whether departed spirits ever have the power of making themselves perceptible to us; a man who thinks he has seen an apparition can only be convinced himself; his authority will not convince another . . ."

He was interrupted by an unearthly howl from the shadowy

corner of the room. All were startled, fearing that indeed an apparition had appeared among them; it was only Levet, upon whose knee the cat had seen fit to sharpen its claws.

"There is, however," continued Johnson, "a not infrequent happening, one I have experienced myself, of being *called* . . . that is, hearing one's name pronounced by a familiar person, but one too far distant for the sound to have been uttered by human organs—"

"Sir, sir," cried Boswell, "I have known somebody to whom this happened. An acquaintance of mine was walking home to Kilmarnock when from a distant wood his name was called in the voice of his brother, who for many years had been residing in America—"

"And I suppose," said Johnson, "that some days later he heard news of his brother's death . . ."

"Why, yes. Exactly so."

"The voice I heard," Johnson said, "was that of my dear mother. I was at Oxford, turning the key in the lock of the college gate when she quite distinctly called *Sam.*"

"And did you then receive news of her death?" asked Mr. Allen.

"No, Sir, simply a letter requesting the sum of two pounds."

Soon after, they sat down to dinner. There was not sufficient room at the table for Levet, who ate in the corner, fighting the cat from his plate. The meal was not lavish yet the cold meats were well seasoned and Mrs. Williams's apple chutney declared delicious. Some months before, Johnson had bought a silver pepper pot which he now passed round the company with a degree of reverence more fittingly accorded to a rare manuscript. When Arthur Murphy made use of it, shaking its contents liberally on his plate, Johnson plucked it from him and, after wiping it on the skirt of his coat, placed it out of reach.

It was when the dishes had been cleared away and a third bottle of port opened that Sir Joshua mentioned his visit to Streatham Park a week before. He had, he said, found Mr. Thrale much altered. His appetite was now so terrible that one could scarce bear to look upon him at table. "At one end," said he, "there was lobster, carp and oysters . . . at the other, hams, boiled chickens, turkeys . . . and in between a quantity of pies . . . all of which he helped himself to in abnormal quantities and fell upon as if any moment his plate might be snatched away . . . and all the while champing with such voraciousness that the veins in his nose turned purple and his eyes threatened to pop from his head."

"To show one's concern," Johnson said, "or to try and stop him, does little good. Mrs. Thrale and I have tried everything in our power to modify his eating, to no avail."

Arthur Murphy said Mrs. Thrale was now back in town and happy to be residing at the fashionable centre of things. He had called on her but yesterday and found her preoccupied with plans for a musical evening she was soon to hold at Grosvenor Square.

"It is curious, is it not," Mr. Boswell remarked, "how fond Mrs. Thrale has become of the human voice uplifted in song."

An uncomfortable silence ensued. Mrs. Desmoulins was not alone in noticing the sly smile that accompanied his words. Then Johnson stood and poured himself a large measure of brandy; every eye turned upon him.

"Sir," Mr. Allen exclaimed, "I did not think you drank."

"For many years I have not done so," he replied, "and have but recently returned to it, though not in society."

"I once remember," said Sir Joshua, "many years ago, shortly before you gave up the habit, you drank three bottles of port, whereupon you found yourself so unable to pronounce a certain difficult word, that, after trying three times to get it out, you put down your cup and left the company."

"The word was *villainous*," Johnson said, "and it was not the word that was difficult, merely that my lips refused to shape it."

Mr. Boswell was in such an inebriated state at the close of the evening that he was unable to walk. Mr. Murphy was obliged to piggyback him into the Court, where, raucously singing, he was tumbled into Sir Joshua's carriage.

Mrs. Desmoulins would have liked to have stayed downstairs in the warmth, but Johnson said she must go to her bed. The wretched Levet was not asked to retire. Indeed, no sooner had Mrs. Williams said goodnight than he rose unsteadily from his corner and took her chair by the fire. The cat followed instantly and leapt upon his lap. Mrs. Desmoulins reckoned it was the odour of herrings about his person that made the animal so fond.

When I am alone and dying, she thought, Sam shall hear my voice calling his name, and weep at the sound of it.

MRS. THRALE WAS determined her musical evening would become the talk of London Society. With the help of Mr. Piozzi she had hired a score of musicians and performers, and instructed Henry to compose a menu of such variety and munificence that it would require twenty-four servants to carry the dishes from kitchen to table. This task, one dear to his heart, visibly appeared to restore the spirits of the Brewer.

Mrs. Thrale would wear a gown fit for an appearance at Court. It was made from material copied from goods brought from the South Seas, of a striped Otaheite pattern, trimmed with crape, gold lace and foil, and ornamented with stones very little inferior in lustre to the most brilliant jewels; the trimming alone had cost sixty-five pounds. When she tried it on for the benefit of Queeney, the girl declared it too *loud*.

Mrs. Thrale had coaxed Mr. Piozzi into beginning the concert with a song of her own choosing. Its words, she said, were particularly apt in regard to her husband. On the opening line, Piozzi must look directly at him—

If the heart of a man is depressed with cares,
The mist is dispelled when a woman appears.

—and then at Sophy Streatfield.

Roses and Lilies her cheeks disclose,
But her ripe lips are more sweet than those.
Press and caress her;
With blisses her kisses
Dissolve us in pleasure and so repose.

—at which it would be provoking if Miss Streatfield did not oblige with an imbecile display of tears.

Mrs. Thrale persuaded Johnson to be present at one of Mr. Piozzi's rehearsals; she said she would appreciate his comments. He sat astride a chair and endeavoured to look pleasant. When the Italian soared into the chorus and, gazing calf-eyed at Mrs. Thrale, sang of kisses and blisses, he stomped from the room.

Later, Mrs. Thrale rebuked him for such ill-mannered behaviour. "You may not like music," she chided, "but you have hurt Mr. Piozzi's feelings." To which he savagely retorted that he did not recall her being so conscious of *feelings*, Piozzi's or those of anyone else, the night they had been guests of Doctor Burney. She stared at him with genuine astonishment. She does not remember the past, he thought, for the present is now all important.

On the night of April 1st, Thrale ate so much that he became comatose and collapsed with his head in the mess on his plate. Mrs. Thrale sent for the physician, Pepys, who, after examining the sick man, said either he must be put under legal restraint or else suffer certain death. Mrs. Thrale could not agree to the remedy.

She declared that as it was Henry's money that was spent on such gastronomic excesses, it was his right to throw it away—but if his mouth could be sewn up, she would pay for the thread herself.

The following morning, at breakfast, Henry again stuffed himself so full that Johnson cried out, "Sir, such eating is little better than suicide." An hour later Thrale went out, left visiting cards at various houses, rode his horse twice round the Square, and slept until roused for dinner. They now dined at eight rather than four in the afternoon as had been common at Southwark. Fanny Burney was present, Mr. Langton, Queeney, Johnson and Mrs. Thrale.

There was an attempt at chat, though it was difficult to shift Mrs. Thrale from talk of her concert on the morrow. Mr. Langton started to recall his knowledge of the Reverend Mr. Hackman who, two years earlier, had gone to the gallows for shooting the mistress of Lord Sandwich, but he was so distracted by the behaviour of Thrale that he soon trailed into silence.

The Brewer's appetite was beyond sensibility—he consumed four bowls of broth, two dozen oysters, two lobsters, three game pies, seven lamb chops and three stuffed capons, the whole washed down with numerous bottles of strong beer. Those around him put down their forks and stared at him aghast; even the servants looked frightened.

He rose before the puddings were laid out, and belching loudly and frequently, quitted the room. Mrs. Thrale followed him to the foot of the stairs. She called out to him, but he merely raised his hand in a dismissive gesture and continued upwards.

Five minutes later Fanny Burney entered his chamber and found him apparently none the worse for wear. "Go, Miss Burney," he bade. "I have a desire to be alone."

"He is less red now," she disclosed on her return to the table, "and perfectly lucid." A half hour after, Queeney went upstairs.

She found her papa sprawled upon the floor, stockings and shoes removed. Terrified, she asked why he was lying there, and received the reply, in slurred tones—"Because I choose it . . . I lie so on purpose." She noticed the dark skin of his bare legs, and the opaque quality of his milky toenails; he has the feet of a savage, she thought, and attempted to pull him upright.

"Leave me be," he ordered, and placing one trembling hand to his livid lips, blew her a kiss. She ran downstairs, emitting small screams.

Pepys was sent for, but could do nothing; it was too late. The dying man was lifted onto his bed, still murmuring that there was nothing to fuss about. Soon after he suffered a rupture of the lungs. Johnson held his hand and wiped the bloody froth from his mouth. On the morning of April 4th, as a rosy dawn leaked above the chimneys in the Square, Thrale died. He uttered no last words, merely let forth a prolonged expulsion of wind.

JOHNSON HAD NEVER thought himself capable of self-deception. Hadn't most of the miseries of his life arisen from too close a scrutiny of actualities? Yet, upon the death of Henry Thrale he had every expectation that his friendship with his *dear mistress* would continue as before. Were they not so joined by affection and past experience, so in accord one with the other that the lift of an eyebrow or the droop of a lip rendered words unnecessary? He was not alone in making such an assumption. Indeed, Thrale had scarce grown cold before the gossip columns of the *Herald* hinted at the likely union between his widow and a certain lexicographer and poet. He did not tell anyone that he had read this scandalous tittle-tattle, nor did he care to acknowledge the vibrant leap of his heart on the reading of it.

As an executor of her husband's Will, he was of great service to Mrs. Thrale, who turned to him for advice and support, and although he sincerely mourned the loss of his master—*the continuity of being is lacerated*—he took pleasure in dealing with the practical details concerning the future of the Brewery; it freed him from the drudgery and solitude of writing. Thrale's five surviving children being but daughters, and Mrs. Thrale loath to burden herself with the business, it was decided it should be sold. Mr. Barclay, the Quaker banker having made a substantial offer—it was agreed his nephew and the estimable Perkins would be in joint charge—the transaction was concluded with satisfaction to both sides.

Thereafter, life continued as of old, Johnson spending the better portion of his existence at Streatham Park, and in between making his forays to Ashbourne, Oxford, Lichfield and Bolt Court. Mrs. Thrale had now moved to a house in Harley Street, where, as always, a room had been allocated for his use.

And yet, circumstances were not quite as before. Several times she had gone against his wishes in the matter of expenditure, and once, at dinner, when he ventured the opinion that the sauce accompanying the goose was not as flavoursome as at Mrs. Langton's, she had rebuked him in the harshest of terms, and in front of company. Some few days later, at Streatham, when he had ordered the carriage to be brought to the door, she had told him it was not convenient, as she would require the use of it herself later in the afternoon. As there were two carriages in the stables, he took this to be a sign that he was no longer of first importance. On seeking the opinion of Queeney and Fanny Burney, they assured him he was wrong in thinking so, but he detected a certain evasiveness in both.

He was poorly with stomach pains when he visited Lichfield, and it did not help that Miss Porter also was broken in health. Worse, she was now very deaf, and it wore him out having to bellow into her ear. Such was his state of dejection that at last he allowed himself to express in words a fear long left unspoken. Hand unsteady, he wrote to Mrs. Thrale—*Do not neglect me, or relinquish me. Nobody will ever love you better or honour you more.*

On his return, Mrs. Thrale noticed a deterioration. She told Queeney that she wondered if he had not suffered a paralytic stroke; there was some drawing down of his mouth on one side, and certain words were pronounced strangely.

"That of Italy, perhaps," said the girl coldly, for Mamma was thinking of going there on an extended tour, Mr. Piozzi serving as guide.

Sir Joshua also perceived a change in Johnson, not least in his outbursts of temper. As he explained to his sister, Frances, though his irascibility was nothing new, indeed an essential part of the man, he had always gone out of his way to ask pardon of those he gored in argument, particularly if they were inferior in intellect—but no longer. It was in his studio that Samuel had all but reduced James Boswell to tears. The conversation was of Bennet Langton, who through his extravagances at the card tables was now in serious debt and in danger of losing his property. Boswell said that to save him, all his friends should call at his house and quarrel with him so fiercely that he would run from London and its temptations, to which Samuel savagely retorted, "It would need but one caller, you, Sir, for if your company does not drive him out of his house, nothing will." Though Boswell was undoubtedly a fool, he was sincerely fond of Johnson and it was not nice to see him treated so roughly.

Mrs. Thrale came to a decision. It had become clear to her that Johnson believed he would reside with her forever. While Henry had lived, he had conducted himself differently, for he was in awe of his benefactor. The Brewer removed, he had more and more taken to behaving as though he was her lord and master. As for her, what with his many illnesses and slovenly ways, she feared she was beginning to regard him much as one would an old and troublesome dog, smelly, wheezing, and constantly under one's feet. Besides, he shambled in the way of her future happiness. Something had to be done.

Searching him out in the Summerhouse one afternoon, she announced she was letting Streatham Park to Lord Shelbourne for a period of three years. She intended, she told him, to retire in the autumn to Brighton and then perhaps journey abroad with her girls. It was for the good of Queeney, who had expressed a wish to travel. He must come too—to Brighton, that is.

He appeared to take it quite well, but then, he did not know what other changes she had in mind. When she left him, doves flew above her head.

On that dreaded last day at Streatham, Johnson rose from his bed far earlier than was his usual hour. His books had already been parcelled up and dispatched, but his desk was to remain, as was his chair, his bed and the little round table at its side. He trailed his fingers along the empty shelves and the surface of his desk in a final caress of farewell. Outside the window crows perched on the black branches of the winter trees. He gazed at the grey and sombre landscape and found it fitting, for it mirrored the desolation in his heart.

He used his chamber-pot before going downstairs, for that too must stay behind; it had a blue border of flowers below the rim and a chip in the porcelain base where his stick had struck it by mistake. As he passed through the quiet hall he saw his reflection in the glass, that of an old, wobbling man, belly bulging, legs swollen with the dropsy. Lastly, he went into the library and gazed upon the books that had been his companions for nigh on fifteen years. "*Templo valedixi cum osculo*," he said aloud, although he was not in church. On the walls hung the portraits of those once dear to him and now dead—Garrick, Goldsmith, Beauclerk, Thrale—and his own likeness hanging between the actor and the playwright. I am not yet gone, he thought, but might well as be.

He composed a prayer before leaving and, head bent, murmured its sentiments for the benefit of Mrs. Thrale and Old Nurse. Queeney would not join in; she stood in the drive, pushing the gravel into small heaps with the toe of her shoe. When the carriage bore them away from the place he had called home, Johnson sat with a book open in front of him, though his eyes were closed.

DURING ONE OF Mrs. Thrale's dinner parties at Brighton, Johnson behaved with such rudeness to her guest, Mr. Hamilton, that the poor man was driven from the house. Mr. Hamilton made the innocent remark that he considered claret to be a very fine drink. Johnson said it was not fine, and that a man would be drowned in it before he got drunk. It was possible Mr. Hamilton was not praising claret in general but simply complimenting his hostess on the wine provided that evening. Anxious to avoid a confrontation, for Johnson was already hissing like a kettle coming to the boil, Mr. Hamilton promptly agreed with him, observing that having drunk three glasses he was beginning to suffer from a head ache. "It is not the wine that makes it ache," Johnson shouted, "but the sense I am endeavouring to put into it."

"How so, Sir?" asked Mr. Hamilton, much puzzled. "A head cannot ache from sense—"

"It can, Sir," roared Johnson, "if the head in question is not used to it."

Two nights later, at a ball in the old Malthouse, he complained so loudly and so bitterly of boredom that Mrs. Thrale told him to his face that he ought not to have come, "as I am sure not one among us gains any pleasure from your company." With respect to Mr. Hamilton's lack of sense, Johnson had spoken no more than the truth, but she was tired of his bullying ways.

Afterwards, he attempted to apologise, but she brushed him aside. She had other matters on her mind, indeed was so disordered by the contemplation of them that she could no longer keep silent. The passion she harboured for Piozzi was now out of control—the mere mention of his name sent her pulses racing—and one morning, dressing in her bedchamber, she made a full confession to her eldest daughter.

She began hesitatingly enough, and with frequent assurances as to the enduring affection in which she held her children. "Nothing I may feel for the man who has captured my heart," she said, "detracts from the love I bear for you."

"How could it?" said Queeney. "Your heart is so big, Mamma."

"My regard for your dear papa," continued her mother, "was of a different degree . . . when he and I met I was ignorant of the world and of that whirling of the senses that betokens p-p-passion. He was a good man, a fine man, one who treated me with kindness and had an understanding of my—"

"Fickleness," supplied Queeney.

"Fickleness," Mrs. Thrale retorted, "arises from a feminine need to fix one's soul to another. If that is denied, a woman may never know the reason for a deep and inner dissatisfaction."

"Now that you know of it," said Queeney, voice chill in tone, "what will you do?"

Mrs. Thrale's plans for the future were comprehensive. She would marry Mr. Piozzi and take Queeney, Susannah and Sophy to live in Italy; Cecelia and Harriet, for the time being, would board with Lady Lade. There was much to be settled. She could not take the children out of the country without the permission of the guardians appointed by Thrale, in particular, Mr. Crutchley.

Queeney went and stood at the window, so that her mother could not read her expression. She looked out at the shore and watched two bathing machines lumbering into the waves. We are all about to be sucked under, she thought, and blinked the angry tears from her eyes. Mamma's feelings for the Italian had not come as a surprise; the soft glances, the signs and smiles that passed between them were the subject of gossip in the drawing rooms of both London and Brighton, and had been for many months. The mention of marriage, however, was unexpected and shocking.

"You will like Italy," said Mrs. Thrale, "and in time, dear Mr. Piozzi."

"I like him now," said Queeney, "as a singing teacher. I would like him less if I was required to think of him as a father."

"His mind is so attuned to the discipline of music," argued Mrs. Thrale, "that a knowledge of harmony precludes any desire for fatherhood."

"Are you asking for my opinion on the matter," asked Queeney, turning from the window, "or simply telling me?"

"I would value your opinion," cried Mrs. Thrale, eyes full of hope.

"Well then," said Queeney, "if you must abandon your children, you must. You may turn us out to fend for ourselves, like puppies in a pond, to swim or drown as Providence pleases. I myself shall look out for a place as a servant, and will never look upon your face again—"

"Nor write to me," said Mrs. Thrale, half smiling, in spite of herself, at such a childish outburst.

"I shall not easily find your address, Madam, for you do not know where you are going—"

"Dearest girl," coaxed Mrs. Thrale, and held out her arms.

"Mr. Piozzi hates you, and has told me so," her daughter shouted, "he is only after your money," and with that she sped from the room and out of the house.

She was running down West Street towards the sea-front when she saw Mr. Johnson coming towards her. He had been swimming, and plodded barefoot, his bathing wrapper dripping water; a strand of seaweed clung to his ear. She would have fled past, but he caught her by the arm and peering into her tear-stained face asked what was wrong.

"Nothing," she said, "nothing beyond the ordinary tussles with Mamma."

He marched back with her to the shore and persuaded her to perch on the rocks below the cliffs, hoping the gentle lapping of the waves might calm her. The day was so limpid that sea and sky merged. A dog came by and sniffed at the girl's ankle, at which she dropped to her knees and endeavoured to hold the animal in her arms. It backed off, kicking up sand, and trotted away.

"You should be less trusting, Sweeting," he admonished. "The beast could have proved savage."

"I am not in the least trusting, Sir," she retorted, "and every day grow more conscious of savagery. There are worse injuries than the bite of a dog." The cynical force of her words, accompanied by a hurt defiance of manner, so disturbed him that he looked about for a distraction, and finding a species of lignite in the sand proceeded to give her a lecture on its properties. He explained it was strombolo, or sea-coal, a composition of sulphur and salt, and recalled an experiment he had once attempted in the hall of Streatham Park, in which he had mixed it with a quantity of iron filings and heated both in a retort.

"To what end?" inquired Queeney.

"I forget," he said, "for there was no end. Your dear papa feared I would blow up the house, and you along with it, and ordered me to stop." Queeney giggled. Pleased he had lifted her spirits, he accompanied her back to the house.

Mrs. Thrale received visitors that afternoon, first Mr. Crutchley and then Miss Burney, though only she had been expected. Mr. Crutchley disappeared into Mrs. Thrale's chamber and descended within the hour grim of mouth and short on words. Johnson tried to question him; beyond a terse comment on the perfidy of women, Mr. Crutchley refused to be drawn, and soon departed.

Miss Burney too went upstairs, even before she had removed her bonnet, and stayed there until dusk. At intervals, those in the rooms beneath heard shrieks, whether of laughter or dismay none could tell, followed by protracted periods of silence. The younger children ran upstairs and came back wide-eyed, complaining that Mamma was not herself. Then, as the candles were about to be lit, Miss Burney appeared on the landing and called for Queeney.

Mamma was lying facedown on the bed, moaning. Miss Burney, eyes sparkling with excitement, said Mrs. Thrale was demented at the thought of giving up Mr. Piozzi. Mr. Crutchley had told her she would not be allowed to take her girls abroad and would most certainly forfeit eight-hundred pounds a year in income if she so persisted.

"What do I care about the money?" cried Mrs. Thrale, voice muffled against the pillow.

"She does not care about the money," interpreted Miss Burney.

"She does not care about most things," responded Queeney, "least of all her children."

"That is not true," Mamma spat, sitting up on the bed, nose red and hair disordered. "It is not my fault that I adore Mr. Piozzi. I did not set out to do so, I did not plan it . . . he is so amiable, his abilities so above his station . . . am I to abandon the hopes that I have cherished, let go the happiness within my reach—"

"You must," cried Miss Burney, and turning to Queeney in some agitation, sought her support. "She must, mustn't she?"

"There is nothing she need abandon," said Queeney, "save

her children," at which Mamma flung herself backwards and writhed about like an inmate of Bedlam. "How am I to choose?" she wailed. "Had I two hearts I might survive. Having but one, it will break between you."

"Had you but one heart," pronounced Queeney, "you would not think there was a choice."

On going downstairs she encountered Mr. Johnson loitering in the hall. She told him that Mamma, tired of London, was anxious to live abroad, and that Mr. Crutchley had advised against it. "Knowing Mamma, as you and I do," she said, "it comes as no surprise she is disturbed at being opposed."

If he knew what she was keeping from him, he gave no sign. Indeed, that night, he was in such good spirits that he diverted the company with the tale of a Newfoundland dog who had behaved like a bird on the nest.

JOHNSON WAS ASLEEP in his bed at Bolt Court, or rather thought he slept, when he was startled by a flash of light striking the side of his face, a light so luminous that he was blinded. A moment later, sight restored, he was aware that he had lost the power of speech, not from a testing of his ability to utter words, rather that in his head he knew the facility had left him. To prove such a calamity, he opened his mouth and dumbly recited, *I wasted time, and now doth time waste me.* Hearing nothing, he reached for his stick at the side of the bed and, gathering what little remained of his strength, banged it repeatedly upon the floorboards.

Some minutes later, Francis Barber, fortunately engaged in seeing to the fire in the parlour, heard his knocking and came upstairs. By means of sign language, Johnson instructed the alarmed Frank to bring him paper and pen, and laboriously wrote, *Fetch me a doctor.* His handwriting, though inclined to wander on the page, was legible.

Soon after, Mrs. Williams rushed into the room and demanded to know what ailed him. Scoring out the words, *Fetch me*, he replaced them with *I need*, at which she, hearing the scratching of his pen, ran demented about the room. In spite of his dilemma, the thought of the mute and the blind conjoined in such a catastrophe struck him as so comical that he succumbed to a convulsion of silent laughter.

He was laid low for four months, during which period, in spite of letters sent informing her of his illness, Mrs. Thrale made no attempt to visit him. It was true she wrote back, effusively wishing him well and emphasising her concern, but she did not come in person.

He remembered the last time he had seen her, some weeks after her return from Brighton, when she had informed Mr. Crutchley and the guardians that she had given up her intention of residing abroad and would retire instead to Bath, where, she vowed, she would establish a household, live economically and devote herself to her daughters. Samuel, of course, would be assured of a room in her new home.

He had visited her house on the eve of her departure and presented Queeney with a Latin grammar and a Virgil. "Dear Mistress," he had addressed Mrs. Thrale, "God go with you," and gazing long and intently into her eyes, kissed her cheek. On his way home to Bolt Court he had been obsessed with the dismal notion that he would not see her again.

Now, frail and pining, he reasoned it was not death that would part them, rather her withdrawal from his life.

MRS. DESMOULINS WAS dusting the parlour when she heard him shout out in the room above. She ran to the foot of the stairs, but no further. He had become so uncertain of temper that it was not wise to disturb him unless summoned. He shouted again, but this time it was a string of words, none of which she understood, followed by a thud, as though a book had been thrown to the floor. As he had been learning the Dutch language for some months, she concluded it was proving difficult.

The anguish Johnson felt was so extreme that he beat his head against the wall. Above him hung a miniature of Mrs. Thrale; snatching the likeness from its peg he flung it to the floor. The recognition of his gullibility, his stupidity, struck him like a hammer blow. That he, who prided himself on his knowledge of human nature, of the vanity of human wishes, should have been so blind as to mistake the hope for the reality, put his mind in turmoil.

When he had partially recovered his senses, he sat down at his desk, and, writing in the grip of such rage and emotion that the quill bent beneath the pressure of his angry fingers, penned a reply to Mrs. Thrale's shameful communication:

Madame, if I interpret your letter right, you are ignominiously married; if it is yet undone, let us once talk together. If you have abandoned your children and your religion, God forgive your wickedness; if you have forfeited your fame and your country, may your folly do no further mischief. If the last act is yet to do, I, who have loved you, esteemed you, reverenced you and served you, I who long thought you the first of human kind, entreat that before your fate is irrevocable, I may once more see you.

She wrote back, rebuking him for failing to acknowledge that she was in search of happiness, a pursuit he had once considered laudable. His reply was less heated, in that he wished her well and said he would not forget the kindness that had soothed twenty years of his wretched life.

Fanny Burney visited him some weeks later. She was apprehensive as to how she would deal with the subject of Mrs. Thrale, should that lost lady's name enter the conversation. Dr. Burney said she need not be anxious, as he was sure Mr. Johnson had shifted her from his mind, and besides, the name was now Piozzi, not Thrale.

Her father was wrong; no sooner had she entered the room than Johnson began to interrogate her on the events of those last months in Bath, for, he said, frowning thunderously, he himself had been left in the dark.

Miss Burney did her best to shed light on the matter. "Mrs. Thrale—as she then was—bending to the wishes of Queeney and Mr. Crutchley, exiled Mr. Pi—"

"Do not mention that name," Johnson roared, striking his breast with his fist.

"She told him," continued Miss Burney, storing in her mind, for future fiction, Johnson's countenance and gestures, "that he must return to Italy. Before he left he called on Queeney and thrust into her hands letters previously written by Mrs. Thrale. Apparently he wept, but she, brave girl, coolly accepted them and showed him the door. Mrs. Thrale shut up the house in Brighton and retired to Bath, but she was not herself."

"Not herself indeed," growled Johnson. He adopted a curious stance, arms spread wide and hands upraised, as though to stop the walls from closing in.

"Soon," said Fanny, "Mrs. Thrale began to show signs of disorder—after midnight she took to roaming the garden singing of love and kisses. Once, she would have wandered out naked had not Old Nurse prevented her. Frequently she cried out, *My heart, my soul, my Pi . . .* my singing teacher. She lost her appetite, her delight in company, her temper, though Queeney claimed the latter had always been unstable. From pecking at her food, she progressed to eating nothing at all. If she was forced, she vomited, and at last was in grave danger of wasting away. A doctor being summoned, and grudgingly acquainted with the reasons for her decline, he urged that . . . *the man* . . . be sent for at once. He vowed he would not be responsible for the life of his patient if his advice was ignored."

When she reached the end of her sorry narrative, Johnson no longer frowned. Now, his expression was so pitiful, his brow so etched with misery, that Miss Burney wished herself invisible. He sat down and studied his feet; she could not help noticing that though his chair was missing a leg, he maintained his seat without effort. Perhaps, she thought, he has always been accustomed to imbalance, though again, it could be the dropsy in his legs that sustained his equilibrium.

The silence becoming oppressive, she searched her mind for diverting topics. She was about to mention the restoration of estates forfeited by Jacobites, when he suddenly cried out, "Did she dwell on me?"

"That she did," Fanny answered, and hesitated.

"Speak out," he cried.

"Frequently she spoke of her break from you, and declared she hoped you would forgive her—"

"I asked for the truth," he said.

"She thought your expectations too high."

"Madame, she was right," said he, and rising from his broken chair, eyes full of tears, gestured for her to leave.

Tiptoeing down the stairs she was waylaid by Mrs. Desmoulins, who enquired of her whether she saw a change in Mr. Johnson.

"No," she lied, for she was past talking.

"Did you not notice his eyes," persisted Mrs. Desmoulins. "They have grown larger, and now carry the gaze of a child."

"I saw no alteration," she protested, though indeed she had.

"He has burnt all her letters," Mrs. Desmoulins told her. "He took them out into the side yard and hacked down the branches of the poplar tree to feed the fire."

"It is perhaps advisable," said Miss Burney, "to consume memories."

"The poplar came as a sapling from Streatham Park," cried Mrs. Desmoulins. "These past ten years he has tended it like a father his son."

Miss Burney pushed past her and made her escape. As she trotted down the steps and into the Court, she could not help smiling, for Mr. Boswell had told her that Mrs. Desmoulins had long been in love with Mr. Johnson; she found it comical that an old woman, plain of features and red of complexion, should harbour such a misplaced passion. But then, was it not a conceit common to another member of her household?

She did not see Johnson again for several months. When he next received her he boasted he was now much recovered in health. He said Dr. Heberden's bleeding of him had given relief, and the prescribed doses of opium he daily took now enabled him to move about as formerly. Only two nights ago he had gone to his club with Mr. Boswell and walked home without distress. She said she was delighted at finding him so well, though it seemed to her that his asthma was worse and his dropsy advanced.

"I will not capitulate," he cried, and next instant brought up the name of Mrs. Thrale, demanding to know what news there was of her. She told him she had been informed by Queeney that her mother and the Italian were at present in Milan. "She writes to Queeney," she said, "but Miss Thrale does not reply to her letters and scarce bothers to read them."

"Poor Sweeting," he murmured. "She has lost her mother."

"They were not close—"

"On the contrary," he said, "they were too close," and added, "a strange thought strikes me—we shall receive no letters in the grave."

"Mr. Boswell," she said, "once told me that upon asking if any man had the same conviction of the truth of an after life as he had of common affairs, you replied, 'No, Sir' . . ."

"I do not recall the statement," he replied, "but perceive the sense of it. If you mean am I serene at the thought of what awaits, the answer must be 'No,' for being rational I regard salvation as conditional. As I can never be sure I have complied with the conditions, I remain afraid of death."

"Why, Sir," she was foolish enough to protest, "you who love God have surely nothing to fear," at which, thumping his stick against the floor, he shouted, "Madame, it is the fear of God that keeps me alive."

When she had gone he sat for an hour or more staring into the flames. Presently, Mrs. Desmoulins stood outside his door complaining that Frank Barber had given the cat the supper cheese. "It will do the dear creature more good than either of us," he bellowed, "for both of us have trouble with our bellies."

He got up, and going to his desk took out a sheaf of papers. After no more than a cursory examination he flung them onto the fire. A page fell to the hearth; he was about to thrust it back into the coals when he glimpsed Queeney's handwriting—

Southwark
24th November, 1772

Sir,

Mamma knows I would have written sooner, but she said you would be troubled no more with my stuff—I left Susan and Sophy well yesterday but poor Grandmamma was bad. Socrates is dead and old Puss like to die. Papa is well and has bought a new horse. Mamma is well too, if cross. I am very much obliged to you for the honour of your letter.

Your most humble servant,

Queen Hester

He wept, and strove to analyse the cause. Age, he reasoned, weakened the emotions owing to a realisation that the light was fading and nought but darkness lay ahead. Suffering, which fell to one's lot in the course of nature, by chance or by fate, did not, *ceteris paribus*, seem so painful when imposed by the arbitrary will of strangers; it was the wounds inflicted by those closest to one that drew blood. In the curling of the burning papers he saw the face of Mrs. Thrale, and seizing the poker, stamped her image into the everlasting flames.

To Miss Laetitia Hawkins,
2, Sion Row, Twickenham.

January 5th, 1811

Dear Miss Hawkins,

Your accusation that I told Miss Burney that your papa stole Dr. Johnson's journal and watch is unfounded. Nor can I be accused of spreading rumours concerning my mother's relationship with Dr. Johnson, for their closeness during my childhood was the cause of much unhappiness. An excluded child has no wish to provide proof of a bond greater than that which is supposed to exist between mother and daughter. I can only believe that Miss Burney, her latest fiction not attaining the approbation afforded to Evelina, has resorted to a regrettable wish for fresh notoriety. It could not have been she who, on plumping up the Doctor's pillows and asking if it would do, received the reply, "It will do . . . all that a pillow can do," for I have a letter from her giving an account of a visit she made to Bolt Court on the 8th December, in which so many people were already gathered in his chamber that he sent word down he was too tired to see more. Nor was your father present that final night, nor Sir Joshua or Mr. Langton, the last two being his dearest friends. The account of his end, which you ascribe to Miss Burney, is erroneous. The seizing of a lancet and the cutting of his leg to release excess fluid, was committed in the presence of Francis Barber, who sent for Dr. Cruikshank to sew up the wound.

When death came the Doctor was alone save for Frank and Mrs. Desmoulins. His stertorous breathing having stopped, they went to his side and observed he had gone.

I have no recollection of a padlock and key which you say my mamma employed to confine Dr. Johnson in his room when the madness came upon him. I regret I shall not be answering any further letters. It is not only the dead who need to be left in peace. I pray you, do not write more.

Yours,

H. M. Keith

Epilogue

TWENTY-FOUR COACHES followed the funeral carriage to Westminster Abbey. It being a Monday and the streets crowded, several officials of the Abbey went ahead to clear the way. Snow fell, but gently, as though to draw a veil across the heavens.

Sir Joshua Reynolds was chief mourner, followed by Frank Barber; the exalted importance afforded to the latter caused Sir John Hawkins considerable irritation.

The burial service was conducted by Dr. Taylor of Ashbourne at one o'clock in the South Close. Edmund Burke and Mr. Langton were among those who bore the lead coffin. James Boswell was not present.

Dr. Taylor lost strength of voice on two occasions, upon which he dabbed at his eyes with the cuff of his gown. He had drunk heavily the night before and his own end could not be long delayed.

A hole had been dug close by the remains of David Garrick. The coffin lowered into the damp darkness, a flagstone was set in place inscribed with the words:

Samuel Johnson, L.L.D.
Obiit XIII die Decemberis
Anno Domini MDCCLXXXIV
Ætatis suæ LXXV

The expenses for the funeral amounted to forty-four pounds six shillings and seven pence, excluding the sum of thirteen shillings and fourpence paid separately to the bellringers.

Mrs. Desmoulins sat alone in Bolt Court, roasting chestnuts in the fire.